Kiet Goes West

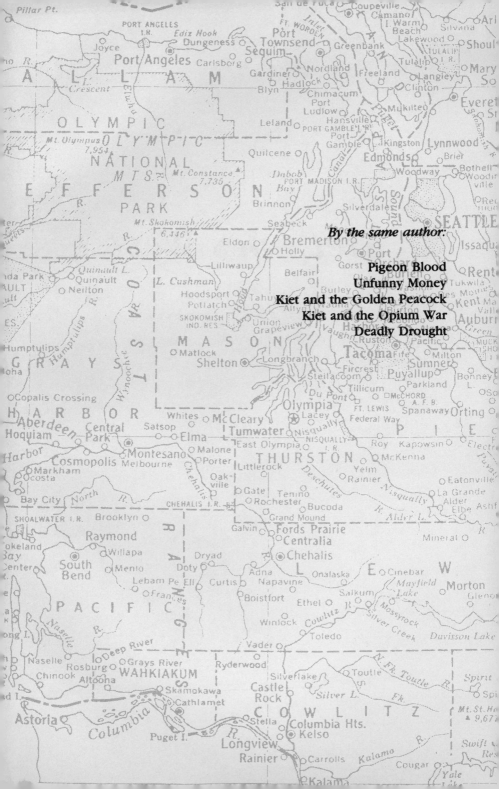

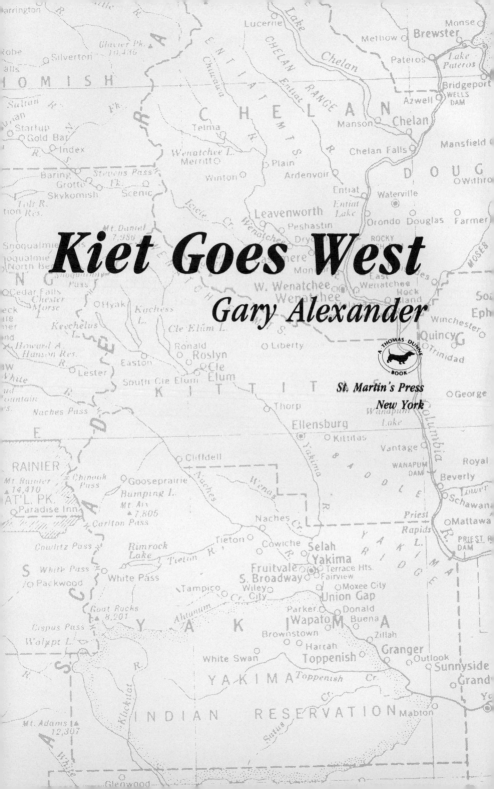

Kiet Goes West

Gary Alexander

A THOMAS DUNNE BOOK

St. Martin's Press
New York

Design by Tanya M. Pérez

Library of Congress Cataloging-in-Publication Data

Alexander, Gary, 1941-
    Kiet goes West / Gary Alexander.
       p.   cm.
    "A Thomas Dunne book."
    "A Superintendent Bamsan Kiet mystery."
    ISBN 0-312-07851-X
    I. Title.
  PS3551.L3554K56   1992
  813'.54—dc20   92-142
                                            CIP

First Edition: June 1992

10 9 8 7 6 5 4 3 2 1

In memory of Roy Duensing

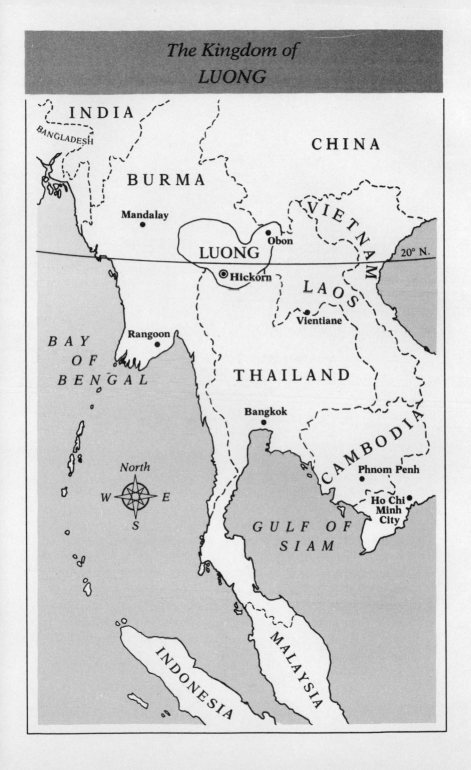

The Kingdom of LUONG

MAJOR CHARACTERS

BAMSAN KIET *(bomb-sawn key-yet)*. Hickorn's superintendent of police.

CAPTAIN BINH *(bin)*. Kiet's adjutant.

DAVID "DAVEY" PETERSON, JR. Computer nerd and crook.

KEN BOLLING. King of paid programming.

DOUG ZANE. Attorney.

MARGE MAINWARING. Real estate super-salesperson.

KEEDENG CHOI *(key-dang choy)*. Restaurateur.

CHICK CHIPPERFIELD. Dealer of preowned automobiles.

MRS. DAVID PETERSON, SR. Davey's mom.

Prologue

The United States of America is a republic of states. The Kingdom of Luong is a constitutional monarchy and a state of mind.

The United States has a gross national product of 4.6 trillion dollars. Luong was founded in 403 B.C. This makes the United States 5,750 times as wealthy as Luong, and Luong 11 times as old as the United States. If asked whether one is related to the other, an American might say, yeah, sure, obviously. Youthful vigor versus stagnation and so forth; just look at the numbers. A Luongan might ask you to repeat the question, but only if you want to.

The American head of state is a president. He is sixty-eight years old and plays golf. The Luongan head of state is a prince. He is eighty-one years old and has a passion for pocket billiards. The prince shoots a good stick. The president needs a better putter.

The United States has 88 times the area of Luong and 157 times the population.

Luong's annual per capita income is $597. The average American brings in $14,595, which is 24 times as much.

This year's federal budget is $1.2 trillion. The Luongan government is spending the equivalent of $134 million. That ratio is 8,955 to 1.

Last year, 22,890 Americans were murdered. During the same period, forty-six Luongans were forcibly united with their ancestors. Adjusting for population, Americans are triply inclined to kill.

A month ago, $20 million was illegally removed from Luong's treasury by an American. It is unknown how many American tax dollars were pilfered, embezzled, or otherwise misappropriated in the same period. Presumably, $20 million would be a slow month.

But $20 million is 15 percent of the Luongan national budget.

Which is why Bamsan Kiet, superintendent of police of Hickorn, Luong's capital, is reluctantly en route to America.

Kiet Goes West

1

Bamsan Kiet had to keep telling himself that the airplane was not on fire.

Kiet's seatmate, a Japanese businessman, noticed his anxiety and told him the same. "Do not be alarmed, sir. It is fog, not smoke. You do not smell smoke, do you?"

Kiet sniffed hot air, sniffed again, then said, "No, but I cannot see two rows ahead of us."

"This plane is Soviet-built," the businessman said. "Its climate control system is designed for Leningrad to Murmansk, not the Hickorn-Bangkok shuttle. The fog and intense heat is the fault of your lovely tropical weather. We are still climbing, you see. Once we are pressurized and at cruise altitude we will be more comfortable. I know. I fly frequently. You, sir, is this your first trip in an airplane?"

"Of course not," said Kiet, who had in fact flown several times aboard Royal Air Luong's domestic hops, on Douglas DC-3s as old as himself. For his first international flight he had chosen this relatively youthful aircraft, a thirty-year-old

1

turboprop twin. Once buckled in his seat by a wing, he had observed missing rivets and a sooty engine nacelle. It was Royal Air Luong's flagship. Ten minutes off the ground and Kiet already wanted to go home.

"Your anxiety is no sin, sir. I too suffered the malady. As a salesman I am compelled to travel by air extensively. The malady nearly terminated my career."

"Malady?"

"Fear of flying. I attended a seminar. It was extremely helpful. We discussed our feelings and were instructed on the sophistication and sterling safety record of the commercial aviation industry. Our final examination was an airline flight. We all passed."

"On Royal Air Luong?"

"Well, no, a different carrier. Are you, sir, going to Bangkok, or is Bangkok just an intermediate stop?"

The airplane jounced over an air pocket. Kiet's stomach fluttered. "America. I am going to the United States of America."

"Wonderful. Is it to be your first trip across the Pacific Ocean to America?"

"And last," Kiet said.

"Where in America, sir, may I ask?"

"Seattle," Kiet said. "A city in a northwestern province called Washington."

"I envy you. I have never been to the States. Their northwest region, I am informed, is scenic and friendly. The mountains are high and the air is clean, and everybody drives a logging truck."

Kiet shook his head in agreement. Captain Binh, his adjutant, had said as much with picture postcards. Binh had been in America for three weeks. It seemed to Kiet like three years.

"Me, I am returning to Kuala Lumpur via a connecting flight."

"Oh," Kiet said. He closed his eyes, hoping the conversation would end.

2

"I am returning without success, but not necessarily as a failure either," the salesman said. "I have garnered a bare smattering of sales during my month in Hickorn. My superiors instructed me to abandon the experiment. The prior two years I was the fourth-leading producer in my zone in Malaysia. I was promoted and sent to open a territory in Luong. That is not indicative of a failure, is it?"

"No," Kiet said.

"I sell facsimile machines. Fax machines. Practically nobody in Hickorn has one. Practically nobody buys from me, from anybody. Hickorn and Luong are—how shall I diplomatically express this thought?—technologically pristine."

"Backward," Kiet said.

"Please do not be insulted."

"I am not insulted," Kiet said sincerely.

"A reliable telephone network is essential to efficient utilization of the fax machine. Frankly, one completed call in four is par in Hickorn. Average one in three and you are having a good day."

"Hickorn enjoys an old French system," Kiet said. "It is satisfactory. Hickornians love to gossip and exchange rumors. If our telephones functioned as they should, everybody would be chatting endlessly about the conduct of their neighbors' spouses and nothing would ever get done."

"I comprehend your, um, logic, sir, but my greatest frustration is not with your private sector, but with the government."

"Excuse me?" Kiet said, opening his eyes.

"Again, no aspersion intended, but the Kingdom of Luong has a rather extensive bureaucracy."

"Indeed," Kiet said. "Layer upon layer of clerks and departmental supervisors and deputy assistant associate ministers. Your point, please?"

"Governmental people yearn to be issued the latest office gadgetry before their peers. Status is the name of the game and high-tech hardware is the means of keeping score. No office product at this moment in time confers more status than the fax."

"Peculiarly, yes. Whether our telephones permit them to be useful or not," Kiet said, nodding.

"Why, then, could I not interest a single deputy minister for materiel control in placing an order?"

"I wouldn't know," Kiet lied. "I don't know how government buyers function."

"Nobody would speak candidly to me, regardless of encouragement."

Encouragement, Kiet thought: money and liquor and whores. He did not reply.

"In retrospect, sir, I don't believe anybody really has the full story. They alluded to budgetary constraints, of day-to-day operating funds being temporarily frozen."

Not frozen, Kiet thought. *Embezzled.* He closed his eyes again, clenching the lids.

"You, sir, your name and face is quite familiar. If I am not mistaken, you are Hickorn's superintendent of police."

"You are not mistaken."

"A quiet rumor whispers that federal money was stolen recently, in one extremely large chunk."

"Rumors," Kiet said, fluttering a hand in dismissal.

How easy it had been, thought Kiet, for that postadolescent monster who had been contracted to computerize Luong's fiscal agencies. David Peterson, Jr. Boy wonder of computers, IQ of 171, hired cheaply, job completed on schedule, paid off, home to Seattle, stopover at Honolulu, numbers punched into a public telephone, instantaneous wire transfers, the equivalent of $20 million U.S., 15 percent of the Luongan annual budget gone, swept by electronic impulses to foreign banks. Twelve billion Luongan zin converted to dollars, gone. Gone.

"Ah, yes, rumors," said the unconvinced Japanese. "July is a lovely time to visit the American northwest, I understand. July and August is their dry season. Are you vacationing?"

4

"Yes."

"An expensive vacation."

"I saved for years," Kiet said, his stomach tightening at the reminder that among the agencies electronically fleeced was the Hickorn Police Department.

Perhaps a dozen people in Luong knew what had happened. His Royal Highness, Prince Novisad Pakse, had begged the intimates to maintain the secret. The embezzlement had diluted already watery revenues. Funds were shifted around to meet the most immediate needs. All taxes were collected quarterly in Luong. The next due date was September 30, a long long time from early July. Fifteen percent of the annual receipts was 60 percent of the present quarter's.

The Kingdom of Luong was close to broke.

In two weeks Kiet would have difficulty meeting his payroll. In order not to further deplete his reserves he had gone on the street to borrow money for this trip from Chinese moneylenders, the shylocks, the usurers he customarily arrested. He deceived them that he was on so miserable a dice and card-playing streak that he must be accursed, and that his seventeen-year-old girlfriend was pregnant.

The loan sharks bought Kiet's story. It was language they understood. Still, he would have to repay on schedule. They couldn't deal with Hickorn's police superintendent as they did their typical delinquent account. They couldn't break his kneecaps, but they could scream. Then the deal would become public and the secret of the embezzlement would be revealed.

The truth would create panic. Civil servants with empty pay envelopes would be on the streets, angry, bewildered, unruly. Kiet did not care to consider how he would deal with such a mess, especially when many of his own officers would likely be on the wrong side of the line.

The salesman nudged Kiet. He said, "Pardon me, sir. We're crossing into Thailand. I thought you would like to know."

Kiet grunted a thank you, folded his arms, and feigned sleep. He imagined a dotted line traced atop the double-canopy jungle. Thailand. He never believed he would leave Luong's borders. Not until twenty-four hours ago.

Captain Binh had gone to America eagerly in pursuit of Davey Peterson. The Seattle Police Department had captured the computer criminal and released him to Binh for extradition. This was a week ago and Binh was overdue.

Then came yesterday's telegram: HELP STOP COME QUICKLY STOP SEATTLE-TACOMA AIRPORT STOP HANG LOOSE STOP PRISONER ESCAPED STOP PRISONER MURDERED STOP I AM A PERSON OF INTEREST STOP.

2

Kiet awakened when the landing gear was lowered. He held his breath until the massive wheel trucks locked into position. He could fly around the world a thousand times and never get used to aircraft hydraulics. Whenever wheels and flaps were activated, they moaned and creaked and whined as if obeying under protest.

He looked outside. Again he had a seat at a wing. It was dark now, but on the last of his frequent checks, all rivets were present and both engine pods were sootless. They should be, he thought. This airplane, a Boeing 747 jet, was gigantic. The Bolshevik death trap could be dismantled and stowed in the Boeing's cargo hold. The Boeing was therefore too big and expensive to be allowed to explode in a ball of flame and plummet into the ocean while its passengers broiled alive in unspeakable agony, shrieking, their skin bubbling, their lungs bursting——

Stop it! Kiet commanded himself. You're almost there; concentrate on the splendid view.

And even at night it was. Directly below were clusters and strings of lights. Some of the strings were moving. Kiet knew of the proliferation of automobiles in America, and that the nation was widely electrified. Beyond, between a horizon as bumpy and tall as Luong's northern highlands, was a body of water that had been waxed glossy by twilight.

"Good evening, ladies and gentlemen," said the pilot. "It's nine fifty-two P.M., Pacific daylight time. We'll be landing at Seattle-Tacoma International in about seven minutes, which will put us on the ground about eleven minutes ahead of our scheduled ten-ten ETA. If I do say so myself, that's pretty doggone good considering how long we've been up in the air. Temperature at the airport is a real mild sixty-six degrees. I hope you enjoyed your flight and you'll fly with us again."

How long had he been traveling? Hickorn to Bangkok to Tokyo to Seattle. Kiet glanced at his watch. It had stopped. He had forgotten to wind it. Including stopovers, he estimated, a twenty-four hour journey. Captain Binh, he thought, if you are not in desperate peril, you shall be.

Kiet cleared customs fast. Since he had never traveled and owned no luggage, he had no suitcases to be searched. The basket that contained his belongings was open-thatched, so the agent was able to inspect it for contraband within seconds.

The airport was remarkably bustling for the evening hour. People scurried toward concourses as if they were late and they knew their airplanes would depart exactly at the minute promised, with or without them. Hickorn International Airport was much more leisurely, Kiet mused. If you were late for your flight, usually no harm was done. "On time" meant that the plane would depart during that day, unless it had been canceled.

Seattle air travelers dressed oddly, too. Informality was a polite word. Many wore only T-shirts and shorts or denims.

8

They were half naked, like aborigines or tropical tourists. True, it was just past the midpoint of the first week of July, early in the Northern Hemisphere summer, but it was also *sixty-six* degrees Fahrenheit. Not Celsius, Fahrenheit.

That the natives pretended they inhabited an equatorial zone was no consolation to Kiet, whose arms were mountain ranges of goosebumps. He was tall for a Luongan, Caucasian height, and thicker than he should be in the waist, but the extra layering of flesh was no protection against the cold. Nor did sandals, slacks, and short-sleeved white shirt prevent the chill air from piercing through to his skin like needles.

Kiet went into a gift shop. Souvenir bric-a-brac filled the shelves. The one wall, devoted to clothing for the most part, offered undershirts and bikini swimsuits. In a corner, however, was warmer garb, which the clerk said they'd just gotten in. The selections were meager. Each article was gaudily colored and printed with logos and names. Corporate advertising, he presumed.

A human billboard or pneumonia? The former was slightly less hateful than the latter. He selected a sweatshirt with orange and blue designs that included the letter *D*, a rearing horse, and a crash helmet. He found a stocking cap. It was white with a black-and-silver patch.

A peculiar combination, yes, a peculiar fashion statement, but warm. Kiet paid, put on his purchases, walked to the main lobby, and waited near the airline ticket counters.

Hang loose. He was presumably hanging loose. Captain Binh had lived twelve months in America several years earlier, studying police science at the constabulary of the American capital city, Washington, D.C. He loved every instant of the experience and devoured American life ravenously. If he had stayed much longer, Kiet felt, he would have gone native. He was insufferably Americanized as it was. Return to normalcy in Luong had not dampened his adoration of the inscrutable West.

Among the informational treasures Binh had brought

9

home were Miranda cards and English-language slang. Kiet had translated a meager percentage of the gobbledygook. Hang loose, he believed, was an instruction to stand by conspicuously until Binh contacted him. Many people were seeing him, looking at him, observing him cautiously as he hung loose, but none was his young adjutant.

An hour later, Kiet gave up. He imagined that he resembled a Siberian trade official, but he didn't quit because he was self-conscious. He was exhausted. He would hang loose tomorrow.

He trudged out of the terminal to the taxicab lineup. Most of the taxis were American-made, spacious and boxy. They had a patchwork appearance and seemed more exhausted than he. They looked to Kiet like military staff cars of the losing side in a global war.

He went to a vehicle whose major body panels were all the same color. The driver took Kiet's basket and said, "That must be kinda hard on the noggin."

"How else would a person carry a basket?" Kiet asked.

"Different strokes for different folks," said the driver. He tossed it into the trunk, slammed the lid shut on the second try, and opened a door for his passenger. "Where to, pal?"

"A hotel, please."

"Which?"

"A hotel close to this airport and moderately priced."

"What amenities you got in mind, you know what I mean?"

"Bottled water and a ceiling fan would be nice."

"Yeah? That's a tall order, them things. They don't grow on trees. How about soda pop machines and air conditioning? Same difference. I can fix you up nice."

They drove from the airport compound onto a four-lane highway that was chockablock with hotels, gasoline stations, car rental agencies, and restaurants. The strip was not quite as brightly illuminated as it would be in daytime, but not for lack of effort by automobile headlights and incandescent

10

lamps and a rainbow of neon. Kiet could not visualize the lumberjack trucks and snowy peaks on Binh's picture postcards.

He pointed at a towering hotel and said, "Here? It's higher than the two leading hotels in my country combined."

"Yeah, I figured you was from out of town. Nah, forget this place. You said cheap. Too rich for your blood. You stay there, you gotta be on an expense account. Trust me."

Kiet sat back and trusted him, albeit with a sense of helplessness. Traffic and artificial lighting gradually thinned. Hotels shrank to one floor. Restaurants served diners in their cars. There were trees and muffler shops. He began to see houses on parallel roads.

He also began to hear gunfire. It was the *pop-pop-pop* of small arms fire. The shots were coming from the residential areas. Could be carbines, could be pistols. That type of weaponry would be consistent with drug gangs. It was commonly known that narcotics organizations battled in the streets of America for the patronage of dope fiends. A multibillion-dollar business.

He sighed. Nothing he had seen thus far in America jibed with tourist brochures he had read on the airplane.

A fountain of sparks erupted behind a house. Evidently a stray round ignited an ammunition cache. The display was beautiful. Kiet hoped it wasn't deadly.

"What, please, is the noise?" he asked the driver.

"Money, pal," he said. "Them stands, they do a land office business. I'd give my left nut to own a piece of the action, but the Indian reservations and the guys who've been setting up in supermarket lots for umpteen years, they've got it all sewed up. A day late, a dollar short. Story of my life."

Money. Kiet's suspicion had been verified. "Are we almost to the hotel?"

The driver stopped at a red light, turned around, winked, and said, "You know, those amenities we was talking about, we never did settle on what."

"I am too tired to care if the room has a ceiling fan or not."

"Look, what I'm saying is are you looking for a room or a good time."

"Room," Kiet said, catching on. "I am a police officer. Just take me to a room."

"Cop? Sure you are," the driver said, laughing.

The light changed. They lurched through the intersection, and turned left between an automobile parts store and a grocery market.

They stopped in the asphalt courtyard of a U-shaped series of connected bungalows. An end bungalow was identified in neon as Office. Atop a pole in neon was: SOFT SPRINGS MOTEL. Below it, a backlighted rectangular sign read: VACANCY—ADULT MOVIES.

The cabbie shut off his meter and said, "Best of both worlds, pal. You got a room and you can make your own party."

3

Next morning, Bamsan Kiet awoke to sunlight throbbing through threadbare curtains. He squinted into vivid yellow outlined with cobwebs—unintentional lace. He groaned.

He reached for Quin. She, of course, was not there. Quin Canh, his lover. Was in Hickorn. Home. Where he should be. Beside her. His exploring hand her alarm clock. Or vice versa.

Kiet wanted to doze but could not. He could not lie still enough. Each fidgety movement, each heartbeat, instigated wave action. He rolled off the bed and onto his feet.

He stood, breathing deeply. Halfway around the planet, six miles above it in an aluminum eggshell, and not a twinge of airsickness. Now, in Binh's words, he was about to lose his cookies. Perhaps it was the shape, he thought, gazing without affection at the circular waterbed. No headboard, no foot, no points of reference for the vagabond sleeper. Disorientation had to be a major factor in seasickness, he decided.

The rhythmic air-intake technique worked. He felt reasonably well, feisty rather than nauseous. He kicked at the arc of the bed, kicked hard. The surface undulated. Surf's up, Binh would say.

He surveyed his unit. Last night he'd lacked the energy. He had paid at the office, two days in advance. He had entered the unit, dropped his basket, and fallen on the wretched, bobbing, plastic-encased pond. He would have snored through a rowboat ride around Cape Horn.

A night's rest had sharpened his senses, but acuity was not necessarily desirable. He hadn't before noticed all the coin slots. The slot on the television receiver, which was incidentally bolted to the wall on swiveling steel plate. The slot on the videocasette machine mounted directly below the television on the same thick steel. The slot on the only chair in the room, a cracking-vinyl recliner. Handmarked on the coin box was "majic fingers fifty sents."

The prophylactic dispenser in the bathroom had two slots, two choices, fifty cents per, which Kiet assumed by the shiny solidity of the machine to be costlier than the fifty sents charged by the dilapidated lounging chair. Pull the left lever for an ordinary condom, tipped and lubricated at no extra expense. The right, illustrated above the lever, was a "tickler." "Crazed pagan ecstasy" was guaranteed.

Kiet looked at the illustration. He doubted the ecstasy guarantee. Fifty years old and no Buddhist monk before he met Quin, Bamsan Kiet had known women with unusual appetites, but none who fantasized sex with porcupines.

The bathroom, and come to think of it, the entire unit smelled of somebody else. Somebody else's cigarettes, somebody else's drunkenness, somebody else's ejaculations.

It was past time to hang loose.

People were inexplicably watching Kiet, staring, rudely gawking, as they had last night. He was in the busiest portion of the Seattle-Tacoma International Airport terminal, near the

14

ticket counters of worldwide air carriers. Of all the strange people buzzing about, why was he drawing attention? He was merely standing, arms folded; he was not obstructing a ticket line, he was not proffering pamphlets; his zipper was zipped, his fingers and hands were not in or on inappropriate parts of his body. He was doing nothing. He was being inconspicuous.

Or was he? It occurred to him that his inactivity was conspicuous. This was America. He was doing nothing, and only public charity recipients and criminals did nothing in public.

He looked for something to do, something to neutralize the nothing. His something was a vending machine. It was freestanding and chest high, so Kiet could pretend serious study while keeping vigilant for Binh, hanging loose.

The machine sold insurance. You pay a small sum. You get onto an airliner. You die a hideous death. The insurance company pays a large sum to the person you chose to enrich.

Splendid, Kiet thought, drumming fingers on the ghoulish machine. A bargain if the policyholder has the foresight to book passage on a doomed airplane.

"Psst."

The source of the whisper was at his side. He was a trim, handsome Oriental man half a head shorter and a quarter century younger than Kiet. He was dressed in a nondescript business suit, blue, with matching tie and white shirt. He wore flat-lens eyeglasses and a glue-on mustache.

The outfit was an extraordinary contrast to Binh's usual starched white uniform. Without golden captain's pips gleaming on shoulder boards as if nuggets, patent leather belt and shoes, and nickel-plated, pearl-handled Colt .45 automatic holstered at a provocative angle, he was a stranger. He looked like an incompetent bookkeeper.

At second glance, though, he strongly resembled the comic eldest brother whose zany movies played at Hickorn cinemas. He looked like an Asiatic Groucho Marx. Kiet smiled.

15

"Superintendent," Binh hissed. "Stop smiling. Cool it. We're not together. We have to maintain a low profile. No shaking hands and hugging either, okay?"

"Yes," Kiet said. "I shall restrain my emotions."

"Superintendent, I have to say this, but I don't want to offend you. I'll be grateful as long as I live that you came halfway around the world to my aid."

"Then don't say it," Kiet said. "You don't have to say it."

"I spotted you a mile away. You stick out like a sore thumb."

"Ridiculous."

"Not ridiculous, Superintendent. The Denver Broncos *and* the Raiders. What are you trying to prove?"

"Excuse me?"

"Your sweatshirt and cap. Even plain, heavy clothing attracts attention. It's the fifth of July. Today's forecast is eighty degrees. And this is Seahawk country, you know."

"I do?"

"Seattle Seahawks. Football."

"Soccer?"

Binh sighed. "No, Superintendent. Football. Seahawk fans hate the Broncos worse than herpes. They hate the Raiders three times as much as they hate the Broncos. You look like you're asking for trouble. You look like you're a wiseass just up from California. We're talking Faux Pas City."

"California is bad?"

Binh nodded grimly. "Being a Californian in Seattle is three times as bad as being a Raiders fan. They have dynamite tans and they buy up all the real estate."

Kiet was thoroughly confused and he was tired of the abuse. "On the subject of low profiling, where, please, is Harpo and Chico?"

"Huh?"

"Never mind. Come."

Kiet led them into a cocktail lounge. Binh ordered coffee. Kiet asked what brands of beer they stocked. Binh told Kiet

16

that it was kind of early. Kiet repeated his "never mind" admonition and asked the waitress if they had Golden Tiger. The waitress had never heard of Golden Tiger. Kiet explained that it was a smooth Luongan brew inexplicably nicknamed "amber death" by foreigners. The waitress said that Golden Tiger still didn't ring a bell, nor did Luong. Binh ordered for Kiet, saying to bring anything as long as it was a light beer in a short glass.

Kiet thanked Binh for his concern, held his baby beer glass in toast, and sipped. "Fizz. No flavor, but a pleasant fizz."

Binh tapped his watch crystal. "Superintendent, it's ten o'clock in the morning."

"In Seattle, yes. In Hickorn it is one o'clock in the morning. A dim, late cabaret hour."

"Superintendent—"

"One A.M. tomorrow. It is Sunday in Seattle, Monday in Hickorn. You're nagging me about morning drinking? Very well. I'm drinking a *day* early. Sin compounding sin. Enjoy your coffee, Captain."

"Superintendent, I met your plane yesterday. I learned from the airline that you were on the passenger manifest."

"Where were you?"

"I came an hour late, which should have been an hour early. I have to stay on the move. This disguise, believe it or not, is not fooling some of the wrong people."

"Really?" Who was the fourth Marx brother? Gummo, the fifth, was an agent. He didn't count. "What people?"

"I'll get to that. At least I haven't seen them yet today. Anyway, I came an hour late and missed you by an hour. Airlines don't run on time. I phoned. They said, yeah, it's on schedule, but am I supposed to buy it? Crapola. I mean, hell, they can't go from Portland to Seattle on time, then they fly nonstop from Tokyo right on the button."

"Eleven minutes before the button."

"Go figure," Binh said. "Well, I'm glad we connected. I missed some work last night. I lose my job, my safe house is history. Marge isn't gonna cut me a whole bunch of slack, the way we've been getting along lately."

"Job? Work? Marge?"

"I'll get to that, Superintendent."

"David Peterson, Jr. Murder, et cetera. Please get to that."

"Well, you know, I flew into Seattle three weeks ago. The arrest complaint on Davey had already been routed through diplomatic channels. I reported in at SPD. That's the Seattle Police Department. They didn't have Davey in custody yet, but they had an APB out on him. They weren't real interested in having me hanging around, actively involved, but they were nice about it. I gave them what input and insights I had. They tried not to patronize me, but I could feel it. I was an out-of-towner on their turf and I could relate to that."

Binh took a drink of coffee and smiled. "Well, in the final analysis, Superintendent, they had to eat a little crow."

Kiet gave his empty glass to the waitress and said, yes, please.

"In retrospect, my most valuable insight was my hunch that Davey would reappear in town. He was born and raised in Seattle, you know. The SPD guys, they said, hey, criminals, they can't go home again. It's sort of like returning to the scene of the crime."

"Criminals don't return to the scene of the crime or go home again," Kiet said. "Intelligent criminals don't."

"Davey's got a 171 IQ, yeah, but in a real-world context, he can be a dipshit, naive and nerdish. Did you ever meet him?"

"No. Our Hickorn Police Department payroll computer apparatus was in a separate building."

"Me neither. In Hickorn, Davey centralized the data of the agencies he ripped off in a mainframe he'd set up in a spare office at the ministry of finance. The dorks whose brilliant idea it was to hire Davey, they were his primary contacts. Glorified clerks who were itching to make names for themselves and move up the ladder by bringing systems analysis

18

to Luong on the cheap. Jesus H. Christ, it was like locking the fox in with the hens! That's why Davey was able to rip off twenty million bucks with a telephone call from Honolulu."

"He did go home again and the Seattle Police Department captured him for you?"

"Indirectly. His mother nabbed him and held him for the SPD."

"Captured him at the family home?"

Binh smirked. "Not hardly. Word was that Davey, when he was in Hickorn, couldn't get laid without paying for it. Fifty percent above the going rate too. Davey's got acne and glasses with Mount Palomar lenses.

"Well, if money talks, like the cliché goes, twenty million smackers screams. Maybe money can't buy happiness, but it sure as hell can rent it. Davey'd been on the lam, but he was back in town, homesick. He called his mother and she said come home, but he wouldn't. She knew what he'd done, how he'd stolen the twenty mil. I'd interviewed her. Nice old widow lady. A bit overbearing, but essentially a decent person. Davey's her only child, so I can relate to her protectiveness. She leads a dismal life. She's an avid bowler. Bowling and Davey, that's her life.

"Anyway, she's badgering him, right, saying he's no good, surrender to the police, act like a man for once in your life, blah blah blah. So Davey tells her to go jump in a lake and then he hangs up on her, right?"

"Right."

"Well, that's what Davey does, although forgetting that he let it slip to his mom where he was staying. There's gotta be a plug on that 171 IQ of his and Davey sometimes trips over the cord. Meanwhile, he'd booked the penthouse suite in a super-fine downtown hotel. His mom somehow cadged a passkey from a desk clerk. Mrs. Peterson can be pushy.

"Well, she barged in on Davey. Her original intention was to lecture him, take him home, and let him make up his own mind whether he was going to do the right thing. That plan went out the window and Davey damn near did too when Mrs. Peterson saw the call girls."

"Plural?" Kiet said.

"Two chickies. Five hundred bucks a night. Each, Superintendent. Plus tip. These were prime foxes. SPD uniforms who answered the squeal said they made Miss America look like a bag lady. Anyway, Mrs. Peterson bops in and one is sitting on Davey's face and one's sitting on his peter. Imagine how you'd feel if you were his mom."

"I cannot," Kiet said.

"Yeah, likewise. Satan asks you what you want for Christmas, this is what you ask for. Mrs. Peterson, well, she's throwing a fit. Davey stealing twenty mil she can semiforgive. Davey a filthy lecher, uh-uh. She grabs him by the ankles and yanks him out from under the babes like he was a tablecloth.

"The girls start getting testy because they haven't been paid. They're calling Mrs. Peterson names. Mrs. Peterson starts swinging her purse. The babes cut their losses and split. Mrs. Peterson calls the law and has Davey arrested."

"This took place when?" Kiet asked.

"Week and a half ago."

"And the prisoner was released to your custody for extradition approximately a week ago?"

"Yep."

"He escaped your custody here in Seattle and was subsequently murdered?"

"Yes and no. He gave me the slip in L.A. He was shot and toasted in his car in Seattle."

"L.A. as in Los Angeles La La Land?"

"Uh, yeah. See, one reason we went to L.A. is that none of the twenty mil was recovered except the cash Davey was carrying to pay the hookers. He said he'd turn the loot in to me if we could fly to Luong via L.A., which isn't that much farther if you figure out the air miles."

"*One* reason?"

"I'll get to that. Oh shit!"

"What?"

"Swivel your chair a little, Superintendent. Not so fast. Play it cool. Those two goons by the drinking fountain. They're faking like they're reading newspapers."

Kiet saw two young men in cutoff jeans and sleeveless shirts. They were cursed with the chemically enhanced physiques of weightlifters. Their heads seemed to be attached to their torsos not by necks but rather by shoulders that sloped upward to their ears.

"They were here last night when I was looking for you," Binh went on. "They stuck to me like a bad smell. I ditched them by getting on a parking garage elevator as the door was closing. I got off on the next level and hid under a car for forty-five minutes."

"Plainclothes police officers?"

"No way. They would've hauled me in for questioning."

"As a person of interest?"

"Yeah. My description was even in the papers. I haven't been charged, but I'm the *número uno* suspect in Davey's death. Davey and I had, well, a little rumble down in L.A., Anaheim to be technical."

"You will get to that, I'm sure."

"Yeah. Later. What do we do about Tweedledee and Tweedledum?"

"Prove to me that they are a menace," Kiet said. "Come."

He took Binh on a circuitous stroll through the terminal. They walked briskly and did not look back. They entered a gift shop and went to the magazines and books. Kiet said relax, we'll take our time. Binh, an automobile buff, said okay and browsed car magazines. Kiet scanned a section of magazines that specialized in true crime stories. Peculiar, he mused. If the publications were a statistical gauge, the favorite American felony was dismemberment of virgins.

"Let's have a peek," he said to Binh.

"There they are, Superintendent. Them and their newspapers. You know they really aren't reading. Their lips aren't moving. Any more suggestions?"

The goons were across the lobby, outside another shop. In a window beside the goons was a sign offering photocopy and fax services. Fax, Kiet thought. Facsimile machines.

"Yes," he said. "Indeed I do have a suggestion. Follow me."

Kiet and Binh walked quickly to an airline ticket counter. Kiet selected one without a line.

"Two seats on your next flight, please."

"To where?" the agent asked Kiet.

"What is presently boarding?"

"What is presently boarding to where, sir?"

"Your next departure," Kiet said.

"You don't care where?"

"We care when," Kiet said.

"Flight 753 to Oklahoma City is boarding."

"Splendid. Two last-row seats, please."

"Can do. Seven-five-three is wide open."

On the concourse, Binh said, "He looked at *us* like people have been looking at you."

"Walk faster. We don't want to miss the airplane."

"Jesus," Binh said. "Oklahoma City? What's cooking, Superintendent?"

"Just do what I do."

They boarded and gave their passes to a flight attendant. Turbines began to whine. One of the goons lumbered on, his face as red as a pomegranate. He went forward to his seat without a glance at his prey.

"You and me and him in Oklahoma," Binh whispered. "The Three Musketeers. Terrific."

Kiet could see the door. The boarding ramp edged away from the threshold. He got up and said, "Excuse me. It is not working."

"I beg your pardon?" said the flight attendant.

22

"Our fear-of-flying seminar. This was to be our final exam, but we cannot go through with it."

"I'm so sorry," she said. "Leon."

Leon, on the ramp, in white overalls, flicked a lever. The ramp rejoined the aircraft.

"This is embarrassing," Kiet said.

"Try hypnosis," the flight attendant said sweetly. "It did the trick for a friend of mine."

In the terminal, Binh, looking around, grinning broadly, said, "Slick, Superintendent. Slick. Bravo. I'll bet the other Neanderthal's heading home to wait for a call."

Kiet snapped his fingers. "Zeppo."

"Damn!" Binh said. "Ten feet behind us. Guess who."

4

Binh assumed charge of the escape. He said pick 'em up, lay 'em down, haul ass, Superintendent, follow me, we'll make the son of a bitch eat our dust. Kiet obeyed, although running on an escalator seemed an affront to the engineers who had, after all, designed the device for speed and convenience. It also seemed futile. The second young goon was striding a parallel staircase, attention affixed on his newspaper. He was nonchalantly holding the paper by a corner that he had wadded into a ball. Blood vessels were raised on his legs, arms, and neck. His mouth was pinched like a fist and he should have been blinded by his beetle brows. Kiet had never seen such a creature.

Outside, Binh grabbed Kiet by a sleeve and steered him into a courtesy van. They took the last two seats. The driver closed the sliding door and crept into heavy traffic.

Kiet saw the goon almost tear the door from a taxi three vehicles behind and lunge into it. He said, "Captain, this van belongs to a hotel. The hotel's name is painted on—"

24

"I know, I know, Superintendent. Determined as he is, he'd stick on us like glue, regardless. This hotel, I know it like the back of my hand. We'll turn Tweedledee around in circles. It's laid out with separate buildings that won't quit, like a high school. I stayed there my first two days in that country. I picked—met Marge in the cocktail lounge. That hotel, I'll tell you, it holds some bittersweeet memories."

Kiet nudged Binh, reminding him that they were not alone.

"Huh? Oops."

Their fellow passengers were trying with difficulty to mind their own business and aim their eyes forward. Upon entering the van Kiet had glimpsed name tags. He and his adjutant were sharing the van with conventioneering members of an association of mortuary cosmetologists. Kiet surmised that these professionals were naturally curious, absorbing every syllable of Binh's chatter.

They rode the fifteen minutes between airport and destination in silence. The hotel was one block and a long curving driveway from the highway. It was a series of low buildings linked by enclosed walkways. The van deposited them under a canopy.

"The lobby," Binh said. "Here's where we lose him. We've got options coming out our ears. Corridors, conference rooms, restaurants, bars. It's a maze."

"I hope so," Kiet said. "Our friend just disembarked his taxi. I didn't see him open the door. Perhaps he did wrench it from the cab when he got in at the airport."

"Steroid City," Binh said. "The son of a bitch is nuclear powered, all the stuff he must shoot and gobble. Thataway, Superintendent."

They quickstepped out a fire exit, into a parking lot, shortcut through a flower bed, trampling somebody's hard work, through a chain-link gate to an outdoor swimming pool, skirted it and went out the other side and into a building.

"Do you believe those people on the van, Superintendent?

This place is crawling with them. Applying makeup to stiffs for a living—that's gross."

Binh was setting a brisk pace. Kiet's legs and lungs ached. "Who are the goons?"

"I'd have to guess. Are you okay, Superintendent? You sound kind of hoarse."

"I am fine. Stop for a minute."

"Good idea," Binh said, peering out the glass door toward the pool. "We'll see if our boy is even lukewarm. Him and his pal, well, you know, figure it out. Everybody thinks I killed Davey. Why did I kill him? Easy. For the twenty million. They played the odds I was hanging loose in Seattle. They lucked out at the airport yesterday and spotted me. I had on the same disguise. How they recognized me, I'll never know."

"Amazing yet true," Kiet said.

"They would've iced me last night except that they came to the obvious conclusion I was waiting for a contact. I wasn't blowing town, bugging out. Ergo, the twenty mil is maybe not exactly in my hot little hands. You're maybe the missing puzzle part, the magic ingredient, the catalyst that'll make them fabulously rich."

"Splendid," Kiet said.

"Add their IQs together and you'd still be three points shy of parsley, but they know we've made them. Discretion is down the ol' crapper. Having us in their sights is the bottom line. You and me, we're the key to the money. Tweedledee will dog us until he can isolate us. He'll kidnap us and tread water till Tweedledum jets in from Oklahoma City. Then the two of them, they'll torture us until we give them the twenty big ones. Then they'll kill us, chop us into pieces, bag us up in garden trash bags, and bury us in some landfill."

"Wonderful," Kiet said. "Is the fact that we do not have the money significant?"

Binh shrugged. "Nah. They don't know that. They'll just torture us longer than they'd planned to and be super pissed off while they're carting us to the landfill. Speaking of Tweedledee."

"Where?"

"In the pool area. He's stomping chaise lounges and swallowing rubber duckies whole."

"You are exaggerating, yes?"

"Slightly, Superintendent. Slightly. He hasn't seen us yet, but he will. Let's go."

They made a left, a right, another left, and came to a conference room, Binh moving like an Olympic race walker, Kiet like a prisoner of war on a forced march. A smiling man was standing by a poster: KEN BOLLING THIN 'N' RICH DYNAMIC DEVELOPMENT SEMINARS, INC. The man had a deep suntan, hair slicked straight back, an expensive pinstriped suit, and a pinkie ring. He was greeting passersby, saying that the presentation was about to commence and that it was free and that it would change their lives.

"Ken Bolling," Binh said, frowning. "The name registers. How come?"

"How come?" Kiet repeated.

"I don't know, but when I saw Ken Bolling, Davey popped into my head. It's perfect, Superintendent. We'll cool it in there. When the seminar's finished, Tweedledee will've given up. He'll be long gone, home, skulking under the bridge where he lives."

"David Peterson, Jr.?"

"I'm not saying there's a connection. I'm just saying that one name associates with the other."

"Good," Kiet said. "I do not wish to die for the sake of a coincidence."

"Nobody's dying, Superintendent. Not if we scoot inside *mucho quicko*. Tweedledee might be in another wing right now, but he can motor. Come on, it's free."

The conference room was crowded with people. Kiet observed that a considerable percentage were overweight and badly dressed. In front was a podium, a chest-type food freezer and a table stacked high with looseleaf binders and audiocassette tape holders. Videotape cameras were mounted on tripods at the rear corners of the room. Camera operators peered into eyepieces while doing a finger dance on buttons and switches, evidently making final adjustments.

The greeter came in, walked to the podium, grinning and waving at the audience. A man by a side door held up a sign: APPLAUSE. The audience applauded.

"He struts," Kiet said.

"He's just sure of himself, Superintendent. He knows who he is. Don't be so critical."

"I don't know who he is," Kiet said. "I know what he is. He is a salesman. He admitted us free to sell us whatever it is he sells."

Binh lifted a shoulder. "No sweat. Hey, if we have to buy to maintain our cover, we'll buy."

The man slapped a flat midsection with one hand and thrust out a wad of U.S. currency with the other.

"Hi," he said. "I'm Ken Bolling. Who wants to become thin and rich?"

Without prompting by the man with the sign, the audience applauded, cheered and whistled.

"Buy?" Kiet said. "How, please? I have barely enough cash to live in this exorbitant country one week."

"Not to worry, Superintendent," Binh said, winking, clapping his hands. "I've got plastic."

5

"In general, Superintendent, Soft Springs Motel sucks, but this is groovy."

Binh's "groovy" was for the circular waterbed. He was seated yoga-fashion in its middle, bobbing up and down, sending swells to the perimeter, a pulsing wash, back and forth, back and forth. Kiet looked away.

"A hot-sheet motel of the grungiest magnitude," Binh said, laughing. "It smells like an Albanian gang bang. I wouldn't be surprised if they rented rooms by the hour. How did you wind up in this fleabag?"

"A taxi driver asked me if I wanted a good time."

"Yeah, I guess you could. You can buy rubbers in the bathroom. I wouldn't go in there to do anything else if I were you. There's probably germs growing on the porcelain we don't even have at home. Those beaver flicks they rent over at the office, I don't suppose, as devoted to Quin as you are, that you've—"

"No," Kiet said.

Binh bounded off the bed and fumbled in a pants pocket. "Well, it still pisses me off that in a dump like this you have to plug quarters into the TV."

"May we watch television later, Captain? We need to talk."

"Sure, but let me warm it up," Binh said, inserting coins in the slot. "It's so old I bet it's powered by vacuum tubes. I guess you have a few questions, huh?"

"Beginning with David Peterson, Jr.," Kiet said. "Your custody, La La Lotus Land, escape, murder, Anaheim brouhaha, et cetera."

Binh sat heavily on the bed and sighed. "A long story, Superintendent."

"Save time and start with you escorting Davey to L.A. for *one* reason."

"Do you know what Disneyland is?"

Kiet nodded. "A vast amusement park."

"Right. You know how I've always wanted to see it."

"No."

"Well, I do. Did. Davey said he'd never been to Disneyland either. He said that he'd converted the twenty mil into cash and diamonds and had it stored in a locker somewhere in Greater Los Angeles. So, hell, I figure, Davey's pretty docile and cooperative and remorseful, right, so what's the harm of killing two or three birds with one stone? He really sold me a bill of goods and 'The Dating Game' was the icing on the cake."

Binh's clichés, Kiet thought. They are blackening the sky like locusts. "Excuse me?"

" 'The Dating Game' is a syndicated TV series where an unmarried person questions three unmarried members of the opposite sex who're on the other side of a screen."

"Interrogation?"

"Sort of. You ask things like 'If your date brought a can of whipped cream along on a first date, what would you think?' The bottom line is that the bachelor or bachelorette who's picked goes on an all-expenses-paid weekend with the picker to somewhere neat like Acapulco. The girls they have on the show are knockouts and the guys are mostly geeks.

"I sincerely believe I'd've had a real shot at winning, and Davey convinced me that a former fraternity brother of his was a producer on the show and could get me on. He'd bump somebody and get me on immediately. Davey said it would take a few days to recover the loot anyhow and I figured I could have him held in a local jail down there while I was on the show.

"I know what you're thinking, Superintendent, but isn't recovery of the loot top priority? I mean, sure, I took some calculating and self-serving risks, but the twenty mil was utmost in my mind."

"The dating program would provide you a girl and send you on an exotic vacation to have sex with her?"

"No, no, no. You misunderstand, Superintendent. Everything's on the up and up. No hanky panky. You're accompanied by a chaperone. Of course, if you and your date happen to hit it off, if that certain magic chemistry occurs and the urge to jump one another's bones is irresistible, well, when there's a hormone there's a way."

Binh paused and sighed again. "Unfortunately, 'The Dating Game' situation is irrelevant. Davey, the two-faced, four-eyed bastard, he stroked me and stroked me good. We did Disneyland before we were to meet his fictional producer buddy. Disneyland was my Waterloo. Specifically, Pirates of the Caribbean."

On the television a professional golfer was squatting, studying the topography of a putting green. Oddly, the announcer was whispering. Otherwise, Kiet would have turned off the set, Binh's monetary investment be damned. He began to ask a question, but stopped himself. Binh's monologue was too rich with non sequiturs. What would he ask?

"I'll save you the trouble of asking, Superintendent. Whether you're aware of it or not, your lips formed a question mark. Pirates of the Caribbean is a super-nifty Disneyland ride. You're in these underground rail cars. You get wet, splashed, and pirates and creatures surprise you as you zip around bends and rises.

"Davey and I loved it. We rated it right up there with the Matterhorn. It was on our third Pirates of the Caribbean ride that he slid out of the handcuffs. He must've loosened them a notch or greased the heel of his hand. He jumped the car and hauled ass."

"Handcuffs?"

"Of course handcuffs," Binh said indignantly. "You trained me yourself. Do you truly think I'd transport a prisoner *anywhere* without cuffing him?"

"Of course not."

"Well, I bailed out of the car too and the chase was on. He had a lead on me and, dollars to doughnuts, he'd done his homework on the internal layout of Pirates. He's a technical genius, you know. I had a hassle or three with employees who didn't like having a visitor running amok backstage, as it were. I somehow made it outside and that's when the ducks and mice jumped me."

Kiet suppressed a groan. "Ducks and mice?"

"Security ducks and mice. They wander around, patting toddlers on the head and stuff like that, but it's not smart to rile them up. I don't think they're really security police, but that didn't do me a whole bunch of good."

"No. I would presume not," Kiet said. The professional golfer's topographical research had been fruitless. The ball halted a centimeter from the hole. Unseen spectators wailed, "Ohhhhhh."

"In retrospect, they were just doing their jobs. They were as nice as you could be under the circumstances. Well, Davey was nowhere to be seen and I kind of went apeshit, screaming and hollering his description at people. Which way did he go, have you seen him, make a citizen's arrest if you do, and so on. This duck carrying a walkie-talkie came up to me and I was explaining the situation as fast as I could, speed being of the essence. He said to calm down, the cops were coming.

"Obviously, the cops were coming for me, not Davey. It didn't click in the heat of the moment, but the handcuffs were hanging from *my* wrist, so you can't blame them. I tried to push by him, saying I had to head Davey off at the main gate. He grabbed me. I swung. My fist's still sore. Those plastic beaks hurt like crazy. I staggered him, though. He released his grip. But then a mouse tackled me. A second duck leaped on my back and rode me down to the ground and they all sat on me. I didn't have a prayer."

"Indeed not." The whispering announcer, the wailing fans, and the distraught golfer had been replaced by dancing soft drink cans. Waltzing carbonated beverages were not incongruous with a duck and mouse constabulary, but the violins grated Kiet's ears. He turned off the sound.

"Disneyland is in Anaheim. They held me for the Anaheim P.D. who hauled me in. I finally got it across to those people who I was and what the situation was. Some Disneyland PR guys came by and they agreed not to press charges, but the guy in the duck outfit I nailed, he went ahead and signed a complaint. Anaheim P.D. didn't have any choice. They had to book me for assault and battery.

"The little twerp said that my punch rotated the duck's head and his too, wrenching his neck. It gave him whiplash. Disneyland is a summer job. He's going to be a senior at USC. Pre-law, wouldn't you know. My attorney said that the assault charge is phony, leverage for a civil suit. My attorney says you can't look cross-eyed at anybody in Southern Cal without giving them whiplash. I settle out of court with the little turd bird, pay him some damages, and he drops the criminal charges. That's a fact of life, the way the ol' cookie crumbles."

"Your attorney?"

"My initially assigned attorney, Superintendent. He works for this huge legal chain. My file's been transferred up here to one of their Seattle offices and reassigned to a different attorney. They had a TV on by the booking desk and I saw a commercial for the law firm and a 1-800 number. Talk about lucky timing. You're permitted one phone call. Two hours later I was out on personal recognizance, owing primarily, I'm sure, to my law enforcement background. But, as I have outlined, I'm in a helluva lot bigger jam now."

"You are a person of interest," Kiet said.

"Yeah, to put it mildly. I was pretty sure Davey would head home where he has friends and family, so I came north. His body was found a couple of days later on an upscale, suburban Seattle golf course. He was in a stolen car. It'd been doused with gasoline and set on fire. There was also a bullet hole in his skull. Him and his car, they were burned to a crisp. There wasn't much left of Davey. The medical examiner hasn't issued a report yet and the police won't put a warrant out on me until there's been a positive ID, but that's a formality, just a matter of time. The local media had some footage and stills of my skirmish at Disneyland. It's died down now, but I was lead-story stuff."

"A golf course," Kiet said, gazing at the resumption of televised golf.

Binh rubbed his stomach. "Are you hungry?"

"No. Too much excitement, too much intellectual stimulation. Please, Captain, don't wait on me."

In a trash bucket packed with ice were Cuisine By Ken frozen dinners. Binh looked at the bucket wistfully and said, "Too bad we're not at the house. It has a microwave and a fridge with an enormous freezer compartment. I could nuke a salisbury steak in three minutes. Ah well. Dutch chocolate ain't all that shabby. If I'm not back in thirty seconds, call an exterminator and the Center for Disease Control."

Binh took a plastic cup and a can of Cuisine By Ken food supplement into the bathroom. He came out, stirring his drink with a finger, raised it to his lips, then said, "Okay. It'd be better with milk instead of water, but okay. Six on a scale of ten."

House? Too bad we're not at the house? Kiet resisted. Earlier confusions took precedence. "Captain, you purchased the Ken Bolling Thin 'n' Rich Dynamic Development package for $699 with a credit card—"

Binh went to the television and switched the dial. "Ken Bolling is king of paid programming, Superintendent. What do you bet he's on at this very moment?"

"King of—excuse me?"

"Paid programming. Half-hour and one-hour commercials. They're known as infomercials. Info-mercials. They sell everything from car polish to food processors to cellulite removal to getting rich quick in real estate. They're listed in the TV schedule as paid programming. You see them on weekends, and in the middle of the night, on independent stations that don't charge much.

"Ken Bolling is the king. He's on the most and he has the slickest gimmick. He sells weight loss and self-image improvement, two of the paid programming biggies. You get two for the price of one. He's inspirational, don't you think? Drop some pounds, feel good about yourself, and you've got the world by the ass. He's a huckster, but he could do some good. Believe fervently enough and Ken'll turn your miserable life around."

"Seven hundred dollars," Kiet said. "A dear price."

Binh gestured at a stack of books and cassettes. "Well, it might be a bargain as I was just saying. You eat Ken's food and you listen to and read the motivational material—"

Binh clapped his hands. "The Ken Bolling—Davey Peterson connection. Yeah, Davey'd talked about the program."

"David Peterson, Jr. had been a subscriber?"

"I'm not certain. Davey mentioned Ken maybe once or twice. Wait, once he let it drop that Bolling was a ladies' man, a big-time lover boy, so it stands to reason that he knew him."

35

"Davey subscribed prior to going to Luong?" Kiet asked.

"Could be."

"I wonder if Davey Peterson paid with a credit card," Kiet said, looking at Binh. "Plastic."

"That's a fascinating story," Binh said, cracking a smile. He removed his wallet and allowed a fanfold of clear plastic to drop. Inside the clear plastic was opaque plastic. Cards. Kiet counted an even dozen. "Bank cards, Superintendent. It's wild!"

"How did you obtain them?"

"You call these 1-900 numbers. They get cards for people with lousy credit or, in my situation, no credit history. Then these fliers come in the mail. They were coming to the house addressed to Occupant or Current Resident. Their computers must've told them that it was an upscale address despite the fact that nobody officially lives there.

"Whether you mail or phone in, you receive your cards superfast. They give you low limits to start with, so that's why I applied for so many. Max one out, move on to the next card, right?"

"Captain—"

"They're all from out-of-state banks. Figure this, a New York bank incorporated in Delaware issuing you your card out of South Dakota. The state of Washington has tough usury laws. Doing it from out-of-state, the banks can really zing you for interest, but, hell, it's only plastic. We'll pay the cards off when we recoup the twenty big ones."

"Captain—"

"Hey, here's Ken, Superintendent."

Handsome, suntanned, glib Ken Bolling was sitting with giddily satisfied customers, backdropped by a tropical beach. Kiet and Binh watched the customers tell Ken how his Thin 'n' Rich Dynamic Development had transformed them from unattractive wage slaves to hot items with Cadillacs, without overhanging guts. Except for the insipid smiles and the Hawaiian shirts, unbuttoned to showcase clunky gold necklaces, they looked remarkably similar to the underclass types in their seminar room. A 1-800 number blinked incessantly on the screen.

"He does weekend seminars like we attended today," Binh explained, "but his biggie is telemarketing."

"Telemarketing," Kiet said, recognizing the North American euphemism. "Boiler rooms. Mr. Bolling's pitch has the tone and cadence of an evangelical missionary."

"Whatever," Binh said. "They were taping today, you know. We may see ourselves on the air."

"Splendid."

"It won't do any harm to listen to some tapes and, essentially, we've got ourselves free grub. Given my druthers, though, I'd opt for peanut butter, white bread, and whole milk. I could live on those groceries."

"Peanut what?"

"Jesus H. Christ! Look, Superintendent."

Flashing brilliantly with the 1-800 number were Ken Bolling's eyes and teeth, and a special, fantabulous, one-time $599 offer.

"How do you like that? A hundred bucks less than I paid. The crook."

"It's only plastic, Captain. Speak to me about your Marge, please."

"She isn't mine. Don't I wish she were. We met in the lounge of that motel, right? Her name is Marge Mainwaring. She sells real estate and is super at it. Her firm runs ads in the Sunday paper and her picture is always in it with the other top producers. For an old gal, Superintendent, Marge's really a fox. I've never been attracted to an older woman before, you know."

"How old?"

"She's forty if she's a day."

"Ancient," Kiet muttered.

"Unattainability might be a factor too. The mind and the libido hook up and play funny tricks on you. I got her up to my room the first night, but no dice. You know why? This is really weird, Superintendent."

"What in this conversation has not been weird?"

"Marge says it goes back to college and a Chinese guy who got her cherry. She's been hung up on Chinese guys ever since. She says I'm a dead ringer for him, how he looked way back in her college days."

"You are not Chinese," Kiet reminded him.

Binh shrugged. "Close enough. We all look the same to Americans. I'm coming on to her, but she's continuing to shut me down cold. We still have a cordial professional arrangement, although that's going to hell in a handbasket, all the work I've been missing."

"Enlighten me."

"Yeah, right, the job. Marge's real estate firm has the exclusive sales rights on this new upmarket tract on the Eastside. I'm night watchman. I stay in the model home and keep an eye on the other sites. Some of the houses aren't done yet. Theft of building materials is an epidemic crime. I initially accepted her offer of the job to have a free roof over my head. My motel bill was adding up."

"Doesn't Marge Mainwaring read the newspapers?" Kiet asked.

"Just the business and real estate sections. I see where you're coming from. Not to worry, I'm kind of incognito. I'm in town on a big law-enforcement-executive conference. I told her it was finished before I went to Anaheim. When I returned, I needed a cover, needed it big-time. I told Marge the conference had been extended. Luckily she hadn't filled my job. Superintendent, you look bushed. Delayed jet lag. It's common."

Kiet nodded. Airliner fatigue? he thought. No. It was a sudden onset of non sequitur and illogic-overdose syndrome. Too much confusion, too fast.

"Why don't I head out? I'll catch a cab to Marge's office. She'll drive me to the house. I'll make some points. Maybe she'll even loan me her Lincoln. Rest and we'll get down to brass tacks tomorrow. We can't accomplish much on a Sunday anyhow."

"All right, tomorrow," Kiet said, raising a finger. "Our mission: Exonerate you of Davey Peterson's murder."

"Uh-huh."

"And do so without consulting the local authorities, who might charge you if we do."

"I can relate to that."

Kiet raised a second finger. "The money."

"Uh-huh."

Kiet lowered the fingers and raised one again. "The two goons. They might be a pathway."

"Granted."

He raised a third finger. "Your lawyer. Perhaps he can assist us."

"Yeah. We'd better check in with him. Their Seattle office says my case is assigned to a Doug Zane. I'll make an appointment first thing in the A.M. Again, thanks a million, okay?"

"Thank me after we have succeeded."

Binh bounced hard on the waterbed, stood, looked at it, and said, "Surf's up. Catch some z's, Superintendent."

6

Binh came for Kiet the next morning in an automobile longer than the motel room. The young adjutant was sleek and casual in denims and rugby shirt. He had discarded the glasses and mustache, abandoning the effort at Marx Brotherdom, saying that if two butt-uglies with the IQ of toejam could make him, what was the advantage?

Kiet was logy from fifteen hours' sleep and did not protest the clothing Binh had brought for him. You insist you're chilly, you insist on dressing like an Eskimo, Binh had said, we're gonna get your act together, you're gonna match.

The stocking cap and sweatshirt fit better than the infamous Denver-Raider combination. Kiet critiqued himself in a mirror and concluded that the green-and-blue raptor's head of the Seattle Seahawk printed on each item was rather attractive. Binh seconded the opinion, saying inscrutably that if the superintendent had to look like he walked away from some institution he at least wasn't gonna be jumped by a demented fan, pissed that the Broncos and Raiders had aced out the Hawks in the AFC West again, in spite of it being the off-season, NFL squads not due to report to camp till later in the month, fasten chinstraps, and play wild-ass take-no-prisoners smashface before early August, but football fans, ticket holders and couch potatoes alike, they live and die for their ball clubs.

Kiet did not ask Binh to decode the marathon sentence. He did thank him for the warm apparel and asked if he had purchased them with the plastic. Dumbfounded, Binh had asked, *how else?*

The automobile was silver and chromium. The interior was lush and fragrant.

"Isn't it gorgeous?" Binh asked. "Eleven hundred total miles. A Lincoln Town Car hot off the showroom floor with all the bells and whistles. Marge paid a bundle. Do you feel anything, Superintendent, hear anything?"

"Excuse me?"

"The ride and the soundproofing. You could run over a pothole the size of Rhode Island and not be disturbed one iota. I'd give my eyeteeth to have a Lincoln dealership in Hickorn. They'd sell like hotcakes. The upper class would glom on to a fully loaded Town Car. Are you making an ostentatious statement or what, right? It's a damn shame our streets are so narrow."

"Marge Mainwaring was generous to loan it to you."

"She was, yeah. We lucked out too. Marge usually takes Mondays off, but she has this prospect. Normally she'd chauffeur him and his family in the Lincoln, but the house she's showing is a ranch-style cracker box. Three bedrooms, bath and a half, one-car garage. It's listed at only a hundred and fifty-five thousand."

"Dollars?"

"Yeah. A cheapie. Houses go for a mint in the States. Marge's taking them out in her '82 Celebrity. It's her second car and she keeps it for these kinds of situations, where you don't want to come on too uppity and ostentatious-like, you know."

"One hundred and fifty-five thousand American dollars," Kiet said softly. "For a house."

"Yup. Imagine what your villa would sell for. Marge and I have speculated about it."

Kiet owned a small home in Hickorn. A wall surrounding a modest courtyard defined the property as a villa. The term was more impressive than the structure, Kiet thought; I have two fewer bedrooms and one less bathroom than Marge Mainwaring's "cracker box."

They were on a freeway, a link in a sixty-mile-per-hour chain of steel, glass, and impatient humanity. Kiet asked, "Where are the skyscrapers?"

"Huh?"

"The downtown office towers. They are in every photograph I have seen of important American cities. They are central, like a cluster of crystals. They strike me as competitive."

"Yeah. Phallic, if you think about it," Binh said.

"When, please, will we be nearing them?"

"We won't, Superintendent. Not today."

"Are not the majority of the tenants in the downtown towers law firms? I read once that American lawyers are multiplying like rodents. They fill the skyscrapers the moment they are built and dedicated. Am I correct?"

"Well, yes and no. Yes, there are beaucoup attorneys. Seattle alone has in excess of five thousand. And, yes, the big boys concentrate downtown."

"Your lawyer?"

"Uh, that's the 'no,' Superintendent. Not downtown."

"When? Where?"

Binh swerved across two lanes to the far right-hand lane. Toyotas and Volkswagens, bullied by the ponderous Lincoln, braked and honked and extended middle digits. Binh went off an exit and said, "Soon, Superintendent. The mall."

"Once upon a time this was farmland," Binh said, as they approached the mall. "Maybe twenty-five years ago they started developing. It's a good example of what you can accomplish when you set your mind to it."

The feeder road went downhill. Kiet could discern, though barely, that the mall was nestled in a valley. That type of terrain could be richly alluvial, an agricultural treasure, but not a solitary paddy was in sight. Not enough unpaved land remained for an urban vegetable garden. The mall's neighbors were industrial parks, factory outlet warehouses, fast food emporiums, multiplex cinemas, and smaller malls.

"Why do the little malls exist so close to the big mall?" Kiet asked.

"They're called strip malls, Superintendent. It's a free country. They're cutting the mustard or they wouldn't be in business."

A peculiar duplication, Kiet thought. Surely there were vendors of blue jeans and furniture within the principal mall. He conjured up a litter of weaned stores, off on their own to grow into mall adulthood. He kept that thought to himself.

Binh parked close to the mall's mock-marble foyer. It was one level of concrete and glass splayed so far and wide that it filled Kiet's field of vision. At far ends were taller and wider brick edifices. Department stores, Binh said, anchors.

"How many market stalls are inside?" Kiet asked.

"They're called stores and boutiques. A hundred. Maybe two hundred. I don't know. Awesome, huh?"

"Since I am in America I should perform the obligatory foreign tourist rituals."

"Such as?"

"Visit the cathedral. Attend a folk dancing show. Bargain for souvenirs at local markets."

They were out of the car. Binh said, "Good luck."

"How much can one reduce the price on native handicraft such as jewelry?"

"Well, native handicraft is usually made in Taiwan except for some Indian stuff that's made in Arizona. And you don't bargain. They get pissed at you for chiseling, call mall security and have you thrown out. You're after a bargain, you watch the papers for sales."

"The law firm is inside with the shops?"

"Nope. Outside entrance. Dead ahead."

Gilded on the door was Baxter Blenheim Pacific Rim Legal Services PS, Inc. They walked in to worn carpeting, a clinging tobacco odor, and cubicles. A receptionist escorted them to a neck-height roomlet and a man Binh's age with long blond hair and residual acne. He was as bulky in the midsection as Kiet. His white shirt was wrinkled and his tie was loosened.

"Yo, you're my Luongan dudes," he said heartily, rising.

Hands were shaken, introductions made. Doug Zane asked them to take seats, easy choices as there was space only for the two folding chairs.

Zane leafed through a folder. "This was just shipped up from our Anaheim office and I haven't had a chance to—oh, man, you coldcocked Donald?"

Binh shrugged sheepishly. "I sort of lost my cool temporarily."

"Whom?" Kiet asked.

"Donald Duck," Doug Zane told Kiet. "Smacking Donald is tantamount to, like, burning the flag or not liking Bill Cosby."

"That bad?" Binh asked.

"But they have to prove it. They've got the burden thing." Zane flipped a page. "Whoa. Red alert."

"That bad?" Binh asked, peering forward. Documents filed on the Davey Peterson murder, he assumed.

Zane looked at Kiet and said, "How do you think the Hawks are going to do this season."

"Excuse me?"

"You have to be an all-time fan to swelter in that outfit in July, Mr. Kiet. I thought you might belong to the booster club and have some insider poop."

Kiet looked at Binh. Binh told Zane, "Well, they should have a dynamite pass rush, but the secondary's vulnerable to the long bomb. On offense, the ball-control passing game is the equal of anybody's. A breakaway tailback wouldn't hurt, and special teams have to be more consistent. Ten wins isn't beyond the realm of possibility."

Kiet, dazed, nodded at Zane and said, "Indeed."

"You can buy tanktops and lightweight jerseys, you know," Zane advised Kiet. "Even on a dude in your age range, they look bitchin'. There's a shop on the north end of the mall that handles NFL—"

"Mr. Zane, your red alert, please?"

"I'm afraid they're homing in for the kill."

"The police are going to indict him?" Kiet asked.

"Shit," Binh said.

"Police? What police?" Zane said. "The plaintiff will drop the charges if we fork over the bucks."

Kiet pointed at the folder. "Are you perusing the correct file?"

"Affirmative, man. Hickorn. I took a year of Japanese in college. This Hickorn place you guys are from. I love old movies. There's this cable channel that shows nothing but Bob Hope, Bing Crosby, Dorothy Lamour. I loved those flicks they made. Did they ever do *Road to Hickorn?*"

"No," Kiet said.

"Too late now," Zane said. "You're the honchos of the Hickorn Police department?"

"Right," Binh said.

"Awesome. You should be able to give me your liability limits."

Kiet deferred to Binh, who better comprehended the arcane idioms of the English language. Binh shook his head no.

"Limits on the liability coverage you carry on your police department."

"Insurance?" Binh asked.

"Oh God," Zane said, moaning. "What do you do when somebody accuses you of brutality or traffic negligence?"

"If they are too loud and disrespectful, we arrest them," Kiet said.

"Insurance is kind of a new concept in Luong, Doug," Binh said.

"The kid in the duck costume is building a case. They learn it young in L.A. They say 'tort' before they say 'mama.' He's already got a grand in bills from a chiropractor and five hundred in physical therapy. This faxed letter from his attorney to our Anaheim people references blurred vision, numb fingertips, and a neurology appointment. Neurologists. Those suckers can rack up a tab faster than the Pentagon does. And you don't have dollar one in protection!"

"I am relieved," Kiet said.

"Relieved. Listen, they'll be whipping a hummer of a suit on us before you can say whiplash and you're relieved? The plaintiff's preparing to finish his USC degree on your tab. Law school afterward. Then he'll retire. And you're relieved?"

"We are merely visiting," Kiet said. "The matriculating duck cannot sue us after we are home in Luong. His injuries are fraudulent, yes? When he realizes we are unavailable to pay, he will suddenly recover."

Doug Zane smiled. "I can dig it. No harm, no foul. So why are you bothering to bop in on us?"

"The murder, of course," Kiet said.

"Murder?" said a bug-eyed Zane.

Kiet groaned.

"Doug, let me explain," Binh said.

And he did.

Zane listened, absently scratching a neck zit, then said, "Whoa, homicide. Davey Peterson. Fuzzy recall. Tweak the static out of the gray matter, Dougie. Yeah. A computer nerd.

A genius. University of Washington dropout. It was on the news. Peterson embezzled money in Asia and was shot in the beanie and roasted in a car on the thirteenth green at Enchanted Lakes. My electives at law school swayed toward the persuasion of civil, but I'm looking forward to the experience."

"Your prior criminal law experience, please?"

"DWI. Possession of marijuana. An alleged assault case, stemming from the goosing of a cocktail waitress and the ensuing brawl."

Kiet closed his eyes.

"If body language could kill," Doug Zane said. "It's me, isn't it? Is it me or the firm?"

"I admit to a certain image of a Western lawyer, Yupster and Postyupster," Kiet said, staring at Zane. The Antichrist of Western religious lore came to mind. This bohemian, he would be to his contemporaries the Antiyuppie.

Doug Zane smirked. "Yeah. I can dig it. Pomp, Circumstance and Shyster. Seventieth floor of the Columbia Center. Won't speak to you unless you're Fortune 500. It's reality-check time, Mr. Kiet. We provide legal services for John Q. Public and you're him."

"Tell me about your law firm, please."

"Rim Legal, as we're known, is the biggest legal chain on the West Coast. Thirty-six offices from the Canadian border to within eyeshot of Tijuana. I could retire on our annual ad budget."

"What, please, is a Baxter Blenheim?"

"Mr. Blenheim was our founder, Lord rest his soul."

"How did he die?"

"You'd have to ask that. Killed in prison by a client."

Kiet groaned.

Zane spread his palms. "I'm making no apologies. Bax may have fallen a hair short in the ethics department, but he was a bitchin' marketing man. You see our ads everywhere. On the sides of buses, on bar napkins."

"On holding-tank TVs," Binh said.

Zane raised a thumb. "There you go."

Kiet looked at the wall behind Zane at a framed diploma. "Your law degree?"

"Eastern Nevada School of Law," Zane said proudly. "It ain't Harvard Law, but you receive a lot of personal attention from the profs. I edited the law review too. You can poke fun at it because we ran it off the last mimeograph machine in captivity, but, hey, what I'm trying to articulate is, murder, it's a trip.

"Qualifications? F. Lee and the hall of famers, they had their first homicide somewhere, sometime."

"True," Kiet conceded.

"Regard it from this slant. I can be as venal and inefficient as the big boys. I've attended billing seminars and I'm lousy about returning phone calls. I can chase ambulances like a fox on a hare. So what's the diff?"

"Excellent points, Superintendent," Binh said.

"Logically persuasive," Kiet conceded.

"I won't screw you as bad on the charges and I'm sort of accessible. Furthermore, this case cries for investigation and I need the practice."

"We intend to investigate," Kiet said.

"Rim legal uses private detectives."

"Private eyes?" Kiet asked. "Good private eyes?"

"Of course not. Cheap private eyes. They give us a volume discount. You're outsiders. They can pry under rocks you can't. I won't formally hire them. You gents don't look like Daddy Warbucks. I'll just pump them for tips. They want Dougie's assignments, they'll do Dougie a favor. I also have connections downtown with SPD and the medical examiner's office. You guys snoop on your own, but stay out of mischief."

"Good downtown connections?"

Zane shrugged. "I might get lucky."

"How about it, Superintendent?"

"Yes," Kiet said glumly. "Splendid."

"This is unseemly," Zane said. "But we gotta address it. It says in your file that your retainer is running on empty."

Binh withdrew his wallet. "Does Rim Legal take plastic?"

Zane smiled. "Does a bear allegedly defecate in the woods?"

7

"I like Doug Zane, Superintendent."

You should, Bamsan Kiet thought. You attended the same linguistics academy.

"Doug's unconventional. He's my kind of guy."

"He is your kind of bitchin' dude," Kiet mumbled.

Captain Binh sighed theatrically. "Is sarcasm necessary, Superintendent? Doug'll cut through the bullshit. He'll get things done. These tight-assed Western corporate attorneys you have this image of, well, they'd trot me down to the courthouse to surrender myself to make brownie points with judges and get themselves on the nightly news, and then they'd slap a bill on us that's twice the Luongan national debt."

"Perhaps. But where are we going? Where are my sky-scrapers?" Kiet asked, half teasing. "Is my tourism experience to be exclusively the freeways? When do I experience the city. I am a city boy, Captain. Malls and divided highways are not my conception of America."

"Well, maybe your conception is wrong. As for the city of Seattle proper, later. Can't be avoided. Business before rubbernecking. Enchanted Lakes is a south-end suburb. The hub is a golf course with a planned community built around it. Beaucoup bucks. You don't get club membership with an Enchanted Lakes home, either. That's an extra fifty grand plus annual dues."

"People pay outrageous sums to live adjacent golf courses and have their windows broken by misfired balls?"

"Yeah. Marge could sell the grottiest fixer-upper for a ton in ten seconds flat. There are guys who'd give their family jewels to live on a golf course."

"Since Luong has no golf courses, I have never been on one. What is so powerful an attraction?"

"To be able to go out your patio sliders, walk onto a fairway, and whack the little white ball around. It's an envy situation, you know. The guys at the office turn green."

"Have you ever played, Captain?"

"Nah. In D.C. I was thinking about it. Then I was driving past a course one day out by Chevy Chase and I saw this golfer flogging a cottonwood to death with his five-iron. I figure, hey, he's having so much fun I don't think I could stand it."

Kiet did not pursue the relationship between recreation and tree mutilation. They rode in silence until they left the freeway and Binh asked Kiet to dig the map out of the glove compartment. Binh meandered in a pleasant residential neighborhood with competitive lawns, map on the steering wheel dangerously impeding his vision, cursing cul-de-sacs and four-way stops.

Finally they passed through the gate of Enchanted Lakes Golf and Country Club. The clubhouse was a plantation-style mansion, an impressive duplicate of the grand residence in that wonderful American movie set in the last century, when the United States government fought a Southern insurgency force. Kiet had seen it at a Hickorn cinema. *Gone something* was the title.

"Pretty spiffy, huh?" Binh said.

"Indeed."

Binh parked in a lot and said, "When we go in—"

"No," Kiet interrupted. "Me, not we. Remember, you are a person of interest."

"Yeah, yeah, I guess," Binh said. "No sense jumping out of the low-profile mode unless we have to. I got us here, but the ball's in your court. What's the game plan, Superintendent?"

"Inspection of the crime scene."

"There isn't anything to see, you know. The cops scoured it with a fine-toothed comb."

"True. We may accomplish nothing."

"But, yeah, okay. You'll acquire a feel for the scene. Can't hurt. Forget the office and restaurant. Go right to the pro shop. The club pros, they know every blade of grass."

Kiet followed Binh's advice and a walkway around the building. The pro shop was at the rear. At close proximity the clubhouse's ambience suffered. According to a brass plaque, the antebellum plantation had been erected in A.D. 1975. The white siding was vinyl and the windows were aluminum casement, double-glazed for energy efficiency. Portico pillars may have been hollow fiberglass, but Kiet was too much the gentleman to knock.

In back, golfers were teeing off on the first hole. Kiet could see the quasi-natural flora of roughs and fairways and sand pits. Split-level homes lined them like cubist spectators. Adjacent a bend in the fairway was a body of water too small to fit Kiet's definition of a lake. Although it would never accommodate boats or crocodiles, it was of sufficient surface area to attract golf balls and consequent cries of anguish. The errant drives disturbed a greenish surface film with a *plop* and disappeared. Kiet wondered: malaria?

He went into the pro shop. For sale were irons of polished

silver, putters with brass heads as elegant as gold, and bulbous drivers made of the richest woods. Kiet immediately fell in love with golf for the craftsmanship of its tools alone.

He was not so enthusiastic about the clothing display. Primary colors were evidently in fashion at Enchanted Lakes, whether they be solids or collisions of plaids and checks. Prices on tags attached to cleated shoes would buy a lifetime of sandals in Hickorn.

"I'm an assistant pro. Can I help you?"

Kiet had been mesmerized by slacks so vibrant a green that radioactivity bombardment occurred to him. The individual offering assistance was a trim Caucasian male in his thirties. He was dressed with relentless informality, like Binh, with the addition of an ENCHANTED LAKES GOLF billed cap so brilliantly orange that Kiet conjured up a tangerine going into nova.

Kiet produced his wallet badge.

"Police," the man said, examining it. "This is on the murder?"

"Yes."

"Where's Hickorn?"

"Out of town," Kiet said.

"Why not? We've answered so many questions by so many cops, my dreams are undergoing the third degree. I didn't think you were a club member."

"Why did you presume that I was not a member, please?"

The assistant pro blushed. "I've never seen you around before."

Kiet detected an incipient racism. Orientals need apply only at the kitchen, thank you. For employment. He smiled and stared into eyes that averted.

"It's what you have on too."

"Excuse me?"

"Don't get the wrong idea, I'm a Seahawks fan."

"Oh, I won't get the wrong idea."

"How do you think they'll do, by the way? Are we gonna see them in the playoffs in our lifetime?"

"Dynamite their pass rush and ten wins is not beyond the realm of possibility."

The assistant pro laughed nervously. "You weren't kidding when you said you were from out of town. I'd okay you to play a guest eighteen after your questions, but what you have on, I'm not rapping it, but we do have standards."

"Standards?"

"A dress code. We don't allow T-shirts and sweatshirts."

"You don't?"

"T-shirts and sweatshirts don't have collars. They don't make the grade at Enchanted Lakes. You can wear T-shirts on public courses. They don't care."

Kiet lifted a shirt from a carousel. "This garment has a collar. It meets your standards?"

"Exceeds them. And it's on sale for thirty-nine ninety-five."

"Pink," Kiet said. "A hue like bubble gum spit out at Chernobyl. But, yes, it has a collar."

"I don't make the rules. Interested in the shirt?"

"No, thank you. I am not playing," Kiet said. "Please, may I visit the murder scene?"

"Sure. Everyone else has."

The assistant pro escorted Kiet outside and into an electric cart that protected its riders from the elements with a canvas awning. They purred away. Kiet noticed that golfers, usually clustered in groups of four, were touring the course in carts.

"Nobody walks," he said.

"Some do," the assistant pro said. "Some pull hand carts. On public courses, lots of guys sling bags."

"Golf is a sport?"

"Absolutely. Ask Henry the Eighth."

Golf *must* come to Luong, Kiet thought. His beloved Quin, a nurse, continually urged him to exercise and lose weight. Should a golf facility be established in Hickorn, he would be at the head of the registration line. Golf was a sport. It was therefore exercise. The exertion participating at golf would burn numerous calories and qualify the participant to consume a hearty, postgame meal.

"Fore," Kiet said, mimicking the oft-heard shout. The assistant pro looked at him.

They stopped at the edge of a rounded, velvety patch of grass. Impaled in a hole roughly at the middle was a bannered pole.

"The thirteenth is our sweetheart hole," said the assistant pro. "It's a two-hundred-and-seventy-yard par-four on a straightaway. You can see the pin from the tee. You'd have to be lame not to par or birdie."

"The grass appears to be in perfect condition."

"Soon as we received clearance from the detectives, we resodded the green. Having it out of commission is like barricading a freeway. You bypass and it screws up your scoring. It's sick, if you ask me."

"Sick" was uttered as a declaration of sacrilege, Kiet thought. "The chain of events as you know them, please."

"I won't be telling you anything you couldn't've read in the papers. The fire department set the time of the fire at between two and three in the morning. We had no guards on duty. That's changed now, I guarantee you.

"The surrounding neighborhoods were asleep. It was a warm night, no wind, so the smoke didn't drift and wake anybody. The thirteenth is the course's dead center, so the trees would prevent the fire from easily being seen from the streets. Whoever's responsible cut a hole through a chainlink fence. The car had been reported stolen the evening before. End of story."

"Peculiar," Kiet said.

"Senseless," said the assistant pro, shaking his head.

"I mean that the perpetrators went to considerable trouble to commit a spectacular crime that would be witnessed only in its aftermath."

"Perverts. Sickos. There are a lot of warped people in the world."

"To shoot and burn a person to death in whichever order," Kiet said, mostly to himself. "Redundant. Repetitious."

"They could have gone out in the woods somewhere and not have damaged private property."

The assistant pro drove them to the clubhouse. Kiet rejoined Binh.

"Snazzy layout, huh?"

"Neo-Colonial," Kiet said. "The gentleman who escorted me to the crime scene did not address me by name or tell me his. At least he did not call me 'boy.' "

"Don't be such a hardass, Superintendent. Discover any exciting clues?"

Kiet related his impressions.

"Yeah, I agree," Binh said. "It feels funny. It happened, but you can't, you know, grip the thing. It's like catching a fish and having it squirt through your hands back into the water. I had the same experience waiting for you, although it's sixth sense rather than your murder scene situation."

"Excuse me?"

"Somebody followed us. Somebody was watching the car. They're gone, but they were here. I didn't see them, but they were here."

8

It was five minutes past midnight, technically the next day, Tuesday. Kiet could not sleep. Last night's fifteen hours had expended tonight's ration.

Binh also could not sleep. He could not sleep because of extreme agitation and the compounding of life's unfair cruelties—a humiliating lecture and a killer case of lover's nuts. Castration City, he said.

Marge Mainwaring had chastised him for keeping her Lincoln so long and for weaseling out of guard duty. In an attempt simultaneously to unruffle feathers and to comfort Marge—who had used up half of her weekly day off on marginal clients who would probably barely qualify for a studio condo anyway, and only had a unsigned earnest money agreement to show for it—he had "put a move on her."

She had once more said no, don't, stop it, don't do that, get your hand out of there. Not because of her usual phantom headache Binh said bitterly. But, so she claimed, for lower back distress caused by chauffering a couple of ringers in an '82 Celebrity that was twenty thousand miles overdue for shock absorbers.

Doug Zane could not sleep. He paid an unannounced call at the Soft Springs Motel. A twelve-can package of beer ("half rack of brewskies, o' thirsty dudes") forgave the etiquette breach.

Zane could not sleep for reasons remarkably similar to Binh's. He had been patrolling singles bars. Although he hadn't progressed far enough to be rejected by migraines and lumbar agony, one young lady perched on a barstool with a miniskirt and legs that went from here to forever answered his gift of a margarita refill by looking him up and down, then yawning. She undressed me with her eyes, Zane said, and she did not dig what she saw. He interpreted this as bad karma and since it was a week night anyhow, to hell with it, Dougie scrubbed the mission.

Captain Binh and Doug Zane dealt with their insomnia by drinking Zane's beer, watching television, and wondering incessantly if they shouldn't boogie on over to the office and rent dirty movies; humping on the tube was no substitute, but what are you gonna do?

Bamsan Kiet vetoed the pornography. Semihooked on a horror movie, he watched as he dealt with his insomnia by cooking.

After their Enchanted Lakes Golf and Country Club investigation, they had gone to a library to research back issues of Seattle newspapers for information on the Davey Peterson killing they might have missed. Nothing. Nil.

They then went to a gigantic mall. It could as well have been the one that housed Baxter Blenheim Pacific Rim Legal Services PS, Inc., except that Kiet thought the book-end department stores were reversed. Binh "maxxed out" two more credit cards. Binh purchased clothing for himself, vividly colored summerwear of a style prominent in beer commercials. He offered to buy Kiet similar articles and long underwear to compensate for his weird thermostat. You can cut off the long-john sleeves and wear them under the casuals, he said; nobody'll look at you and think dork, dufus, dweeb.

Kiet had replied no thank you, buy me items for my contentment, not yours. Binh sighed heavily but did. These items of contentment included: electric wok, bottled water, kitchen herbs and condiments, peanut oil, Vietnamese *nuoc mam* fish sauce which was a satisfactory substitute for the unavailable Luongan *nic sau* sauce, and Pepto Bismol.

Binh dropped Kiet at the Soft Springs. Kiet spent the early evening perusing Ken Bolling's Thin 'n Rich Dynamic Development seminars material. In his view, it was illogically eclectic and superficial, and not a little silly.

Audio cassette tapes of ocean waves, purported "subliminal turbochargers of the mind." Manuals that implored the reader to stand before a mirror and chant, "I am, I can, I will, I am, I can, I will . . ." Kiet was not, could not, would not.

Ring binders and accompanying audio cassettes on buying foreclosed real estate without money. On making a fortune in direct mail marketing. On the techniques and advantages of improving one's memory. On the value of nutrition and exercise, with cursory specifics on the four basic food groups and the body's aerobic demands.

Ken Bolling was quoted frequently, in bold type, extolling his "comprehensive approach to total success." He appeared frequently in photographs taken on tropical isles, at palatial homes, in curved driveways amidst luxury cars. His suntan was remarkable for a Caucasian. He seldom appeared without a twenty-four-tooth smile and a tennis racket.

Enough, Kiet thought. He felt neither thinner nor richer. He felt a spot of mild gastrointestinal distress and he felt homesick. He felt an overwhelming yearning for Quin. The ocean wave tapes, he decided. There were no ocean waves in landlocked Hickorn. There were no ocean waves in the Soft Springs Motel. But Hickorn was halfway around the world, so wherever the ocean was was closer to Hickorn and

Quin than he was now. He felt oppressively sorry for himself.

Binh had hitchhiked to the motel just when Kiet was at his emotional nadir. Binh told his tale of being automobileless in America and in sexual torment. Not to mention his continuing and unsubstantiated hunch that he was being followed. His self-pity was so richly agonized that Kiet's own faded. Melancholia yielded to hunger.

Kiet broke the contents of a frozen Cuisine By Ken Salisbury steak dinner into chunks and dropped them into the hot wok. Ground beef, mashed potatoes, and julienned green beans sizzled and popped in peanut oil. He sprinkled the stir fry with salt and pepper.

"Superintendent, Cuisine By Ken meals are designed to be low sodium, you know," Binh said. "You're defeating the purpose."

Kiet was not listening. He was peering over and beyond the two young thirsty dudes guzzling brewskies, engrossed in a televised movie.

The plot was advancing to a crucial stage. Crabs had been drenched in toxic waste. They grew to the size of pedicabs and developed foul dispositions. The humans were fleeing.

Kiet tasted his food. Bland. He poured in *nuoc mam,* stirring rapidly.

Doug Zane held his nose. "Whew! Smells like clients I've had."

Binh drained his beer, crushed the aluminum can, and said to Doug, "We saw a microwave on sale, you know. It was under a hundred bucks. You could do popcorn and TV dinners and stuff like that in it. The superintendent said no dice."

"Shhh," Kiet said. He dished up his stir fry and poured a glass of bottled water. A cranky, toxic crab snapped a parking meter in two as if it were a cocktail straw and sidled toward a stalled Buick.

"This flick," said Doug Zane. "What else is on? Where's Morton Downey, Junior, now that we really need him?"

"Lighten up on the superintendent," Binh whispered. "I don't think he's well. He refused a beer, you know. And he's in the can every ten minutes."

"Whoa," Doug Zane whispered back. *"Turista* in Seattle?"

Kiet, overhearing, flushed. To change the subject, he said, "Mr. Zane, what have you done to earn your retainer since our meeting?"

"That's principally how come I landed on your doorstep without an invitation. I've been one busy bee. This Perry Mason thing, it's a helluva lot funner than drawing up wills, I kid you not. The autopsy results being held up for so long, something goofy is afoot."

"What?" Binh asked.

"I put my ear to the ground and got this from an acquaintance of an acquaintance. It's the toxicology thing. Like the results are reading out Tilt. They're running the tests again or they're rechecking the original results."

"Davey Peterson was also poisoned?" Kiet asked.

"The dude was overkilled," Zane said with a shrug. "Blasted and roasted. Why not tincture of hemlock too? Why not go for the hat trick?"

Binh belched and opened another beer. "That's disgusting. That's really gross. I think, Superintendent, that Luong has a better class of killer. You whack out your victim once, using adequate force, and get on with your life."

"Life," Doug Zane said. "This sucker who offed Peterson, he's a sadist. He's got no sanctity for human life."

Two beers, perhaps three, Kiet observed, and they were already departing the world of the coherent. Speaking fast, to acquire information before Zane stumbled on his tongue, he asked, "When will you learn the results?"

"Beats me," Zane said, belching. "Hey, one of your countrymen in Seattle, what's his name, Keedeng Choi. Know him?"

Binh shook his head no. Kiet said, "The name is faintly

familiar. A restaurateur by that name owned a nice café in Hickorn. He moved away or closed the café."

"Has to be the same dude. He has the hottest restaurant in town. The Hickorn Café. His reviews have been four stars across the board. I've heard the word of mouth and I was reading a review in a paper while I was waiting at the dentist today. The food is bitchin', to die for. La de da. Trendies line up around the block to get in. He has other irons in the fire too, I've read."

Splendid Luongan cuisine in Seattle? A miracle. Kiet would seek out Keedeng Choi and his eatery. This tourist goal would supersede the cathedral and folk dancers, regardless how colorful their native costumes were. "Seattle has a Luongan community?"

"I'll have to be honest with you," Zane said. "Before you guys and the Peterson thing and the Hickorn Café publicity came along, I didn't know Luong from Jupiter. You said Hickorn to me, I'd slap you on the back and say 'Hold your breath, that cures me when I get 'em.' Has to be one, though, probably in the south end. We have big Vietnamese and Cambodian and Laotian populations."

"Vietnamese, Cambodians, and Laotians were refugees," Kiet said. "Luong is known as the fourth Indochina, yes, but we were granted independence from France in the 1950s. We did not fight for it. Nor did we endure a war of national liberation fought between indigenous communists and Americans. Prince Pakse steers a neutral course that has kept Luong out—"

"Superintendent," Binh said.

"Excuse me?"

"You're being di-di—"

"Didactic?"

"Yeah, pedantic."

"Sorry."

"No sweat," said Doug Zane. "I liked history in school. I

had a flair for it. C-plusses and B's. No false modesty about Dougie."

"Our money?" Kiet asked.

"No bona fide headway, but primo general info."

"Swiss banks?" Kiet said.

"That's traditional. Like fine old wine. Launder your dirty money through Zurich. Thing is, they're getting leaned on and they're caving in to the pressure and cooperating with the authorities some, whereas they didn't used to.

"You've got other routes these days. You deposit your loot in offshore banks and then receive it back in some form. A loan, for instance. You're borrowing your own money, except nobody knows except you and your banker. He doesn't care. It's your little secret. They don't give a damn about a foreign government's tax laws. What goes on between you and the IRS is like the consenting adult thing.

"Another diddle they do is phony sales and purchases. The bread is illegal, drug money or scam money, or whichever, you rig it so it's revenue. You didn't buy anything, but you did on paper. Hey, you pay taxes on it. No biggie. What doesn't go to Uncle Sam is gravy."

"Impressive," Kiet said. "Your private detectives briefed you well."

"Wasn't them," Zane said. "Haven't been able to reach them. They're all out in the field, as it were, trailing hormone carriers to motels not unlike the establishment where we sit at this very moment."

"At least somebody's getting some," Binh said morosely.

Kiet chewed his stir fry slower, then stopped chewing altogether. He set down his plate, satiated. The chemically polluted crab had shelled the Buick (by tearing off the driver's door) and was enjoying the meat, a hysterical gentleman in coveralls. "Your detectives did not brief you. Who did? Another client of yours?"

"Gross," Binh said, watching the televised gore.

"Uh-uh. Our clients are low-rent. No offense, dudes. Their

idea of getting over on the IRS is not reporting hitting the daily double for two hundred bucks. My dentist."

"Excuse me?"

Doug Zane lifted his upper lip with a thumb. "Filling fell out. Shee. Rethilled it."

Kiet groaned.

"My dentist lost his shirt on oil leases in the eighties. He's gotten gun-shy. He goes for the sure thing now. He's an old fart, forty or forty-five. He's awful sick of having his hands in your mouth eight hours a day. He's thinking nest egg."

"Old fart," Kiet muttered. The crab finished his snack and the action paused for a commercial break.

"Customers he trusts, yo, Dougie among them, he drills and fills at a bitchin' discount if you pay cash and don't get personal and mushy and ask for a receipt. He jets to a Caribbean island twice a year and it's not entirely for the sun and fun.

"He deposits and borrows his own money through that bank's branch in another country, like Holland, to buy gold and silver that he doesn't buy. He hasn't done a gold crown since dental school. You audit his books, he's losing his butt. He's paying a fortune in fake interest on these fake loans. He's in real life netting two hundred grand a year if he's making a dime, and the IRS mails him tax refunds like he's a kid working at McDonald's, he's so poor."

"David Peterson, Jr.'s ploy too, perhaps?"

"I'd say yes. What was his IQ? I read it, but I forgot."

"One-seventy-one," Binh said.

Doug Zane tapped his temple. "With his brainpower, Mr. Kiet, it's a cinch."

"By himself?"

"Davey wasn't really in business. He did free-lance consulting like he did for Luong, but he made peanuts. It's easier when you're in business. You phony a bunch of income and outgo. You have these write-offs, depreciation and things, for your mad money on phantom goods and services. Corporate mattresses are plumper."

"A partner," Kiet said, thinking; a partner who through the act of murder became a sole owner.

"Jesus H. Christ!" Binh said, jumping to his feet and pointing finger, arm, and body at the television set as if he were a hunting dog.

A chunky man in a red devil's costume was grinning and chattering at the camera. Satan, Kiet thought. That was the character's formal name. A Western Christian mythological terror. The custodian of the nonbeliever's eternal afterlife. Hot climate, zero humidity, low threshold of pain.

Although this Satan was holding a pitchfork, he was cordial. He was waving the pitchfork at rows of automobiles. The automobiles were not new, but to a car they were low-slung and sporty.

The man pointed his pitchfork at a car, raised it above his head, and cackled insanely.

"Have I got a *h-e*-double hockey sticks of a deal for you!" he yelled. Then he slammed the car's hood with the pitchfork.

"Chick Chipperfield!" Binh exclaimed.

"Chick Chipperfield!" Kiet exclaimed.

"Chick Chipperfield, Seattle's most obnoxious car dealer," Zane said. "So what?"

9

"Once upon a time," Binh said, popping the top of the last brewsky. "Once upon a time, Chick Chipperfield came to Luong. How long ago would you say, Superintendent?"

The crab movie had ended in favor of the humans. In the next to final act, the army mobilized tanks, paranoiac generals, and nuclear weapons. But the scientist, his daughter, and the daughter's muscular yet sensitive boyfriend had killed the monsters with a hastily constructed radio wave device, thus saving mankind without wreaking further environmental damage.

Afterward, Kiet relented to semidrunken nagging and permitted Binh and Zane to rent a pornographic videotape. It was playing, the sound turned off at Kiet's insistence. The tape had a large cast, which was thrashing on a bed. Kiet was counting legs. Recounting legs. Recounting legs again. Each time he came up with an odd number.

"Superintendent."

"Excuse me?"

"Chipperfield and his crony, how long ago was it?"

"Three years, three and a half years."

"Okay, that's about the time frame. Chick and his attorney brother-in-law came to Hickorn, right. Ex-brothers-in-law. They were married to sisters who dumped them. Ex-attorney too. He'd been disbarred."

"I remember," Doug Zane said. "Chick got stepped on by the attorney general for rolling back odometers and stuff. The attorney brother-in-law defended Chick and got disbarred for falsifying documents and bribing a witness. A pair of bad-news dudes. I remember because we covered the thing in law school. The funnest case study I ever had, I kid you not."

"Their ex-wives operated a travel agency," Kiet said.

"That blonde," Binh said, leering.

"Yo, blondie. Which blonde?" Zane asked.

"The one straddling the guy with the tattoos. She's got a sweet face. She doesn't seem the type."

"Bad childhood, that's probably the thing," Zane said. "Too much junk food and TV."

"Chipperfield and his disbarred cohort operated a television station in Hickorn," Kiet said. "They also sold package travel tours of Luong."

"The ex-attorney was offed, wasn't he?"

"Smashed over the head in the national museum with a stone Buddha," Kiet said. "At night, presumably in the process of burglary."

"Migraine City," Binh said.

"A Luongan national treasure, wasn't it."

"*The* national treasure," Kiet said. "A headdress. The Golden Peacock. An incredibly beautiful antiquity fashioned of gold and gemstones."

"The attorney was in cahoots with the museum curator, the minister of tourism, the former mayor of Hickorn, and Vietnamese diplomats," Binh said.

"But you let Chick off the hook," Zane said.

"We couldn't prove his complicity."

"He turned stool pigeon for us," Binh said. "We let him walk."

"The golden pheasant thing, you rescued it?"

"Indeed," Kiet said. "It is safe in the national museum."

"They were going to dig out the jewels and melt it down?"

"Initially," Kiet said. "The attorney and the museum curator struck a bargain. The curator owed gambling debts."

"The peacock flies. The curator gets to keep his kneecaps intact," Binh said.

"The minister of tourism learned what was happening and invited himself to the conspiracy," Kiet said. "His motivation was political."

"That blonde," Binh said, sighing. "Marge, twenty years ago."

"Political, how?"

"It symbolizes Luong's last military victory."

"When?"

"One-fifty-four B.C."

"Whoa," Doug Zane said, crushing his empty beer can. "Fred Flintstone was still in diapers then."

"That blonde. Marge's daughter. I wonder. Nah. Couldn't be. Marge's been married and divorced three times, but she never had kids."

"Yeah. We didn't concentrate on that aspect of the thing too extensively," Zane said. "The case study was mainly on how hard it is to disbar a lawyer. A good news and bad news shot. Good news if you're a slimebucket attorney, bad news if you're the general public. You can pull a lot in this state before they yank your ticket. I can dig where you're coming from. No pheasant and the peasants are carrying torches, rioting in the streets."

"Luong is stable and mellow, but we are tiny," Kiet said. "A coup d'état is as imminent as a crazed mob under the control of a cunning leader."

"Speaking of cunning," Zane said. "Chick Chipperfield landed on his feet after you gave him a pass, didn't he? You just saw for yourselves. He's back in the used car business and is even stronger than before his hassle. Chick Chipperfield's Preowned Automotive Elegance. He sponsors the late movie on channel forty-six and does that devil thing with the pitchfork. It's made him a local celebrity. He's not going to be elected mayor or anything on account of it. It's more a two-headed calf kind of thing, but I'll tell you what, the dude sells cars."

"Groovy cars," Binh said. "That was a cherry 300ZX he whacked with the pitchfork. I liked to've cried."

Zane nodded and said, "No question, Chick's moved up in the world. In the old days he owned beater lots. Biggest collection of rolling junk in town. Now he sells late model and sexy, exclusively."

"Yeah," Binh said. "I saw Corvettes and a Porsche 911 Targa."

"His market is the middle-aged midlife cuckoo. The male menopause deal. Dude turns forty, can't get it up anymore, and buys a 'vette."

"This is an omen, Superintendent," Binh said.

Kiet counted fifteen legs again and shook his head. "What, please, is an omen?"

"Us seeing Chipperfield on TV."

"It is not an omen, Captain. It is a coincidence."

"Whoa," Zane said. "Scope the schlong on the sport with the amputated leg. We're talking Louisville Slugger."

Ah, Kiet thought, the solution to my mathematical impossibility.

"It is an omen," Binh said. "We declined to prosecute him. We protected him from his partner's fate and we deported him. We could have sent him up the river and we could've hung him out to dry."

Kiet groaned and closed his eyes. Binh had overloaded his

capacity for English language slang. We had charitably declined to waterlog Mr. Chipperfield *and* dehydrate him?

"He owes us," Binh said.

"Owes us what?"

Binh shook a fist and grinned. "Wheels."

10

"I am confused, Captain. Are we traveling in circles?"

"No, Superintendent."

"Isn't this the highway to the airport? Didn't we pass the airport?"

"Yes. We passed the airport. We're south of the airport."

"Then it isn't the highway to the mall where Zane's law office is?"

"No."

"It isn't the highway to Enchanted Lakes?"

"No, and now I'm the one who's confused. How can this highway be the highway to all those places?"

Kiet gestured outside. "The same businesses."

"Huh?"

"McDonald's, Midas, Goodyear, Pizza Hut, Texaco, Kentucky Fried Chicken, Firestone, Burger King. I see the same businesses."

Binh laughed. "Superintendent, they're franchises. You have them everywhere."

Kiet blushed at his own ignorance. "I knew that. I meant they were the same franchises. Each is subtly distinctive, yes?"

"Well, I guess," Binh said. "If you squint your eyes and look real close."

"Will we soon see Seattle skyscrapers?"

Binh moaned and wiped perspiration from his brow. Kiet knew that because of the brewskies consumed with Dougie, Binh was not at his chipper best. Kiet, on the other hand, thanks to the spicy stir fry and the bottled water, felt fine. His head was clear and he was not on a constant lookout for a bathroom.

"Aren't you well, Captain?" he said, thinking that a bit of verbal torment would be beneficial for the lad's character.

"No comment, okay? Lighten up, will you?"

"Please, a single simple question. When will the Seattle skyscrapers come into view?"

"Not today, Superintendent. We're going in the opposite direction. Chick's lot is on this highway, in a south suburb." Binh sighed and added, "We're going downtown, yeah, eventually."

"South, a south suburb," Kiet said. "I am beginning to believe that Seattle and its rugged, surrounding scenery is merely the trick photography of travel promoters. Will we see mountains and forests and salmon streams and logging trucks?"

"No, Superintendent. We are going to the burbs, not the boonies."

"Forgive my tourist enthusiasm," Kiet said, answering Binh's snotty tone.

"This is a bummer. I wish I had a dollar for every time this bus has stopped."

"Stopping is what buses do, Captain. They must stop in order to load and unload passengers."

"We should have gotten a schedule. We should have caught an express bus. If you have to ride a bus, at least ride one that gets you where you're going before you forget where you are going."

"What is wrong with this bus?" Kiet asked, having fun. "Half the seats are empty. We had our pick. This bus, this Metro, it smells nice, too. Compare it to Hickorn coaches. Not one fellow passenger on this Metro has brought live chickens aboard."

"Number one," Binh said slowly, "there are no live chickens in America. They're all cut up and chilled in supermarkets and restaurants. Number two, half the seats are empty because nobody in America wants to ride the bus when you can drive a car."

"Who in America would prefer to drive a car in maniacal traffic when a bus driver will drive for them?"

Binh muttered something unintelligible that might have been "get a life" and stared out the window.

"We could already be at Chipperfield's if not for our intermediate stop at a uniform supply store for your disguise," Kiet needled.

"Spur of the moment," Binh said. "Trust my instincts for a change, okay? Okay!"

"Okay," Kiet said, aware that he had reached the boundary between ribbing and persecution. He would ease off. If he ignited a tantrum, the mutual loss of face could imperil the mission, not to mention their friendship.

"I didn't say so then, but I'm pretty sure we were being followed," Binh said.

Kiet swiveled his head.

"No, between your motel and the uniform store. They broke off surveillance there."

"They? The neckless thugs?"

"Well, again, I didn't see anybody. It was a sixth-sense situation. I think it was something higher on the food chain than the goons. The one you suckered onto the plane, he's still trying to find somebody at Oklahoma City who'll read an airline schedule for him, and his buddy's still prowling the

motel where we ditched him. Nah. They'd be snorting fire.
They wouldn't be following us. They'd be after blood. We'd
be dead meat."

"Who?"

"That's the scary part. He, she, they—it's out there but it's
invisible. Me being in a disguise again is a step in the right
direction. I can be out on the front line with you, where I
ought to be, assisting in the investigation. That and the hot
set of wheels we squeeze out of Chick, somebody gets on
our tail, if we can't fake them out, we'll sure as hell outrun
them, blow their doors off."

"A comforting strategy," Kiet said grudgingly.

"Hey, speaking of the devil, pun intended," Binh said,
yanking the bell cord.

The bus stop was a short, convenient block from Chick
Chipperfield's Preowned Automotive Elegance. A rotating
board on a tall pole read: RIDE IN, DRIVE OUT. LEAVE THE DRIVING
TO U. 0 DOWN. EZ PAYMENTS.

They walked by a doughnut shop and an enterprise that
promised to change your oil while you waited, and onto
Chick Chipperfield's car lot. The property was paved with
extraordinarily black asphalt.

Kiet wondered whether it had been painted to veil the
tarlike drippings of dying engines and transmissions. He
scuffed a sandal, the detective in him examining for grease.
He slipped, caught his balance, and turned to Binh. Binh was
gone. Where?

There. There, at a row of gaudily metallic cars, the front
row. It paralleled the highway, ten or twelve automobiles,
each with its hood up. They struck Kiet as baby birds in a
nest, beaks opened wide. Chipperfield the psychologist, Kiet
thought. It was like Ken Bolling's oceanfront subliminal
tapes and his mirror chanting. Shout your message or slip it
under the door of one's subconscious. No difference. A sale
was a sale. Bottom line, Binh would say. Feed me. Buy me.
Feed me, buy me.

Binh was peering into an engine compartment. Peculiarly, thought Kiet, there was more shiny plating on the motor than on the outer body.

"A Maserati," Binh said reverently. "Twin intercooled turbochargers. Then somebody tricked it out with the brightwork. I'll bet it's been souped up too. Chipperfield may be a royal dipshit, but he's super classy where groovy cars are concerned."

"Come," Kiet said, gently dragging him by an arm. "We're looking for Chick, not chromium interchargers."

"Wheels," Binh persisted. "We came for wheels, Superintendent. Don't forget."

They negotiated an obstacle course of dangerously powerful cars and smiling, helpful salesmen and were at the steps of a mobile home identified as Office when Chick Chipperfield walked out.

Chipperfield was as Kiet remembered him, though ten kilograms heavier. Late forties, wispy reddish hair grown long and combed back, ruddy complexion, gin blossoms on nose and cheeks. Most of all, Kiet recalled Chipperfield's unique fashion statement. Today he obeyed it extravagantly: maroon-and-white checked slacks, black shirt, algae green sports jacket, white tie, white patent leather belt and shoes.

Chipperfield clutched his heart and said, "Kiet, you pretty near shocked the ol' ticker into a dead stop. Not in a jillion years did I figure we'd lay eyes on each other again. A déjà vu overdose is what this is. Talk about your coincidences."

"This is no coincidence," Kiet said. "This is an omen."

Chipperfield frowned warily. "I'm not catching your drift, Kiet. Okay, fine. You Luongans, I said it before, I gotta say it again, you fuckers *are* inscrutable. Oops. Wash my mouth out with soap. Sorry, padre."

Chipperfield was apologizing to Binh, whose disguise was the flat-lens eyeglasses and mustache, and a Roman Catholic priest's attire. He had purchased the clothing with plastic at the uniform store after grousing about selections in his size.

No way, he had told Kiet, am I gonna be some waiter or bellhop or a drum major.

Binh, an undevout Buddhist, crossed himself and said, "You are forgiven, my son."

"This is Father Quoc, our Hickorn Police Department chaplain," Kiet said.

"My pleasure?" Chipperfield said, shaking Binh's hand. "I *don't* have a *h-e*-double hockey sticks deal for you. How'd you boys find me?"

"Channel forty-six last night," Kiet said.

Chipperfield smiled. "Yeah, the devil routine made my comeback. That costume, I ain't recommending it for everyday wear. It don't breathe. I'm hotter'n a popcorn fart during tapings. You liked the flick?"

"Indeed," Kiet said.

"This is critter week. Killer bees are on a rampage tonight. You watch it and you won't eat honey for a month. Next week is slumber parties from hell week. The party crashers wear hockey masks and tote chain saws."

"When is Marx Brothers week?"

"Never," Chick said firmly. "People don't stay up late to see funny little guys running around handing out exploding cigars. They stay up for blood and guts. They stay up for T&A."

"Nice cars," Kiet said, scrutinizing the lot.

"Nice and quick, too," Chipperfield said. "I don't floor no station wagons. A trade-in don't scat zero-to-sixty under eight seconds, I wholesale it. Come on inside and take a load off, fellas. Kiet, you got a bug in your ear. You didn't come ten thousand miles to talk Seahawk football with me. I like your outfit, by the way."

"Gentlemen, I presume you do not require a representative of the church," Binh said. "May I instead browse?"

Not browse, Kiet thought; salivate.

"You betcha, padre. You see something that lights your fire, I'll throw in a St. Christopher's medal."

Chipperfield led Kiet through the trailer to an inner office and shut bifold doors for privacy. The wood-grain wall paneling was covered with plaques and photographs of youth sports teams.

"That's me donating myself to my community," Chipperfield said.

"Generously," Kiet said.

Chipperfield laughed and sat at his desk. "Kiet, is that sarcasm?"

Kiet sat on an edge of the desk and stared at Chipperfield. "I know you, Chick."

"I belong to every service organization in a ten-mile radius. Chick Chipperfield's Preowned Automotive Elegance is plastered on soccer and baseball jerseys in all the leagues, all the age groups. I attend the luncheons, I flip pancakes at the Saturday morning breakfasts, I donate the lot for car washes, I sponsor a little honey for the big annual beauty contest, I'm on all the committees and boards. I'm a member of the Lutheran church. They draw big turnouts. I sing in the choir."

"Do you play golf?"

Chick Chipperfield winked. "The links is a gold mine. I start lessons this fall."

"I've heard of the phenomenon you described," Kiet said. "Boosterism, is it?"

"Kee-rect. Maybe I was a bad apple in my past life, maybe I ain't exactly an angel, but being active in the community—the *hombre* they call when they need something done—it erases memories. I know you too, Kiet. What gives?"

"I am in Seattle for a police superintendents executive conference convention," he said, paraphrasing Binh's fabrication to Marge Mainwaring.

"Don't bullshit a bullshitter," Chipperfield said. "I don't read the papers, but I watch the news. This little cutie reporter on one of the stations, I'd follow her anywhere. C'mon, man, what's the program?"

Kiet smiled in spite of himself. He did not reply.

"Your number-two guy, Binh, he stepped on his own pecker, didn't he?"

"A misunderstanding," Kiet said.

"Okay, fine. What I'm misunderstanding is what possessed him to shoot the computer nerd and roast him like a weenie or maybe the other way around. While he was at it, why didn't he just pound a wooden stake through his heart for good measure? Binh was a nice kid. He reminds me a little of the padre. He's enjoying himself, by the way, isn't he?"

Chipperfield poked a thumb at the window. Binh was in the driver's seat of a long, black sportster, shifting gears. A 200-mile-per-hour fantasy, Kiet surmised.

"Jaguar XJS," Chick said. "Too rich for his blood. We had a priest in once, wanted a '90 Mazda Miata so bad he could taste it, but he didn't qualify. The Vatican, I don't think they even pay minimum wage. But who's buying and selling cars today? I'm not, not while you and me are sitting here smokin' and jokin'. You know what I think Binh's problem is?"

"Please inform me."

"It wasn't the murder of the computer nerd. People know how poor your little country is. The kid robbed you blind. He deserved what he got. Maybe he didn't deserve being killed as much as he was killed, but Binh would've had everyone rooting in his corner if it wasn't for his attack on Donald Duck.

"You're a foreigner, Kiet. I don't expect you to grasp what I'm saying, but Binh beat that poor kid within an inch of his life. Donald Duck is like Mom and apple pie. Binh was pissed. Okay, fine, but is that any reason to go nuts? He was whaling on him like a mad dog."

"Captain Binh is, yes, a person of interest, but he has not been charged with a crime," Kiet said evenly.

"His days are numbered," Chipperfield said, shaking his head. "The story's been fairly quiet recently, but on the news last night, my favorite little honey, she said that the autopsy results on the nerd was gonna be made public any second.

In the next story they interviewed the lawyer representing Donald, the kid entering his senior year at Southern Cal."

"Did you know that Binh thrashed him so bad that his whiplash pain and suffering is the exact same as if he'd been rear-ended by an eighteen-wheeler doing fifty?"

"No."

"This lawyer, whiplash is his specialty. He oughta know. On account of headaches and numbness, the kid may never get back in school. Or hold down a job. It's serious, man. It's not some duke-out in an alley. You screw with a man's earning power, it's bad news. It's like a crime against property. The holy father out there, you oughta get him to say— what do they call them absolution prayers?—a novena on Binh. He'll need it."

"We want to borrow an automobile."

Chipperfield puckered his lips and nodded knowingly. "I owe you a biggie is what you're laying on me?"

"Indeed."

"You could've tossed me in the pokey. I'd still be there, eating fish heads and rice. Or you could've thrown me to the wolves. Next day I'd've been floating in the river. Instead, you protected me and sent me home."

"Yes."

"Kiet, what you're doing is appealing to my sense of gratitude and decency."

"Yes."

"I hate that," Chipperfield said, whining. "I don't come through, I feel guilty as hell. You got any idea how hard it is to make me feel guilty?"

"I can imagine."

"My mother used to be able to make me feel guilty once in a blue moon. Kiet, you're under my skin from the git-go."

"Hopefully."

"Just outta curiosity, a dumb question, how come you don't rent a car?"

Not a dumb question, Kiet thought. Binh could pay with

plastic money. If he, a person of interest, could risk exposing his name in a transaction, why not automobile rental also? Kiet would have to ask. He said, "Rent? Our good friend Chick Chipperfield, I knew, would not hear of it."

"Okay, fine. I don't know what you're up to, but I'm not nosing into your business. No sir. This is too weird. My lips are sealed. How long you need it?"

"A week, two weeks. Three at the utmost."

"Are you picky?"

"Excuse me?"

"Like the padre out there, drooling on the stock. Does it have to be cherry?"

Cherry? Not in the context of virginity or fruit, Kiet was certain; perhaps in the context of bitchin'. "No. Cherry is unnecessary. Reliability *is* necessary."

"Got the perfect unit for you," Chick said, clapping his hands. "Almost forgot about it. Came in yesterday. It's behind the office. We haven't had a chance to take it out to the auction."

"It is reliable?"

"It don't quite fit in at Chipperfield's Preowned Automotive Elegance, but this little buggy's reliable with a capital *R,*" Chick said sincerely. "It's a one-owner. A CPA about our age. His wife traded him in on a twenty-four-year-old ironworker so he said, fuck it, cleaned out the joint savings and IRA before she could get her paws on it and traded up to the sweetest Mercedes 450SL this side of Stuttgart. You should've seen him peel outta here. He was wearing shades and driving gloves. Makes you feel good when you can upgrade a man's life-style for him. C'mon, let's have a gander."

On the porch, Kiet heard a *psst* that sounded like a ruptured steam pipe. Kiet excused himself to tend to the padre's hissing and waving. Chick said okay, fine, meet you out back.

"Well, how'd it go?" Binh said from the driver's seat of the sleek, black roadster.

"Mr. Chipperfield is showing me a possibility."

"I know Chick wouldn't spring for this Jag, but the Z-car he creamed with the pitchfork, the damage to the hood is minor. You have to be looking for it to really notice. We could live with that. The car he's showing you, if it's a roach, request the Z, okay?"

"Yes," Kiet said, walking away.

"The Z has leather and a CD player, Superintendent. Options are important. Don't accept a 'plain Jane.' "

Chick was leaning on a fender, arms folded. "Kiet, before you bitch, lemme explain some of the finer features—"

Kiet smiled, raised a hand to interrupt, and said, "No bitching. No complaints. It is splendid. It is perfect. We'll take it."

11

"Mark my words, Superintendent, kids on skateboards will be zooming by us. Little old ladies from Pasadena will be zooming by us. Hay wagons will be zooming by us. I'm flooring it and we're doing forty-five. Turn around and look at the blue smoke we're belching. Christ, a Yugo with a sick engine, that's like being born crippled, then catching cancer."

Binh's words were the first he had marked, or spoken, since departure from Chick Chipperfield's Preowned Automotive Elegance. Kiet had instantly pegged Chick's donation as sluggish, and the claustrophobic, Yugoslavian-manufactured hatchback did not disappoint him. The young adjutant would not send Kiet to his ancestors at high velocity.

"Reliability is our prime consideration, Captain," Kiet said, patting the dashboard. "The low mileage persuaded me. A paltry eleven thousand. The automobile is barely broken in."

"Superintendent, Chick's up to his old tricks. He's rolling

back odometers. Even this roller skate wouldn't burn oil at eleven thou."

Binh, though obviously displeased, was suspiciously not hostile. He was speaking matter-of-factly, not whining, not demanding that the injustice be righted. His attitude toward the Yugo was of grim acceptance. Further, he had taken the keys from Chipperfield hurriedly and without complaint. They were headed somewhere in a rush and Kiet did not know where. Peculiar behavior, he thought. Extremely peculiar.

But he would restrain his curiosity. He would be patient. Binh was troubled, fidgety. Information was being concealed. This enigma was building in the lad like steam in a boiler. When the pressure reached the red line, Binh would release it in a guilt-ridden burst.

Meanwhile, Kiet savored the scenery. The sky was cloudless. The day would have been pristine except for the subarctic temperature, which Kiet gauged at seventy-five degrees Fahrenheit.

A yellowish haze of industrial prosperity clung, but it was thin and odorless. Through it, to the south, Kiet had earlier glimpsed an immense ice cream sundae identified in travel literature as Mount Rainier. It was a volcano, supposedly dormant.

They were eastbound on yet another freeway. Ahead was the Cascade mountain range. The summits were substantially lower than the potentially deadly Rainier's. Winter snow had melted and the peaks were a spiky green.

Kiet wondered if the mountainous region was their mysterious destination. Seattle's elusive skyscrapers were to their rear. Perhaps today was the day they would see loggers, alpine meadows, and streams full of frisky game fish.

No. Not to be. Binh took the last exit before the freeway began ascending. "Um, Superintendent."

Ah, the needle quivering at the red line. "Yes?"

They stopped at the base of the exit, at a traffic light. The brakes squeaked like a choir of rats.

"Well," Binh said, "You know, when you were in Chick's office with him and I was out in the lot, I was sort of messing around in that Jag XJS, which was loaded and then some, including a cellular phone, they cost a lot less than they used to, you know, like computers and VCRs and everything when they come out, likewise the per-call service fees, so I didn't figure it was much skin off Chick's nose if I called Marge, and, this is sort of bizarre, I caught her on *her* cellular phone in the Town Car and she said she was hoping she could reach me because there's a situation at the model home and I'd damn well better meet her there if I knew what was good for me, her saying it so even with the static you have in one car phone talking to another car phone I knew she was brutally pissed, and, Superintendent, I realize that holding out on you is a crummy thing to do, but remember when I told you that in my relationship with Marge I was kind of incognito——"

A horn drowned Binh out. The blast startled Kiet, who had been counting the words in Binh's guilt-ridden burst of a sentence: 203. The light had long since turned green. Binh replied with a middle digit and drove through as it changed red, swung left, then right, then up a winding hill.

"Kind of incognito, you know," he went on. "I did what I had to do. The resolution of the Peterson case is the bottom line, Superintendent, and whatever deceptions I had to create were instigated with the case the top priority. Marge says anything to you that sounds off the wall, no matter what it is, play along like everything's normal, okay? Please?"

"What manner of incognito deceptions?"

"That's kind of irrelevant unless Marge initiates a conversation that doesn't make sense, right?"

Kiet suppressed a groan. "We are en route to the model home?"

"Yep. You'll love it."

"Not a protracted visit, I trust," Kiet said. "The investigation—"

"No sweat, Superintendent. We won't be long. From here on, you call the shots and we'll get to the heart of the situation. I couldn't guess why Marge is so bent out of shape, other than me slacking on the job, but I can sweet-talk her in short order. Besides, Marge has been my cover, so we're therefore working on the investigation. Indirectly."

Kiet digested Binh's logic in silence. They came to a plateau. Binh took a side road. A semiwilderness of conifers, mailboxes, and gravel driveways suddenly transformed into a denuded landscape of voluminous houses. They were markedly similar: two stories, shake roofs, arched doors, leaded windows, brick veneers. Although of common parentage, they appeared proud, as if ready to swell out of the confines of their tiny plots. Kiet gathered that they had bathrooms and as many as four private bedrooms. A three-generation Hickorn family could live comfortably in these scale-model mansions and have space to take in a cousin or two.

"You like?" Binh asked. "Pretty spiffy, huh?"

"Yes. Expensive?"

"Your typical monthly payment would choke a horse. With enough left over to choke the jockey, too. Three hundred grand buys you a fixer-upper if there is such an animal, which there isn't because in a neighborhood like this, nobody has peeling paint, nobody has cracked glass. Christ, if I found a dandelion I'd probably be paid a bounty for it. This is a competitive, upscale life-style that carries over from business to home. It's hard for a Luongan to conceive, but that's how it is in America."

"Golf green," Kiet said. "Is there a golf course nearby?"

"Naturally."

"A question. Where, please, is the originality?"

"The what?"

"These upscale, prideful palaces are not identical, but they are alike."

"It's the style. French Château."

"Seattle is also a former French colony?"

"No, no. French Château is popular. It's classy. Understated elegance. It looks like you have more money than you do."

"It looks across the street, thinks it is looking into a mirror, and this simulates wealth?"

"The BMWs and Volvos in the driveways are looking at each other in a mirror situation, too, and they're smiling. Not to worry."

"So you are saying that people live here who cannot afford to?"

"Yeah. Some. These eastside suburbs are thick with wannabes."

"Why do they not live in housing they can afford?"

"Drop down a notch? Uh-uh. No matter where they live, people will think they're living over their heads, so if they're living where they can afford, people will think they make less money than they really do. See?"

"Yes," said Kiet, who didn't, not entirely.

"The best is yet to come," Binh said. "And here we are."

They drove through an arched entry constructed of white brick and flanked by marble fountains. It looked to Kiet like a war memorial. With one exception. The bronzework was not a plaque enrolling the battlefield dead. In cursive letters it read Swan Lake Acres.

"Marge's real estate firm's pride and joy," Binh said. "Swan Lake Acres is platted for about eighty units. Thirty are done, about fifteen sold. Ground's been broken on the majority of the other lots. It's a going concern. Marge makes a sale and when it goes through, she pockets in excess of fifteen grand in commissions. She's a fox, Superintendent, *and* she's loaded."

Kiet looked out at French châteaus in stages of progress

ranging from skeletal to complete. Sod was stacked in rolls, eager to become instant lawns. "Where is Swan Lake?"

"Well, that's kind of a problem. They were planning to divert a creek into this low spot. Take out some trees and you have a natural basin. They wanted to trap some swans in wetlands up north by the Canadian border and resettle them in the lake. The EPA and the Audubon Society, they had cows. That was the end of that tune. Don't say anything around Marge. The way she feels about environmentalists, she'll bite your head off."

"Swan Lake Acres without a Swan Lake?"

"Marge sells it as symbolic. She says it's the name of a famous opera or something. Sales haven't been hurt, so—oh hell."

At the head of a cul-de-sac to their right was a French château designated by a sign staked in the front yard as Model Home. Parked in the three-car-garage driveway, nosed against an arched, brick-veneer garage door, was Marge Mainwaring's elephantine Lincoln. Beside it was a King County sheriff squad car. A slender, blond woman in a navy suit and ruffly white blouse stood on the veranda. A uniformed police officer stood with her. The woman was several inches taller than the man, and she was doing the talking.

Binh said "Deep Shit City" and drove on. At the end of a curving block they came to a vacant plat and a copse of alders that earthmoving equipment had inexplicably spared. Binh hopped the curb, and the Yugo shuddered to a stop just deep enough in the miniature forest to be invisible from the street. Binh said he would find an observation post where Marge and the officer could be seen and he couldn't. He returned soon and reported that the patrol car was gone.

Marge's Lincoln had not moved, however. Binh parked next to it, checked his hair in the rearview mirror, and, winking, asked Kiet to sit tight until he could go on in and chill her out.

Kiet sat tight. Chill her out. He contemplated the terminology as he sat tight. He presumed the technique to be a peculiar blend of machismo and psychological refrigeration. Binh returned sooner than soon, flustered, himself in need of cooling. He opened Kiet's car door and said, "Superintendent, please, as I asked before, play along with whatever Marge says, okay?"

"Marge is not chilled out?"

"Marge is not a happy camper. You'll go along with the program, okay, Superintendent? My incognito situation, right?"

"Okay. Right," Kiet said, groaning, getting out. "Okay, fine."

Bamsan Kiet, a professional police officer, appraised the cause of Marge Mainwaring's foul temperament. The doorless veranda was not a doorless veranda. It was a porch minus a door. The door had been kicked in and was prone and splintered and hingeless on the tile entryway. Captain Binh, Kiet thought; professional police officer and errant night watchman.

"I sort of dodged the bullet," Binh said in a low voice. "Just juveniles busting in to drink and screw and party. There's two thousand bucks worth of copper plumbing alone in that partially framed unit across the street. I'm thanking my lucky stars it was a bunch of kids, not pros."

Kiet nodded, wondering, was it the goons, the neckless psychopaths from the airport? The kicked-in door was a solid assemblage of hardwoods; it would not have given way readily. A special type of mentality would batter in a sturdy door rather than manipulate the lock. The young gentleman who had jetted to Oklahoma City might be a candidate. He would logically be in a proper mood; he would be in an extraordinary rage.

"Marge is in the guest bedroom past the kitchen off the den. You can make it a family room too. That's where I sleep. The other bedrooms are upstairs."

Kiet followed Binh, observing the damage. Cigarette burns on polished oak flooring. Overturned tables. Wall splatters, the foreign substances unknown. Perhaps not the goons, he thought. The mess appeared exuberant and careless instead of malicious. Perhaps kids after all.

"Ick," said Marge Mainwaring, pointing at a condom on the shag wall-to-wall carpeting with the toe of a stylish black shoe. "Safe sex. Icky-poo."

"Marge," Binh said, "this is the gentleman I was telling you about."

Marge Mainwaring extended a hand. Her grip was firm and dry, yet feminine. She didn't wash dishes regularly, but she probably changed her own flat tires. She was tall, blue eye to brown eye with Kiet, and attractive for a Caucasian. She made no attempt to putty the netting radiating from her eyes—crow's-feet as it was known in America—nor had she tampered with the gray streaks in the blond hair that hung freely below her shoulders. She had good teeth and unblemished skin. If Binh were compelled to be infatuated by a woman ridiculously inappropriate for him, Marge Mainwaring was a splendid choice.

"I admire you coming this distance from Asia to assist at the police leadership conference," Marge said.

"My pleasure," Kiet lied. The woman was regarding him strangely, squinting, as if he were vaguely familiar to her.

"The sheriff's deputy dutifully took my report," Marge said. "He was a realist and I'm a realist. They won't make an arrest and my company won't recover a penny of restitution. In your country, is your police department bothered with senseless vandalism?"

"No," Kiet said. "Criminals do not burglarize houses to party and to be messy. They burglarize to steal money, food, and jewelry. Our criminals are not senseless."

"We live in a land of plenty," Marge said, planting hands on nicely rounded hips and shaking her head. "We take too much for granted."

"Peanut butter. Wonder bread. A gallon of milk. Gone! The little creeps!"

Binh was in the kitchen. Marge responded to his lament to Kiet, in a low, husky voice, "You have to be careful what you say. I know how it is in your culture. Offend the wrong person and you could lose your head. Literally. But isn't he awfully young for the responsibility he carries on his shoulders? He dearly needs a mentor. Rank shouldn't be a handicap. Age is venerated in your society. I know this to be a fact."

"Excuse me?" Kiet said.

Binh brought an empty peanut butter jar, complaining, "It wasn't a third gone."

So this was peanut butter, Kiet thought. The residue on the jar was disgusting. It looked like pureed fecal matter. Binh, he feared, was indeed going irreversibly native.

Marge said to Binh, "Be a dear and run upstairs. I didn't see any serious damage, but we ought to double-check before we send in the cleaners."

As she watched the departing Binh, out of the side of her mouth, she said, "A priest suit, gag glasses and mustache. Why on earth that silly getup?"

"To excommunicate a used car dealer who unfortunately was a Lutheran."

"You people are droll. Him, Charlie Chaplin at the seminary, and you, a Seattle Seahawks Chinese superfan. I thought Bamsan dressed funny to amuse me to fall back into my good graces. I should fire him, but I can't. The little dickens, he's too likable."

"Bamsan?"

Marge had moved closer to Kiet, into perfume proximity. "Bamsan has a one-track mind, you know. Sex, sex, sex. To function as police superintendent while his head is cluttered with naked ladies is an ordeal, I'm sure. He must be a trial for you, Captain Binh."

"Yes," Kiet said. "Yes, he can be."

90

"Bamsan speaks very highly of you, Captain."

"I am honored," Kiet said, bowing.

"You do have influence over him, don't you?"

"Perhaps."

"You'd be doing him a big favor if you'd use that influence to talk him into listing his villa with me. It sounds absolutely palatial. I'd coordinate with a realtor in your town. It might take time, but we'd eventually receive lucrative offers."

"Where would Bamsan then live?"

"Oh, he could rent. I don't know what the per capita income is in your corner of the world. Not very high, I suppose. Bamsan could invest his equity in the United States and live comfortably on the dividends."

"Sensible," Kiet said.

"Sensible is putting it mildly, Captain. I could steer him into a tax shelter. Don't believe what you read. They still exist."

"Indeed," Kiet said. His mind was drifting to this break-in, wavering again on the goons as candidates. No, he decided. The carnal appetites of that pair might believably encompass both sexes and several species. Appetites would be satisfied without the introspection and patience required to don a contraceptive.

"Captain, you remind me of somebody in my past."

Marge Mainwaring was regarding him peculiarly. There was a playfulness in her eyes he had not seen before and her perfume was the atmosphere he breathed.

"Oh? Whom, please?"

"A naughty, naughty boy."

Kiet did not reply.

They heard Binh's footfalls on the stairs. Marge whispered, "I've seen *The Last Emperor* eight times."

12

It was in any language, any society, the silent treatment. It was passive torture, torment not by doing or saying but by not doing or saying. The Silent Treatment. The technique was innate to Luongans, Kiet thought. Our principal weapons are our mouths. We open them to wound with malicious gossip, we close them to slash deeper, to wound with anxiety. Might the silent treatment have originated in ancient Luong, our major contribution to the advancement of civilization?

Binh was aiming the Yugo westbound on the interstate. The speedometer needle flickered at fifty and the motor howled as if it had been scalded. Kiet had not spoken since ordering Binh where to go.

"Go ahead, Superintendent," Binh said. "Keep it up. I deserve it."

Kiet acquiesced silently and motionlessly and expressionlessly. I shall maintain verbal celibacy unless absolutely necessary. I shall be a stone Buddha, he thought.

"Well, you can draw any conclusion you care to, but like I said without actually saying what I did, I did it for the case, the cause. The incognito deception situation, you know. Yeah, maybe I was playing the bigshot to jump Marge's bones, which hasn't happened lately as you know and I think that's punishment big-time, but you should take it as a compliment, me pretending to be you, imitation being the sincerest form of flattery, and you'll have to admit, it worked out best in the long run, Davey betraying me in Disneyland like he did and me being a person of interest, I'd be in even hotter water if my true identity became common knowledge."

Of course Davey Peterson, Jr., betrayed you in Disneyland, Kiet thought. He is—was a criminal. A criminal who does not betray a police officer when the opportunity occurs is abnormal, perhaps criminally insane.

"That kind of ties in with why I applied for and was mailed the plastic in your name."

"*My* name?"

"Superintendent, I'm from out-of-state and I'm just a captain. Yeah, these credit-card outfits are in other states such as South Dakota, but they prefer you to be stable. That failing, you ought to draw a hefty salary. Everybody knows that superintendents earn more than captains."

"True, but my salary is not hefty. How much did you state I—you earned?"

Binh smiled. "It was kind of a little white lie by omission. I stated the right number. They assumed I was talking Yankee dollars, not Luongan zin. It was a misconception I did not correct. As far as they're concerned, I, you, we, we're Daddy Warbucks."

Kiet could not prevent himself from laughing. Binh also broke into laughter. Five minutes and four teary cheeks later, the laughter played out. The Luongan flair for the silent treatment evidently had been genetically lost on Bamsan Kiet.

Finally Binh said, "What did you think of Marge?"

"Inscrutable."

"Did she say anything about me?"

Kiet still required vengeance for the "incognito deceptions," but he was no longer angry. He would exact it in the spirit of fun. "Oftentimes it is what a person does not say."

"Talk about inscrutable, Superintendent. What the hell does that mean?"

"She is concerned about you."

"That's nice. What I mean is did she indicate she had the hots for me at any level? What do you mean *concerned?*"

"We confided in one another regarding the deliberateness and viciousness of the burglary, in particular the strength and anger required to rip the front door from its jamb."

Binh gulped. "The goons?"

"I didn't confide our experiences with them to Marge, but yes."

"Do you really think so?"

Binh was as pale as a Caucasian. Goosebumps stood his scanty arm hair upright. Splendid. Sufficient vengeance, Kiet thought. He smiled and said, "No. I think adolescents broke in to eat, drink, and have safe sex. I have been teasing you."

"You're lying, Superintendent. You're just trying to make me feel good. Those scumbags somehow located me."

"Honestly, I was merely teasing."

"Sure, sure. Sure you are. I'm damned if I do, damned if I don't. I can return to night watchman duty and be a sitting duck or I can quit. In Marge's eyes I'll have a yellow streak down my back a yard wide. I do appreciate you trying to soothe my fears, though."

Kiet closed his eyes and shook his head. "My pleasure."

"What do you figure on accomplishing by interviewing Davey's mom?" Binh asked.

"I don't know. You interviewed her once, didn't you?"

"Yeah. Prior to Davey being picked up."

"Was she asked to identify the body?"

"Considering the condition it was in, no, but I read in the paper that she knew it was Davey. A mother knows when her child is dead, stuff like that. You're wondering about the twenty million, aren't you?"

"Indeed."

"Whether her life-style's skipped upward a notch? Whether a blue-collar widow's become a Swan Lake Acres prospect?"

"Yes. There! Skyscrapers!"

They were in Seattle proper, climbing a hill. Suddenly, to the north, a flat industrial area was exposed. Beyond was the downtown vertical cluster. The setting sun cast a pinkish glow on the tallest of the buildings, a stretched black ziggurat.

"It's as if it is on fire," Kiet said excitedly.

"The Columbia Center," Binh said. "Seventy-six floors. Tallest building in the American West. Pretty awesome, huh?"

Binh took a side street and the panorama vanished, obscured by trees and small, boxy houses. He said, "Now you see it, now you don't. But put your happy face back on, Superintendent. You'll get your skyscrapers. This town is one hill after another. Beaucoup view property. You just had the moving equivalent of what Marge and the real estate profession call a peek-a-view."

"Has suspicion been directed on Mrs. Peterson?"

"Not that I'm aware of. If Davey left the loot stuffed in her mattress, she's playing it pretty close to the vest. What did Marge say about me?"

"That you're too likable. What, please, is *The Last Emperor?*"

"It's a movie about the last emperor of China. You're not making any sense."

"Good. Are we near?"

"Next block, second house on the right."

The boxes were as conceptually uniform as the French

châteaus. Paint schemes and choice of fencing material, wood or chain link, distinguished the dwellings. Flowers bordered them. The lawns, while neatly mown, were parched. According to travel literature, Seattle was entering its dry season.

"I'll park around the corner, right?"

"Wrong," Kiet said. "Two Asian strangers, one a mustachioed priest and the other a football hooligan. On your sidewalk. What would you think?"

"Yeah, right," Binh said, stopping. "No lights on. She's not home. What should we do?"

"The curtains on the largest window are open."

"The living room. We're gonna snoop? What do we say if we're confronted by neighbors?"

"That you've come to provide spiritual comfort for the bereaved."

"What about you?"

"Explain me to them in Latin."

"I don't speak Latin."

"Neither will they. Improvise."

"Whatever's fair."

Before peering into the large window, Kiet led Binh through chain-link fence gates and around the house. The rear lawn was shaggy and dotted with dandelions. A barbecue on wheels was the lone furnishing on a tiny concrete patio that was spidery with cracks. Meat residue on the grill was green and furry. Draperies and curtains were drawn. The corner bedroom, Binh said, was Davey's; he had more computer gear in there than the Pentagon.

They went out the gate on the opposite side and stared into the living room. Dusk light was bad, but the sun was low and bright behind Kiet's shoulder like a flashlight. The furniture was nondescript. A stone fireplace caught Kiet's attention, or rather what was on the mantle and hanging on the wall above. Oranges, reds, and pinks from the dying sun glinted on peculiar brightwork that occupied the mantle from end to end.

"Dark, solid, glossy bases. Unreadable inscriptions on metal plates. Human shapes fastened on the bases. Figures stooped awkwardly, clutching spheres," Kiet narrated. "What are they? Religious icons?"

"Bowling trophies," Binh said. "Davey's mom is an avid bowler, remember?"

"Yes. You mentioned that. The framed photograph above the trophies. Davey?"

"That's his mother's all-time favorite. It was taken three or four years ago."

"Hearty smile," Kiet narrated. "Moon face. Thick glasses. A homely lad."

"Yeah. The retouchers blotted out the zits too. Acne City. A pizza face only a mother could love and the personality of a world-class dork. Do you wonder why he couldn't score with the chickies? I look at that picture, I almost feel sorry for the treacherous son of a bitch."

"An accurate likeness?"

"Semi. Davey had lost a lot of that baby fat. Him and Ken Bolling knew each other, you know."

"Ah," Kiet said. "Ken Bolling's Thin 'n' Rich Dynamic Development Seminars, Incorporated. He certainly grew rich. Perhaps Mr. Bolling thinned him also. Affirmation chanting, ocean-wave listening, and correctly microwaved Cuisine By Ken. Slimming is conceivable."

"Cynical as you're coming on, Superintendent, you might be on the mark. Davey's mom, maybe I know where she is. She bowls most weeknights, even in the summer when there are far fewer leagues."

"I have never been in a bowling parlor," Kiet said.

"Of course you haven't. We don't have any in Luong. And it's bowling *alley*. South End Lanes is Davey's mom's hangout."

"You roll a heavy ball at pins in an attempt to topple them, yes?"

"Right on. One roll per frame or two rolls, depending on you knocking them all down, which is a strike. Second shot if you don't. Then you sit with your buddies and smoke cigarettes, drink beer, and eat junk food till it's your turn again."

"Bowling is a sport?" Kiet asked.

"Yep. Pro bowlers go on tour and get paid big bucks if they win. The matches are on TV."

Ah, Kiet thought. Hickorn Golf and Country Club. Hickorn Lanes. I shall be Luong's most avid sportsman.

South End Lanes was between an auto body shop and a convenience store. Kiet suggested that Binh wait in the car, citing exposure in a public place as needlessly risky. Who'll see me, Binh asked? It wasn't very public, anyway, not really, not when you counted parked cars. Davey's mom wouldn't recognize him, either; Chick Chipperfield hadn't. You aren't a person of interest in the death of Chipperfield's son, Kiet said. Sit tight.

"Superintendent," Binh called out cheerfully. "How will you recognize her?"

Kiet groaned and motioned him to follow. Binh scurried alongside and said, "Not to worry. I'll keep a low profile. I'll bless the snack bar or something."

South End Lanes smelled to Kiet as foul as his Soft Springs Motel room. Signs posted at the cocktail lounge entrance admonished No Minors and No Firearms. Kiet walked by, thinking of wild saloon shootouts in the black-and-white American western series that were the staple of Luongan television.

Ten of thirty bowling lanes were in use. Stolid black balls rumbled along hardwood strips and pins clattered. The noise irked Kiet. There was no rhythm, no cadence. It was a harsh continuum of cavernlike echoes.

"No leagues tonight," Binh said. "Open play. That's how come it's kind of dead. In league play, you wear bowling shirts."

"Team uniforms?"

"Yeah, sort of. You know those golf outfits they wear at Enchanted Lakes? Bowling shirts are in the same range of colors except they're shinier and have stuff sewed on. There's Davey's mom. Bowling by herself on the lane at the far wall. The old gal in the bowling shirt. Maybe she never changes. I think she was in one when I talked to her. Good luck. Mario and I will be doing a number on Pac-Man."

Before Kiet could request a translation, Binh faded into an alcove illuminated by video game machines. Kiet took a seat in a spectator row behind Mrs. David Peterson, Sr.

Her bowling shirt was voltaic blue with KEGLER KUTIES stitched in yellow. Mrs. Peterson took her game seriously. Her concentration was so intense that Kiet wondered momentarily if the configuration of the hardwood lane changed, warped or otherwise altered by design, requiring tactical adjustments.

He noticed patterns in her play. As she crouched before rolling, she tapped her right toe once and rotated her left heel against her right. Her first shot at the ten pins was taken with a cigarette in her mouth. The second at the remaining pins was taken sans cigarette, evidently because of the increased finesse required to topple the stragglers. The ritualism and the minimal physical exertion appealed to Kiet.

Hickorn Lanes.

Mrs. Peterson wore her gray hair in a style Kiet believed to be permanent wave. She was fifty-five to sixty years of age. From the rear she seemed mannish, the breadth of her hips gone to her shoulders, but her movements and her face were not masculine. She was bland and inoffensive, neither attractive nor unattractive. She was eminently forgettable. Kiet could picture her as a mother, but not his own.

Shortly, she brought a bottle of beer and her cigarettes to a seat once removed from Kiet. She lit up and said, "You're not a new Seahawk mascot, are you? Prancing on the sidelines like the village idiot."

"No."

"You didn't come to watch an old bird like me bowl and try to pick me up. You're here about Davey. A mother knows."

"Yes." Kiet showed his police identification.

"Bowling is my release, how I'm dealing with it. I can lose myself bowling a few lines," she said, exhaling smoke. "I loved bowling when Mr. Peterson was alive, too. We were in mixed leagues. With Davey gone too. . . . On nights when I don't have league, I bowl a few lines. I like the wall. You have bowling etiquette on only one side of you to worry about. Should you bowl, should you let him bowl first? It's like an uncontrolled intersection. Loony as it may sound, I practice in my team shirt. I concentrate better."

Without saying that it was her only remark that did *not* sound goofy, Kiet said, "His Royal Highness, Prince Novisad Pakse, is an avid billiards shooter. He competes in international tournaments. He practices at the royal palace in tuxedo for the identical reason."

"How long have you been in town?" Mrs. Peterson asked.

Kiet had to think. "I flew halfway around the world on Saturday, although I landed in Seattle on Hickorn Sunday. Three days? Four days? Two days? Five days?"

"You're helping the Seattle police hunt whatshisname?"

"Yes," Kiet lied.

"Whatshisname was a nice boy. Davey could be a brat. He shouldn't have pulled his shenanigans at Disneyland, but that was no call for whatshisname, your bounty hunter, to murder my boy."

100

Bounty hunter? "Captain Binh is merely a person of interest, not a charged fugitive."

"Oh well, I'd expect you to stick up for him. It's the money you're after too, isn't it?"

"Yes," Kiet admitted.

"Well, you're barking up the wrong tree. I ain't got a dime to my name. You should see my house. If I can't scrounge the cash to have a new roof put on by fall, I'll have to be looking for a blue light special at the K mart on buckets."

"I am not implying you have the twenty million dollars, Mrs. Peterson," Kiet lied.

"Did you know that Davey had a 171 IQ?"

"Yes."

Mrs. Peterson coughed and said, "I don't know where it came from. Not his father or me. The mister passed away in his sleep four years ago come November. He worked at Boeing in a tool room, I'm in my third year at Boeing myself. In spares. Inventory control clerk. We were married late. Davey came late. I was a housewife. Mr. Peterson wasn't a real strong or bright man, but he was a decent man. The mister's death hit Davey harder than he let on, I think, but he was never one to open up. When he didn't have a computer job, he was cooped up in his room working on his computers. He never had a girlfriend. I suppose you being a cop, you heard about the harlots in the hotel. If Davey was alive, I'd still be awful steamed."

"I am sorry," Kiet said. "I am sorry about everything."

"Sorry won't raise Davey from the dead," Mrs. Peterson said, getting up. "It's not your fault. I ain't blaming you. I hope your money turns up. Stealing money, it wasn't like Davey."

"Why did he, then?"

Mrs. Peterson shrugged and lit a cigarette. "I don't know anything about your money. Davey was a genius, but you could sell him the Brooklyn Bridge. Never mind me rattling

101

on. I don't know much about money, period. Look at me. I'm not any high-society debutante swimming in the bucks."

"Could your son have been influenced by somebody?"

"By who? Davey was a loner. He didn't have any close friends. I carry a 166 average. Not bad for an old bird, eh. Better get going. Somebody might be waiting for this lane."

Mrs. Peterson resumed bowling. Kiet watched through several frames, watching without seeing.

He was thinking, wondering. Her grief was too measured, too unemotional. Davey, Jr., her only child, had, after all, died just days prior. A Luongan mother would still be wailing and pounding her breasts. But perhaps, to the contrary, it was correct what some said, that life was cheap in the West.

Then, too, the money. The loot. Mrs. Peterson was less than forthright. Had Davey taken it to the grave with him?

Kiet was thirsty. He went to a drinking fountain, then hesitated. No. His lower tract was functioning smoothly. No silly risks, thank you. He changed a piece of U.S. currency for coinage that a soda machine would accept. The contents of his wallet reminded him that international traveling was more expensive than he had anticipated. He hoped that Binh's Bamsan Kiet plastic would hold out.

He took a cup of cola from the machine and went to the video game alcove to retrieve Binh. The throbbing neon colors on the screens and the warlike noises were surreal. Binh was the only player over fourteen years of age. Monsignor Groucho was cursing a ravenous dot. Kiet took him out of the bowling parlor before they both went mad.

13

"What, please, is STD?"

"Superintendent, what the hell are you reading?"

"Classified advertising in the newspaper Mr. Zane brought. Men and women are advertising for the company of men and women in amazing combinations of gender, race, sex, and age. These people who are demanding an absence of the STD consistently state a preference for dancing, walks on the beach, sitting by the fireplace, and nurturing. They are unanimously attractive, professional, outdoorsy, successful, and nurturing. What is nurturing? Am I missing the idiom?"

Doug Zane laughed, popped a beer can top, and said to Binh, "He's reading the personals."

"STD is sexually transmitted disease," Binh said. "It's a big-time no-no. Nurturing I'm not sure about."

"I think it's the thing you're whispering in their ear while you're talking them out of their britches," Zane said.

"Too bad you can't bottle it," Binh said, sighing. "I'd buy a five-gallon jug of nurturing for Marge."

They were at the Soft Springs. Binh had driven Kiet there, had decided to stay, had proposed they discuss the case in detail and develop a "viable game plan." Kiet suspected he was stalling to avoid duty at Swan Lake Acres and an encore staged by the nonexistent goons. Kiet was in favor of the proposition and, if he were not, he would not have objected. To do so would have been to indirectly accuse Binh of cowardice, to deliver a crushing loss of face.

Doug Zane knocked on the door not five minutes later, bearing the newspaper and another half-rack of brewskies. The paper was a local weekly tabloid that featured precious writing on arcane subjects and advertising of BMWs, Rolfing, and condominiums. It impressed Kiet as a publication for lonely pseudointellectual materialists. Zane had bought it and the beer, had seen a review of the Hickorn Café. The motel was closer than his pad and, what the hell, the beer would have gotten warm if he'd taken it home, so, hey dudes, here I am, bright-eyed and bushy-tailed. Kiet suspected that Doug Zane was as lonely as the STD-phobic nurturers.

Kiet thumbed to the review while his companions switched on the TV and channel-hopped. He read: "The Hickorn Café is in a fringe downtown area in a former gastronomical wilderness. Owner/chef Keedeng Choi, a full-blooded Luongan from the Kingdom of Luong and pride of Seattle's burgeoning Laotian community, has overnight virtually transcended the Southeast Asian restaurant scene that was fast becoming a dreary cliché of mediocre predictability."

The praise did not abate. Choi's fare was lauded as "incandescent," "elegantly unpretentious," "layered and textured in the interminable heritage of the mysterious East," and "just plain yummy."

Kiet read aloud the critic's favorite entrées. "Sautéed peppered endive, mixed fish grill in tarragon-currant sauce, chicken wings flambé over rice cakes."

104

He looked at Binh. "Orthodox Luongan cookery at its zenith, they conclude. Four stars. The dishes cost fifteen to eighteen American dollars a la carte. What, please, are they?"

"Beats me."

Doug Zane said, "That grub's not Luongan?"

Binh wrinkled his face and continued twisting the tuning knob. "No way. Sounds like cat food."

"There it is, the restaurant scene in this town," Zane said. "I was sold on the hype too. They say he cooks nectar of the gods, you say it's fake and cruddy. This Choi dude's gone into a gentrified location with an oddball thing everyone's got to say they're the first to try. You have the instant crowd syndrome. They'll be lined up around the block waiting for a table. Two months from now he'll either have a solid, regular clientele or he'll have gone belly up. A new guy'll come in. Burmese, maybe. Monkey meat on a stick. Different grub, same cycle."

"The Keedeng Choi I remember owned a small café," said a puzzled Kiet. "He served good food at a fair price. What is endive, what is currant?"

Zane said, "Well, you can take the boy out of Luong but you allegedly can't take the Luong out of the boy, except in his case."

"What does that mean?" Kiet asked.

Zane burped and slapped his belly. "I don't know. I think it means I've had a brew too many."

"Jesus!" Binh said. "Superintendent, do you see what I see."

If what he saw was a beaming Chick Chipperfield on television, yes. Chick was at his used-car lot, dressed as he was earlier except for the red carnation in his lapel. Kiet imagined that viewers by the thousands were reaching for adjustment knobs in an effort to correct the color malfunction.

A pert Causcasian woman stood beside him, speaking into a microphone. The word LIVE blinked on the screen.

She said, "I'm live with flamboyant used-car dealer Chip Chickerfield for an exclusive development on the yet-un-solved, brutal execution-style slaying of computer genius David Peterson, Jr., whose incinerated, bullet-riddled body was dumped on the unlucky thirteenth green on Enchanted Lakes Golf and Country Club. Mr. Chickerfield, according to you, authorities from the isolated Laotian principality of Luong arrived in Seattle to assist in the manhunt for the prime suspect, a missing police captain by the name of Binh, who had taken David Peterson into custody in an extradition situation. How was this information relayed to you?"

"Straight from the horse's mouth, Annabeth Marie. I'm a greater believer in civic involvement. I spent time in Luong. I was associated with one of those mutual-benefit business deals that did a lot of good for those poor folks down there, putting them on the map with a travel industry they didn't have before. It wasn't Peace Corps, but it was in that ball park. I got to know the muck-a-mucks in Hickorn, their capital. Bamsan Kiet, chief of police, me and him were like brothers. I helped him solve some tough crimes."

Kiet groaned.

"Chief Kiet came to you?" the woman asked.

"Yep. Hopped off the plane and beelined it to yours truly this very afternoon."

"How were you able to provide assistance?"

"I gave him a car free of charge, in the name of law and order. I gave him some tips on the whys and wherefores of our Emerald City. Captain Binh, he used to work for Kiet, so Kiet has a personal, intense interest in wrapping this up without a whole bunch more muss and fuss."

"We can presume that Chief Kiet is planning to coordinate the manhunt with the Seattle Police Department, but an SPD spokesperson has denied to our station that Chief Kiet has reported in with them and also that Captain Binh has not yet been charged with the grisly homicide."

"Well, I don't know what to tell you, Annabeth Marie. The

first thing I said to Kiet was, Bamsan, in the interests of protocol and mutual understanding, hustle on downtown and have yourself a powwow with Seattle's finest."

"Chief Kiet was reportedly accompanied by a Roman Catholic priest."

"The Archbishop of Hickorn. They didn't spell it out, but you can read between the lines. Binh's a devout Catholic. When Kiet corners him, the padre'll be on hand to talk him out of doing anything dumb."

"I'm a goddamn Buddhist," Binh yelled.

"Our hopes and prayers are with Chief Keet and the Archbishop of Hockorn, that they can avert further bloodshed. The world is a global community, but Seattle's Luongan settlement is reputed to be insular and tight-lipped. The chief and the archbishop may make the difference. They may be able to access Seattle's Luongans and gain information that will bring Captain Binh out of hiding where the American authorities can't. Wherever they are. Wherever Binh is. Thank you, Mr. Chickerfield."

"Okay, fine."

"This is Annabeth Marie Tetwell-Moodey reporting live for the 'Eleven O'Clock Action News Hour.' "

"Tetwell," Doug Zane said. "They say she's moving up to the network."

Binh changed the channel. Bees covered the face of a screaming, writhing man. Binh shut it off and said, "Bee Breath there has it made compared to what they'll do to me. SPD will take that newscast as a challenge and hunt me down like an animal."

"Not to worry. Dougie and Rim Legal are in your corner and will defend you and the constitutional rights you don't have to the full extent of the law and your retainer."

Binh and Kiet looked at him.

Zane grinned and warded off figurative blows with his forearms. "Just getting on your case. Seriously, truly. A levity thing. I'm in for the duration. Listen. My peers who went to

Harvard and Michigan while I was at Eastern Nevada, they're uptown, driving Beamers and Benzes and not the four-banger stickshifts either. Pinstripes and fifty dollar haircuts. Park the Yupmobile in the garage and ride up forty floors. Corner offices and partnerships before they turn thirty-five. Fucking *A* I'm jealous. My don't-give-a-damn counterculture facade is that. Till I met a pair of bitchin' dudes named Kiet and Binh. Those constipated, blow-dried, fast-track turkeys, hey, they ought to be jealous of me. I'm *doing* something and I'm having fun."

Binh slapped Zane's palm, said all right, then offered the same palm, which Zane slapped. Evidently a gesture of solidarity, Kiet thought as their eyes shifted to him.

"What next, coach?" Zane asked.

Kiet lifted a dripping Cuisine By Ken dinner from the bucket. Ice refilling had been neglected. The Chicken Divan inside the carton was soft. The plastic sealant was bulging.

His stomach growled. He said, "What is next is food."

14

It took Kiet ten minutes to convince Binh that Chick Chipperfield had not necessarily betrayed him, not precisely, not
with malice aforethought. Chick's groin was doing his thinking. His motivation was the reporter, Tetwell-Moodey, with
whom he desired to have sex, safe or unsafe. Binh said he
understood, sort of, but it isn't gonna do him a helluva lot of
good when a SWAT team blows him away in some alley,
right?

Doug Zane, behind the wheel of an aging, dinged, oxi-
dized BMW, a yupmobile caricature, was bound for the
Hickorn Café. "Hey, what's done is done," he said. "What's
uppermost is taking the thing a step at a time, the next step
being a change of wardrobe. You, Superintendent Kiet,
you've been in that Seahawk sweatshirt so long you'll soon
be smelling like one. After a three-hour practice. On an
August afternoon. And, you, Binh, the priest's habit—"

"Is getting old," Binh finished. "I know, I know. Secular
City, here I come. Any bright ideas?"

"Yo, affirmative," Zane said. They had to pass through downtown en route to the Hickorn Café and they had to pass through the Pioneer Square–Kingdome area en route to downtown. "Pioneer Square," he explained, "is a rehabbed, boutiqued, condominiumized section of old, old, old Seattle, old defined as a century. It used to be skid row, and they've left just enough drunks for color. Despite my sarcasm, it's pretty neat for us locals, and tourists totally flip over it. The Kingdome—you may've seen it from the air coming in, it's the thing that looks like a humongous gray orange-juice squeezer—the Mariners and Hawks play there, it's a hop, step, and jump away. To make a short story even longer," he went on, "in between Pioneer Square and the Kingdome is industrial property that you can get into for much less than you can farther uptown, although the dumps aren't what you'd call cheap and the artists have been pretty much priced out of their lofts, but as a commercial enterprise, that's where my buddy who dropped out of law school in his second year—going straight, getting religion, as it were—comes into the picture."

"Please, do we enter the picture this evening," Kiet asked.

"Whoa, I thought us white devils were supposed to be the impatient, type A, eager beavers," Zane said. "Matter of fact, my man has a combination vintage-clothing store and es-presso bar in a piece of that distressed real estate. Weird combo, you say? Radical? It's funky, and people love funk. He stays open late in the summer to oblige the tourists."

Binh said he thought it sounded cool. Kiet said he would reserve opinion on funky and/or funk.

In the establishment named Zoot Suit Cappuccino, Kiet examined a Nehru jacket. Following a chat with his owner-friend and a cup of *latte,* Zane rushed to him and advised, "Kiet, man, you can overdo funk."

"I refuse to freeze to death," Kiet retorted.

"No sweat," Doug said, leading him to business suits. A

lightweight, shiny blue, double-breasted number best satisfied requirements of warmth and size.

"Bitchin'," Zane said approvingly, "You're a hybrid of Fu Manchu and Al Capone."

Binh perused the uniforms. He told Kiet and Zane that he liked uniforms. That is news to me, Kiet almost said, removing a sailor suit from a rack.

"C'mon," Binh said, "I'm an officer, a captain, I don't wanna be an enlisted man."

"Try it, you'll like it," Zane said in a Groucho Marx voice. "Girl in every port and so on. Besides, the insignia patch on your arm, the chevron under the eagle, you're a petty officer third class."

Kiet summoned travel data from his memory and informed Binh that Seattle was a maritime city. Smart, Zane agreed. Anonymity. You'll blend into the background. Not a good time to hit the street decked out like MacArthur, Zane added further.

Binh sighed and departed to a changing room. He emerged smiling, looking jaunty and heroic, white cap pitched to an eyebrow. He had primped in the mirror, Kiet knew. He had sold himself.

Binh did voice a concern inspired by movies in which unfortunates wearing enemy uniforms were shot as spies. Kiet thought it was the other way around, spies being shot if they *weren't* in uniform. Zane said he didn't know diddly about military law. Binh tried to pay with a credit card. The clerk's computer instructed her to confiscate the card and destroy it. Binh said not to worry and presented another card. It was accepted, but Kiet wondered how much longer they would be privy to the miracle of plastic money.

Zane drove them into downtown along Fourth Avenue. It seemed to Kiet to be a principal thoroughfare of business, commerce, and hostelry. Kiet leaned out his window, sniffing. They were half a kilometer from the waterfront, Elliott Bay. Kiet felt the unfamiliar coolness and smelled the unfamiliar smell of salt water. He craned his neck until it should have hurt, but he was too fascinated to feel pain. He gawked upward at skyscrapers, at the sampling of yellow glowing rectangles and squares. Office lighting was his visual reference to the fantastic altitude of the monuments.

"Superintendent, please retract yourself before you're decapitated by a parking meter."

Zane laughed. "How come I'm reminded of large dogs in Volvo station wagons on nice days?"

Kiet refastened his seat belt and asked Zane, "Why are so many lights on? Do Americans work at their desks all night?"

"Nah," Zane said. "They forget to turn 'em off."

"Wasteful," Kiet said. "Electricity in Luong is expensive and unreliable. Hickorn neighborhoods black out for hours. It is so common nobody complains."

Doug Zane shrugged. "You got it, you don't think about it. I guess it's like those Arabs burning natural gas off on their oil wells."

"Gentlemen, could we discuss energy conservation later?" Binh said. "We've got a ticklish situation. We, especially me, should be maintaining a low profile, yet we're headed for the most popular restaurant in town."

"We have to eat," Kiet said, rubbing his tummy. "Keedeng Choi surely can prepare genuine Luongan food. His menu cannot be restricted to the endive currant inedibles. Ah, fresh shrimp fried in peanut oil and sesame seeds. Cold bottles of Golden Tiger. I shall order for us."

"Superintendent, if we get busted, we're all going to jail. It's late. I don't think they'll be holding dinner for us."

"I had a client," Zane said. "He told me the King County jail serves a bitchin' S.O.S."

"S.O.S?"

"Creamed chipped beef on toast," Zane said.

Kiet could not reconcile the initials to the words. Before he could request clarification, Binh said, "Come on, this is seri-

112

ous. It's my neck that's on the line. We can eat anywhere. Anywhere quiet and dark. My treat."

"Hey," Zane said. *"No problema, amigo.* You're incognito."

"Keedeng Choi may be important to us," Kiet said.

"How do you figure that, Superintendent?"

"David Peterson, Jr., was awarded the computerization assignment by somebody. A person in America who either was Luongan or had Luongan contacts. Who?"

"The Luongan consul in L.A. was the go-between. We don't have a Seattle consulate," Binh said.

"So whom, please, married Davey Peterson to our L.A. La La Angeles consul? Davey was socially stunted, a mama's boy who, when not on a computer job, lived in his bedroom with his own computers."

"Who. I don't know," Binh said. "When Davey and I were in Southern Cal, I phoned the consulate. The bastards stonewalled me. They were, you know, covering their tails. They denied ever hearing of Davey Peterson. The consul, his deputy, and their three clerks. A unanimous wall of bullshit. I wouldn't be surprised if the consul defected. I would if I were in his shoes."

"Presuming the consul is lying, an individual from Seattle introduced Davey to him, yes?"

"Yeah," Binh said. "Nobody put an ad in the papers for a computer consultant, nothing like that. Feelers were put out to Luongan-Americans to keep their eyes and ears open, I assume. But how come Keedeng Choi? He slings hash."

"He is a Seattle Luongan," Kiet said.

"Yeah. Him along with hundreds and maybe thousands of others. You're laying money on Choi as the intermediary, Superintendent, you're betting on a long shot."

"No gambling improbabilities," Kiet said. "Keedeng Choi is not my intermediary suspect. Keedeng Choi is Luongan. Name another Seattle Luongan."

113

"Well, not off the top of my head, I can't, not at this point in time."

"Keedeng Choi is an outstandingly successful resident alien. It logically follows that he is a leader in the Luongan community. We shall speak to him and he will lead us to the infamous liaison, who will perhaps lead us to the stolen money."

"A good theory, Superintendent, but what if Choi doesn't cooperate?"

"He is Luongan," Kiet said. "He must cooperate."

"The severity of the embezzlement is hush-hush. You know, how our government departments are damn-near broke. If he doesn't know anything, we'll have to tell him what's going on before he can steer us in the right direction. We're talking big-time security breach."

"No," Kiet said. "He is Luongan and his homeland is in jeopardy."

"What's on the tip of Binh's tongue is that a dude's head can be turned," Zane offered.

"Excuse me?"

"Our boy Choi, he's emigrated to the land of the big PX. He's settled into a nice, big, sweet, livable city. We ain't New York, but we don't want to be either. Andy Warhol said everybody ought to be famous for fifteen minutes. It's a kind, sentimental, unrealistic notion. None of us in this car will get a shot, but Choi fell into it. He's the toast of the town, a notable restaurateur, making moola hand over fist, and his fifteen-minute timer is ticking. He's no dummy. He's grabbing what he can while he can."

"You are arguing that he has gone native?"

"Yeah, I guess you could say that. He's into other things in the Luongan district, too. A new strip mall, I think. Luong Square rings a bell. Dude's moving up in the world."

"A strip mall," Kiet said. "Real estate, Captain. If we're in a position where information is needed, your realtor friend Marge—Captain."

Binh was looking out the rear window.

"Captain, are we being followed again?"

"Could be. There was a car five cars back. I don't see it. I thought I saw that car—aw, hell, I don't know. I'm getting so paranoid, I can't believe it."

"Paranoia is a useful emotion," Kiet said.

"We're approaching Belltown," Zane said. "It's directly north of downtown and is being gentrified to the nines. Used to be auto body shops, grungy hotels, and second-rate office space. Now there's fresh paint on everything and new owners and the rents are going through the ceiling. Condos, restaurants, galleries. It's kind of an interesting contrast with the scuz who haven't been pushed out yet. The winos are drinking 1968 LaFrog Rothschild out of their paper bags."

Kiet looked at him.

"A joke," Zane said.

"The Hickorn Café is in this Belltown?"

"Yeah. Once upon a time it was a corner tavern. I'm looking for it. A bitch to find. There it is. The little neon sign in the window."

The sign was smaller than little, the artsy cursive letters spelling Hickorn Café were barely visible. "Why would a café owner deliberately conceal his place of business?"

"So customers who can find it think they discovered it. Like they tripped over a gold nugget."

"Of course," said an uncomprehending Kiet.

"Given the café's current publicity, it's irrelevant and immaterial. I see people inside eating. The Mariners played in the Dome tonight. He's probably serving dinner late for the baseball crowd."

They were met at the door by a harried Asian man with an armload of menus. "Do you gentlemen have reservations?"

Kiet peered around him. The café was dark and crowded and noisy. Diners sat at rough-hewn tables. Inset in the back wall was a counter and a grill. Keedeng Choi was holding tongs, barbecuing fish fillets. He was fortyish and of average

Luongan height: about five-foot-five. Choi was slender, also a norm. His graying hair came to a widow's peak. His brow was distinctly and permanently furrowed, as if his life were a seamless series of surprises. "No. No reservations."

"I'm sorry. Nobody is seated without reservations," the man said in an excruciatingly bored monotone. "Phone tomorrow. Next week on a weeknight, early, we can try to fit you in."

"Are you Luongan?" Kiet asked.

"Yes. This is a Luongan restaurant. Did you not notice?"

"You are not Luongan," Kiet said. "You are Vietnamese."

To Binh he said, "He is not a northerner, a Tonkinese, is he? He is not dark enough."

"Nope," Binh said, frowning at the maitre d'. "The cheekbones aren't kosher for a Saigon southerner. I'd bet Annamese. Vietnam's central highlands. Pleiku, Kontum, Ban Me Thuot."

"Is he correct?" Kiet asked.

The man was crimson. "Pleiku."

"You are a Vietnamese headwaiter. Do your job, please, oblige your patrons, and tell Choi that we wish a table."

"Who should I say is requesting a table, sir?" asked the thoroughly subdued headwaiter.

"Do not say. Just ask him to look at us."

The headwaiter went to Choi. Doug Zane said, "Man, you dudes were giving him the whammy like anthropologists inspecting a skull. I really want to ask how you can tell the difference, you all looking alike, but I guess that would be in bad taste, huh?"

Binh laughed and Kiet could not arrest a smile.

The headwaiter was whispering at Choi and Choi was looking at Kiet. His lower jaw plunged and his tongs clattered on the grill. The headwaiter returned and asked, "Smoking or nonsmoking, gentlemen?"

They chose the nonsmoking section. Though their waiter (wait-person, per Binh) was Cambodian, they did not challenge his racial authenticity. Kiet glanced at the menu, saw endive, shut it, and shook his head. Their waitperson recited the specials of the evening. After the braised pork and mango, Kiet said, "Cease. Please. Ask the chef, Mr. Choi, to fry a large plate of shrimp and bring us bowls of sticky rice on the side. And a trio of Golden Tigers."

Binh circled thumb and index finger, and told Zane, "You'll love it. You'll flip."

The waitperson said, "Sir, the dish you ordered is not on the men—"

"Mr. Choi will oblige us," Kiet said genially.

"I will ask him. What, sir, is Golden Tiger?"

Kiet groaned.

Binh said, "Make that a round of Coronas."

"No Corona. Dos Equis?"

"Sí," Zane said.

The shrimp was delicious, the cold dark Mexican beer likewise. Kiet could no longer see Keedeng Choi behind his grill. Nor could Zane or Binh, who said, "He took a powder. I wonder how come. He saw you, Superintendent, he saw a ghost."

The Cambodian waitperson brought the check and three fortune cookies. He handed out the cookies. When he left, Binh said, "Fortune cookies. Gimme a break."

"Next thing you'll unload on me is that Luongan restaurants don't have chop suey," Zane said.

Kiet read his fortune: "Pike Place Market. 10:00 A.M. tomorrow. Produce stalls. Come alone."

He handed it to Binh, who read, saying, "Bingo. Maybe you're right about a Choi link to Davey."

They paid the check and went outside. A muscular bearded man in jeans and T-shirt stepped out of an alley and blocked their path. Binh was walking ahead of Kiet and Zane. He raised his hands, but before his lead hand curled into a fist, the bearded man thrust a folded document into it.

He proffered a salute, said have a nice day, went into the alley, and drove off in a yellow Toyota.

"A summons and complaint," Zane said, taking it. "Bummer."

He unfolded it and said, mumbling, "County of Orange, state of California, grievous and malicious bodily harm, et cetera, et cetera, twenty-five million. Dude's a process server. The duck filed suit on you, Bunky."

"Twenty-five million *dollars?*"

"In damages. Yeah. They always ask for umpteen bucks more than they expect to be awarded."

"Swell," Binh said.

"Don't lose any sleep," Zane said. "You'll be ten thousand miles away and middle-aged before the case comes up on docket. This is a civil suit, not criminal. No one's throwing a net over your head on this thing."

"Captain Binh is at liberty despite being a person of interest, of intense interest," Kiet said to Zane. "A civilian apprehends him, in a sense, while law enforcement officers cannot?"

"Easy," Zane said. "Poachers work on a fee basis. Piecework."

"Evidently the process server is the person following you."

"Uh-uh," Binh said grimly. "Not the last tail. It was a dark car, blue or black. Not yellow."

15

They stayed the night at Doug Zane's West Seattle apartment which, judging by the rise of the sun over Seattle proper the next morning, was indeed west of downtown.

Zane lived in a two-tiered square doughnut of a structure. It surrounded a swimming pool and a community room that contained a bulletin board, billiards table, and a row of vending machines. Zane termed the room a "cabana" and his abode, in the aggregate, a "singles complex."

Peculiarly, when they arrived, at the brink of midnight, the pool was occupied. Young residents in bathing suits and shorts were shuttling between the pool area and the cabana's ice machine, refreshing the liquor in their plastic cups and beer cans in insulated chests.

Zane said that the revelers were "playing the role" and that anybody serious about heavy breathing, they were inside, getting it on. A bitterly envious response, Kiet thought, although he did not doubt its accuracy.

The night sky was star-speckled, the air windless, the temperature frosty, no warmer than sixty degrees Fahrenheit. Remarkably, these sexually desperate young people maintained a pretext of contentment. Everybody was smiling and nobody was shivering under a blanket. The saving of face was positively heroic.

Kiet felt sorry for them. They should be Luongan. They belonged in rural Luong and to a lesser extent in the cities. Their parents would have arranged marriages in their adolescence. There would be no need to play any role. They would be inside, warm, getting Doug Zane's "it" on.

Zane's austere apartment had one bedroom and a living room sofa that pulled out into a bed. The lone wall decoration was a pennant: EASTERN NEVADA U FIGHTING CACTI. On latticed wooden shelving that separated the kitchen from the living room was a beer mug collection. Binh said the pad was groovy. Kiet collapsed on the rolled-out sofa and said good night.

In the morning, on his way to Baxter Blenheim Pacific Rim Legal Services PS, Inc., Zane drove Binh to the Soft Springs Motel and the Chipperfield Yugo. Binh was to see Marge Mainwaring, concoct excuses about last night's absence at the model home, and mend his tattered fences. Especially, he was to ask her assistance in ascertaining Keedeng Choi's financial status.

Kiet rode a Metro coach into downtown for his appointment with Choi. The bus was crowded with morning commuters. None were transporting live chickens this time, either. Two bus rides, no poultry. Binh's implausible assertion that American live chickens were extinct might be true.

They crossed a tall, modern bridge that linked West Seattle to the main city. Below was a brackish river where a century ago aborigines had speared and netted salmon. He could see the marvelous skyscrapers and the sprawl of industry. In the vicinity were numerous cranes, enormous orange-steel praying mantises that plucked containers from cargo vessels. Seattle was a city both pretty and muscular. It smelled better

120

than Hickorn, but like any large city, Seattle had dirt under its fingernails. The municipal water supply had been proclaimed safe for drinking, but no thank you—for Kiet this was an unreasonable test of faith.

It occurred to him that water also posed an altogether different problem. Bodies of water, that is. The sound, the bay, rivers, lakes, creeks, sloughs, ponds. Land masses seemed to be compulsively linked by bridges, two of which actually floated on a lake named Washington. Natural land barriers had been eliminated. A coup d'état could be sprung. Insurgents could roll across the bridges and seize key positions before they could be detonated.

The Kingdom of Luong had been blessed with political tranquility. She was nonaligned, teetering since independence on a neutralist high wire thanks to the deft political touch of Prince Pakse. But His Royal Highness was old. After he passed on to his ancestors, then what?

Anybody grabbing for power would, however, be severely inconvenienced. Luong had one highway, which joined Hickorn to the northern highlands and its second city, Obon. Rebel troops or communist guerrillas from the north could be ambushed at the outskirts of Hickorn like targets in gunnery school.

The Ma San River was Hickorn's lone body of water. It lazed from no place to nowhere, petering out into malarial tributaries. A two-lane bridge tied Hickorn to Savhana Island and a second spanned the other waterway, from the island to slums and double-canopy jungle beyond. It would be a suicidal bridgehead. The only other way in and out of the capital was up.

The United States of America, Kiet thought. The world's strongest, richest nation. Ample atomic missiles to annihilate friend and foe. Natural resources that often rotted on the vine for the sin of superabundance. Geography that extended through four continental time zones and from the subtropical south to the Martian climes of Alaska. A citizenry who could

121

afford Mercedes-Benzes and the highest-clarity Japanese stereos.

Yet, inexplicably, they left themselves exposed, vulnerable to insurrections. Revolutionaries could storm the radio stations. Within twenty-four hours a self-appointed president-for-life could be haranguing the masses from a balcony. As Binh would put it, go figure.

Kiet contemplated this complacence, this strategic myopia, until the Metro fell under the shade of skyscrapers. He got off and followed Doug Zane's directions to the Pike Place Market. His travel literature had informed him that this bazaar was Seattle's original farmers' market, a significant asset which nearly died in the 1960s. A bureaucratic monolith known as urban renewal attempted to raze it in sacred homage to progress and erect in its place parking garages and luxury hotels. The citizenry revolted and drove off the pathological boosterites, and saved the market. Kiet saw it and silently cheered the victory.

Old buildings, some enclosed, some only roofed, paralleled a brick road already loud and teeming with customers. Stores and individual peddlers sold food, crafts, and an unimaginable assortment of merchandise. The market radiated a wonderful aromatic blend of fish, spices, ripe fruit, perspiration, flowers, and exhaust fumes. It was the aroma of Hickorn.

Kiet thought of home, he thought of Quin. So that tears did not flow, he forced himself to think of anything and anyone but.

He saw Keedeng Choi at a vegetable stall. A young man with a notebook was smiling as Choi and a burly vendor haggled in fractured English shouts and wild gestures. Choi wielded a bunch of scallions like a club. The vendor was snarling and cracking his knuckles. Tourists in short pants and floppy hats gathered round. Everybody seemed to be having fun, particularly Choi and the produce seller. A photographer recorded the spectacle. Kiet retreated to a chicken stand and ate fried wings, livers, and drumsticks until they were through with Choi.

"Thank you for coming," Choi said with a toothy smile. "How long has it been?"

Kiet accepted his hand. "You tell me. We were never formally acquainted."

"You ate in my café periodically. I remember. Everybody knows Hickorn's superintendent of police. I was honored whenever a VIP patronized my humble café."

And you are patronizing me in return, Kiet thought. "Why, please, did you emigrate to Seattle?"

"I had won the grand prize in the national lottery, the equivalent of eight thousand dollars. My wife had just divorced me and my children took her side. I worked eighty hours per week in my little café. I was never home, so the divorce was my fault, too. My astrologer said I was predestined. My horoscope said it was an auspicious moment for travel. I always dreamed of going to America. I closed my eyes and touched Seattle on a map. If I were right-handed instead of left-handed, fate might have deposited me in Boston or Richmond."

"You have a successful restaurant," Kiet said. "A strip mall too, I am told."

Choi bowed his head modestly. "I am a hard worker and I have been blessed by further luck."

"Those people were journalists, I presume."

"Interviewing me for a regional magazine. I am known for buying fresh ingredients at the market every day. That is to be their editorial slant."

"Don't all restaurateurs buy their food at a market?"

Choi hoisted the plastic bag of scallions and smiled. "Some yes, some no. This isn't Hickorn, Superintendent, where you walk to the central market. In America you can have truck deliveries. The prices are lower but purchasing food by telephone order is not romantic. Tony gives me a deal on fresh vegetables. We split the difference between wholesale and retail. The bargaining was for the benefit of the reporter."

"The Pike Place Market also sells fresh Luongan endives and currants?"

"I adapt to what is the freshest on a given day. I make no apologies. Do you know what winter is?"

"Of course."

"Like me, only from books until I came to North America," Choi said. "Seattle has mild marine weather, but it does have a winter. You cannot conceive of winter unless you have lived in one. Leaves fall from trees. It rains and hails and snows. You freeze and it is terribly dark in the daytime."

"I can imagine," said Kiet, who could not.

"In winter, fruit and vegetables do not grow. They are flown in from the South. Your choices aren't the best. One January day, Tony's endive looked good. Julio, two stalls to my right, had nice currants. Recipes were born. I'm Luongan, Kiet. I create a dish in Seattle, it is a Luongan dish. Seattlites love my food. Did you enjoy the shrimp?"

"They were splendid. Golden Tiger and *nic sau* would have been ultimate complements."

"*Nic sau* is coming. It has been shipped," Choi said. "No possibility on Golden Tiger. It's been banned by the FDA, the Department of Agriculture, and the EPA."

"Peculiar," Kiet said. "Why, please, were you and the vegetable vendor shrieking in pidgin English."

Keedeng Choi shrugged. "Tony's Italian, I'm Luongan. We screw up conjugation and tenses, we sound ethnic. Can I ask you a question?"

"Perhaps."

"That was your adjutant, Binh, in the sailor uniform, wasn't it?"

"Did the reporter interview you about him?"

"No. Why should he? Because I am Luongan? Me and hundreds of others. His world revolves around food and wine. I'm not happy that you brought Binh into the Hickorn

124

Café, Superintendent Kiet. Everybody is searching for him. A SWAT team could have stormed in. People could have been hurt and killed by stray bullets."

"You were looking at me when you dropped your tongs at your mixed fish grill."

"Your eyesight tricked you. I laid them down."

"Your waiters were Vietnamese and Cambodian. No Luongans work for you?"

"A Luongan chef assisted me in the kitchen. My Luongan waiters happened to have the evening off. Will you quit interrogating me so I can explain why I asked to meet you?"

"I am curious."

"The computer thief Binh murdered, how much money did he steal? Rumors are spreading that Luong is approaching bankruptcy."

"Captain Binh killed nobody," Kiet said calmly. "He hasn't been charged. He is a person of interest. The money? A moderate sum. The kingdom is in no danger. I nevertheless have every intention of recovering it."

"I'll have to take your word for it, but the figure I heard was twenty million dollars U.S."

Accurate rumor, Kiet thought. "Who supplied you that outlandish number?"

"I don't remember. Gossip in a letter from home. I don't know. Superintendent, I'd like to cut a deal with you. I've cultivated influential friends in Seattle. An assistant police chief and two—not one, two—senior deputy prosecutors eat at the Hickorn Café. Bring Binh to me and I'll surrender him to my friends. It'll go much easier for him."

"Aren't you listening? He has not been indicted yet," Kiet said.

"That's inevitable and you know it. They just have to re-solve a problem with the autopsy. If he turns himself in to high-ranking law enforcement in advance of an arrest war-rant, it will go easier for him."

"Assuming the unlikely event of his indictment, he will be

charged with shooting David Peterson, Jr., to death and burning him to death and vandalizing an exclusive private golf course. How can anything go easier for him?"

"Think about it," Choi said. *"Please* think about it."

"Why are you generously volunteering your services?"

"I'm Luongan, Superintendent. Binh killed a man who stole Luongan money, but killing is killing. He crippled a young Disneyland worker for life too. He has dishonored our Luongan community. He has dishonored me."

Kiet suppressed a groan. He knew Choi was seeking press attention. The write-ups on his café had evidently transmogrified him into a publicity-crazed egomaniac. He asked, "What is the population of Seattle's Luongan community?"

"Six hundred and seventy at last count."

"You are Seattle's richest and most celebrated Luongan, yes?"

"I'm not the poorest."

"David Peterson, Jr., and our Los Angeles consulate were presumably introduced by a Seattle Luongan. Who is the liaison?"

"Not me."

"Use your influence and find out who. Whom."

"A deal." Choi extended his hand. "I deliver the liaison, you talk to Binh."

"Deal," Kiet said.

"Where can I reach you?"

Kiet withdrew his hand. "Never mind. I will contact you."

16

The taxicabs conveniently available to Kiet were painted, respectively, yellow, yellow, yellow, yellow, and yellow. He selected the second from last yellow because it was shiny and dentless. The driver started his engine and Kiet was tempted to bolt. It had suddenly occurred to him that severe collision damage on American taxis was inevitable. This vehicle was therefore overdue for a tragic crash.

Kiet shunted the thought aside. He was ashamed. He was not a superstitious man. There was no harm, though, in pointing out potential hazards. Driving in urban America was a complex and dangerous undertaking. You could never have too many vigilant eyes in a moving automobile. Accordingly, he alerted the cabbie to upcoming stop signs and motorists who wandered in their lanes.

At the Soft Springs Motel, Kiet paid the meter charge. His cash was depleting fast, but he added a fifty-cent tip. The driver rolled his eyes and told Kiet that he couldn't fucking accept such a big-hearted fucking tip because the sheer fucking pleasure of his congenial fucking company had made his fucking day, thank you very fucking much.

Contrary to what he said, the driver kept the fifty cents and accelerated onto the highway, leaving as a farewell black patches of rubber. Kiet contemplated the man's oddly volatile behavior until he saw a greater enigma.

Marge Mainwaring's silver-and-chromium mastodon was backed to his unit. Captain Binh, the dashing seaman, was loading Kiet's luggage basket into the trunk.

"Superintendent, dynamite timing. How'd it go with Choi?"

"What is happening?"

"Take off your jacket. The forecast says it'll hit ninety today. What's happening is you've been evicted," Binh said, slamming the trunk lid. "You're two days in arrears, you know. The manager jumped me on the situation when I was going into your room. I could've paid. They take plastic, but hey, I'd be exposing your identity and you're the link to me, right? Your name is on the credit cards, you know."

"I indeed know, and my identity was exposed when I registered."

"Well, you'd worn out your welcome anyway. This shit-hole, they'd rather rent rooms by the hour if you catch my drift. The only thing I'll miss is that circular waterbed. I didn't create a fuss. In our situation it wouldn't've been wise. You can stay at the model home. Marge won't mind."

"Why do you have her car?"

"The Yugo wouldn't start. I called and had it towed to Chipperfield's. Doug ran me to Marge's. They hit it off fine. She was real nice to me. I think, Superintendent, that maybe this swabbie suit is gonna be my breakthrough. I told her I was on loan to the navy for a week, working undercover on a classified situation I couldn't talk about on account of national security. I slipped Choi in at that point, kind of hinting that whatever she could dig up on his financial situation could be sort of crucial to my case."

"Splendid."

"Everything's groovy again. She was eyeballing me like I was a slab of raw meat. Doug ran Marge to her office. I've got her cellular. She'll buzz when she needs her wheels."

Kiet sat in the Lincoln, leaned against soft, lush leather, and sighed. The lad's machinations were exhausting. It was not yet noon and he felt ready for a siesta.

Binh got in and repeated his question about Keedeng Choi. Kiet related the encounter in detail.

"Wow, a prince of a guy, isn't he?" Binh asked. "He'd take valuable time from his business empire to give me up to police bigwigs. As notorious as I am, they'd probably award him a key to the city."

"As he said, he is Luongan."

"The rancid son of a bitch," Binh said, shaking his head. "He knows Davey skipped with twenty mil. The exact number's not common scuttlebutt, so his ear's to the ground. He can probably finger the middleman for you, but will he?"

"Perhaps."

"I wouldn't trust him as far as I can throw him, Superintendent. The smarmy little scumbag. If he'll sell a fellow Luongan for a press conference, he's capable of anything. Let's run over to the model home and dump your stuff, okay?"

"I do not trust Choi either. He is, however, a Seattle Luongan, one in 670."

"Yeah, I guess we play that situation by ear for a while," Binh said, turning the ignition key. "Choi's a helluva lot surer shot ransacking the haystack for the needle than us."

"Excuse me?"

"Duck!"

Kiet ducked. Binh was peering above the dashboard as if it were a ledge.

"I knew it," he said. "I knew it. Knew it. You can look up now. To your right, Superintendent. It's the same car. Same same."

129

Kiet looked out at the highway traffic. "Which same car, please?"

"The car that tailed us to the Hickorn Café last night. It's the same color."

"Which car? Which color?"

"The dark car in the right-hand lane. The slow one everybody's passing."

Kiet saw a maroon compact sedan. There was a lighter colored rectangle on the front passenger door.

"Are you certain, Captain?"

"I wasn't till I saw it behind me today, creeping along super slow, just before I turned into here. Two guys in it. Young guy driving, older guy next to him."

"A goon?"

"Nah. Which is good news and bad news. Good news that it isn't one of the goons. Bad news that you have to wonder how many guys are tailing us."

"What is the object on the passenger door?"

"I couldn't tell you," Binh said. "I only saw the front of it well. Then we ducked and now I'm seeing it from the rear. I'll tell you this. I've had a bellyful. We're turning the tables on them. We're through playing defense. The offensive team's coming onto the field."

"Translate, please."

"In two words, Superintendent. Buckle up."

Kiet did. Fast. Binh tromped on the gas pedal and shifted into drive, producing a *clunk* that sounded to Kiet like an appliance falling off a truck. The Lincoln bolted onto the highway, turning hard right, fishtailing, rear tires spinning. Binh corrected and they raced under a yellow light.

"He has an eight- or nine-block lead, Superintendent, but he's just poking along. Not to worry."

"No hurry," said a perfectly rigid Kiet.

The next light was red. Binh weaved between crossing cars. Kiet closed his eyes.

130

"Christ, that was a close one! This mushbucket of Marge's handles like the Queen Mary."

"Please do not hit an iceberg."

"Superintendent, this is a piss-poor time for a nap. I'd sure appreciate you opening your eyes and IDing the vehicle and occupants, okay? We'll be in range *mucho pronto.*"

"My apologies."

The next traffic signal blurring overhead was a miraculous green. Kiet was not necessarily consoled; the numerals on the digital speedometer were fluttering sevens and eights.

"Okay, Superintendent, we're homing in."

Traffic in their lane, the inside, was thickening. Fours and fives displaced the sevens and eights. Kiet muttered "thank you" to nobody in particular. Binh yelled "drive it or park it" to the same abstraction.

They were gaining rapidly on the surveillance car. Impatient drivers followed it, bumper to bumper. Kiet estimated their speedometer numerals as twos and threes. The turn-signal lights of each blinked, but none were foolhardy enough to confront the prow of the speeding Town Car.

Kiet could and did ID the vehicle and occupants, IDing orally for Binh. "Adolescent male driving. Hunched forward. Tense. Middle-aged male with him. Talking. Rectangle on driver's door too. A sign—"

"A sign? Superintendent?"

"Ah," Kiet said.

Binh was leaning, craning his neck, reading:

BOB'S DRIVING ACADEMY
Teenage Driver Education
Insured

"Shit," Binh said as they struck the median.

When Binh's attention wandered, so had the Lincoln. It climbed a six-inch-high cement barrier that optimistically separated northbound and southbound motorists. The

131

unique grinding of steel on concrete was remarkably loud inside the soundproofed luxury automobile.

Binh regained control before they bounded into oncoming traffic and disaster. Digital numerals registering in the ones, they limped to a gasoline station, *thump thump, thump,* left front corner of the vehicle undulating.

Binh folded his arms on the steering wheel, rested his head on a forearm, and said, "Superintendent, I'm coming unraveled. I'm going paranoid crazy. We're not being followed. I'm seeing bogeymen."

"Your stress is justified," Kiet said. "You are being hounded unjustly. You made a mistake now, but the goons were not imaginary, were they?"

"No."

"Is it not preferable to be overalert than to be taken by surprise?"

"I guess so."

"Of course it is. We are making progress, are we not?"

"Yeah. Kind of."

"We shall prevail."

"Superintendent, thanks a lot, I mean it, thanks for everything, but don't overdo it, okay?"

The telephone rang.

"That'll be Marge. Please get it. I don't wanna talk to anybody just now, especially her."

Kiet picked up the receiver. "How?"

"Push that button and say hello."

"Hello."

"Bamsan?"

"No," Kiet said. "Captain Binh speaking."

"Captain, Marge Mainwaring. Is your boss with you?"

"He is temporarily indisposed."

"Oh well. You're the man I should talk to. Bamsan said he was so busy on the *ecretsay avynay asecay* he was giving you the *oichay* assignment."

"Excuse me?"

132

"Pig latin," Binh whispered. "Marge's way of maintaining telephone security. Say yes."

"Yes?" Kiet said.

"I have you-know-what per Bamsan's request."

Kiet looked at Binh. "You-know-what is pig latin too?"

Binh sighed. "She has some poop on Choi."

"Splendid," Kiet told Marge.

"Are you boys staying out of mischief in my car?"

"Oh yes," Kiet said.

"I'll be tied up at the office until midafternoon. Why don't you come by the condo around fourish for drinks and munchies? I'm fifteen minutes from Swan Lake Acres. Bamsan knows where I live. I'll cadge a ride home. Today promises to be a scorcher. My deck overlooks the lake and the breeze will be marvelous. Ciao."

Kiet replaced the dead telephone and said, "Did I accept her invitation?"

"That's an automatic, Superintendent. Nobody says no to Marge Mainwaring."

17

The mechanic at the gasoline station raised Marge Mainwaring's Lincoln Town Car on a hoist, gazed at its undercarriage, flashlight held like a torch, and said, nasty, but it could be worse. Binh asked, are you saying it's bad or what? The mechanic said it wasn't looking too great and Binh said, what are we talking about in terms of, you know, the bottom line? Hell, I drove it in here. It's drivable, you know, not on the end of a tow hook, and you're acting like I ran it off a cliff or something. Could've fooled me, said the mechanic; keep your shirt on and I'll phone up the dealer for some prices.

He emerged from his office with a clipboard and an estimate sheet. Total cost of repairs: $1,003.94. Binh said you gotta be joshing me, a thousand bucks for a flat tire and a little wobble in the steering. The mechanic thumped a grease-encrusted fingernail on the estimate, line by line, saying—tire, wheel, shock absorber, lower control arm, knuckle, tie rod. Payment in advance too; it's mostly parts, which I gotta pay outta my own pocket up front. And I'm giving you a break 'cause I was in the service myself, the army, the motor pool at Fort Ord and Bien Hoa, dodging bullets.

Binh paid with his last valid plastic, using two cards, putting 50 percent on each. Bank-card computer operators informed the mechanic that the amounts exceeded available credit. Charges were trimmed to those limits, and Binh and Kiet pooled their cash to cover the balance. The mechanic wrote two charge slips for Binh's signature and a cash receipt, and said that if he'd wanted to grow up to be a bookkeeper he'd have gone to college.

Binh said they had an appointment around fourish, and would the car be done around three? The mechanic laughed and said this is Wednesday. The control arm is on backorder. How about Fridayish around fourish?

On the Metro ride to Chick Chipperfield's Preowned Automotive Elegance, Binh sulked, but did not complain about all the stops by the bus. Kiet prudently reserved sanguine observations on the absence of live poultry. They had counted their money, had counted forty dollars altogether. The trip to Chipperfield's was a diversion from the case, they agreed, but a mandatory one. The tony Eastside suburb of Swan Lake Acres was not easily accessible by bus—the natives' multiple ownership of automobiles rendering Metro transportation superfluous, Kiet presumed—and a single taxi fare would gobble their nest egg.

They separated at the bus stop. Binh took Kiet's basket and Marge's cellular phone across the highway to a self-service laundry, a basket being a pretext, a natural smoke screen for idling in a laundry. He'd wash Kiet's Seahawk sweat outfit and read the bulletin board. Kiet tossed his suit jacket into the basket and went to Chick's lot. The temperature on a lighted board above a bank registered eighty-six, hardly Marge's "scorcher," but it was edging upward into tolerability.

Chipperfield's used cars had been rearranged, creating

135

space in the center of the lot. There seemed to be a disturbance, people assembled—no, they were an audience, an audience watching a man with a camera on his shoulder, a boom microphone attached to it, videotaping Chick Chipperfield in his devil's outfit.

Chick was blabbering at the microphone and lens, punctuating with pitchfork jabs at selected cars that had been priced with white foam numbers sprayed on their windshields, prefaced by LOW LOW LOW. In his other hand he waved a small booklet. Kiet was fortunately too distant to hear the spiel. Perspiration cascaded from Chick's face onto the shiny red costume; Kiet was pleased.

An audience composed of passersby, customers, and employees, Kiet surmised. Vulgarity aficionados? He hurried into the mobile home/office. Nobody there. Splendid. Kiet peered between the venetian blinds. Chick was approaching his finale, lips moving faster, pitchfork raised with both hands above the Yugo, like a pagan priest conducting a human sacrifice. He smashed its hood. Kiet retired to the inner office and a walk-in closet, leaving the closet door ajar.

Chipperfield came in minutes later, panting and lurching, peeling off the costume, grunting, perspiration droplets spraying. He wore nothing under it. He smelled like a mix of carpet store and gymnasium. He looked like a careless sculpture made of yeast dough with an overripe tomato for a head.

Kiet came out of the closet and said, "I thought *I* was repulsive naked. Put clothes on, please."

Chipperfield gasped, stumbled against his desk, and lifted the telephone receiver. "Kiet, you're bound and determined to gimme a heart attack, ain't you? I've had a bellyful of this happy horseshit. How's about I call the fuzz?"

"I am the police," Kiet said serenely, latching the door.

"Negative. Not in Seattle, the U.S. of A. Some third world hell hole, yeah, but not here in the land of the brave, home of the free. Far as I'm concerned, you can go take a flying fuck at the moon."

136

"Third world," Kiet said, clucking his tongue. "A demeaning label."

"Tough nouggies," Chipperfield said. "Gimme one good reason why I don't punch nine-one-one."

Kiet touched the folded papers in his shirt pocket.

"What's them?"

Kiet unfolded the documents, the estimate itemizing damages to Marge's car and the stapled receipts. "Extradition papers."

"Yeah? Lemme see."

"When you physically take them from me, Mr. Chipperfield, you are legally served. You are in my custody. We shall go without delay to Seattle-Tacoma International Airport."

Chipperfield shielded his face with his palms. "Wait a sec. No rush. I thought I was free and clear on that stolen whachamacallit."

"The Golden Peacock."

"Yeah. It was the other guys, Kiet. You know it was. Furthermore, it's ancient history."

"A higher court has decided to reopen the case," Kiet lied. "There is no statute of limitations on a matter of this magnitude."

"Kiet, I'm innocent."

"I too am confident you will be exonerated. By a Hickorn magistrate. In due time. Eventually."

"You didn't come to Seattle to catch Binh? You came for me?"

Kiet did not answer.

"Okay, fine. What do you want?"

"Initially, to put some clothes on. Please."

Chipperfield dressed in tangerine slacks, white patent leather belt and shoes, green shirt, and lemon tie—a marginal improvement to his nudity. Copies of the small booklet Chipperfield had brandished at the camera were strewn on his desk. They were coupon books, tear-out script entitling the bearer to free food items at a chain of hamburger restaurants. Binh and he were paupers, yes, but they would not starve.

"Help yourself," Chipperfield said, cinching his tie. "Come in for a test drive and we give you five bucks worth. No obligation."

Kiet gathered in the booklets as if card game winnings and stuffed his shirt pocket until it was taut.

"Or . . ." Chipperfield said thoughtfully, "Or your extradition deal is bullshit, a bluff. You're jerking my chain. Your boy Binh is the real deal and you need something else from ol' Chickeroo."

Kiet stared at him until Chipperfield looked away, then said, "Your lips were sealed, yes? You and I were like brothers, crimebusting brothers."

Chick cleared his throat. "Oh, that."

"Was your betrayal of me rewarded by sex with the reporter, Mr. Chipperfield?"

"You make me out to be a prick with ears, Kiet. No. You'll be happy to learn I struck out cold. Me and Annabeth Marie, we wrapped up the interview and I asked her out. She's divorced. She hangs onto that hyphen to discourage undesirables. Coupla drinks, I was thinking, dancing, midnight snack, and who knows what. She says she can't. She has to shampoo her dogs. Golden retrievers. I say okay, fine, and hit her up for her phone number. She gives it to me and I'm thinking later on, no point doing tomorrow or next week what you can do today. I don't sell cars because I let a prospect boogie off the lot without giving him my best shot, so I call her up. I can bring a bottle of vino over and help her shampoo the mutts and maybe me and her, we can drink the vino and hop in the tub and shampoo each other.

"The joke's on me, Kiet. This phone number, it's a recording. This preacher is ranting and raving about the Seventh Commandment. Thou shalt not commit adultery. How'd she know I was remarried? You can't trust nobody. You can't even trust your own judgment of people. She's the last person in the world I'd of picked as a religious fanatic.

"By the way, where's the padre?"

"Proselytizing Baptists," Kiet said, fingering the repair papers. "Mr. Chipperfield, your unsealed lips, your betrayal of my trust in you, has caused me grief."

"Kiet, I'm sorry. I'm a salesman. I run off at the mouth. I'll keep it zipped from now on. Honest true."

Kiet stared at him. He doubted Chipperfield's sincerity, but his eyes were wide with fear. Splendid. Terror was more reliable than conscience.

"Goddamn it, man, will you quit looking at me like I'm something you stepped in! Word of honor. Cross my heart and hope to die. I'll make it up to you. Hey, the Yugo. Bruno, my service manager, he checked it out. You must of flooded it. He adjusted some doohickeys and it runs like a top.

"I'll sign the title over to you. It's all yours. I was gonna have it towed to a wrecking yard to be put to sleep anyhow."

"Thank you."

"That ain't all. You're still staring. You're giving me the heebie-jeebies. Ask and ye shall receive. I want you outta here and outta my life."

"One question, Mr. Chipperfield. You spoke to Tetwell-Moodey about the case. Did she speak to you?"

"You whisper in my ear, I whisper in yours? Yeah. She has a contact at the medical examiner's. She said it's a rumor and she can't use it on the air till it's official."

"Rumor?"

"The crispy corpse," Chick said, smiling. "They about-faced. They don't think it's the Peterson kid any longer. They think it's someone else."

18

"What's shoe-horned in your pocket, Superintendent?"

"Coupon books."

Binh fanned pages, smiled, and said they made him feel kind of semiprosperous. They could live on fast-food breakfasts, lunches, and dinners for a week. *Big* meals. Double burgers, jumbo fries, beverages galore; no need to economize, to leave the restaurant hungry. Which freed a chunk of their cash reserve for evening snacks at the model home. Which they ought to pick up at a supermarket now on the way to lunch, a big lunch, he advised. When Marge said "munchies" she meant trendy hor d'oeuvre stuff, not real food. About as many calories as you'd get in a refugee camp, except it'll look nicer.

An American supermarket. Kiet couldn't believe it. Reality surpassed legend. It was an immense emporium air-conditioned so frigidly that nothing could spoil but the customers' respiratory systems. Row upon row of shelves were stacked with foodstuffs, household cleansers, and pet supplies. The meat case ran the length of a wall and was a slaughterhouse of livestock parts, not the least a section of dead and plucked chickens.

Binh selected a half gallon of whole cow's milk, a loaf of white wheat bread, a bottle of gelatinous fruit extract labeled grape jelly, and—Kiet grimaced—a jar of peanut butter. Kiet chose one item, a shaker container of flaked red pepper. He hoped the spice would neutralize the bland, greasy coupon food and prevent a relapse of *turista*.

Bill's Blitz Burgers was a regional six-store chain, kiosks in shopping center parking lots. You ordered at a window and ate in your car. On the kiosk roof, BILL'S BLITZ BURGERS outlined an ovoid American football. Bill had played linebacker for the 'Hawks, Binh said, till he blew out a knee. Blitzing was what linebackers and safeties did to quarterbacks.

Binh described the blitz process further as "to take the quarterback's head off." A homicidal assault in any city's ordinance book, Kiet mused. But the hamburger, a Red Dog (bacon and Swiss and fried onion) treated with pepper flakes, was tasty. Bill had evidently mellowed in his miniscule kitchens, frying ground meat and potatoes.

Binh also opted for the Red Dog, two of them, with Nose Tackle Fries, Cornerback Onion Rings, and Tailback Milkshake. Kiet envied the lad. The fats and starches and sugars would slide right through him. He wouldn't gain a kilogram.

They were eating in the Yugo, looking out at a moonscape of a hood so warped and dinged by pitchfork blows that it had to be secured by a coat hanger. Earlier, Kiet repeated Chipperfield's rumor. Binh had said something was fishy, but that he'd mentally debate it between the supermarket and the hamburger stand.

"Who won the debate?" Kiet asked.

"A no-win situation for me," Binh said. "Look, Superintendent, the days shortly after the torching, you know, the media was saying that identification was a formality. There wasn't a helluva lot left but the remains. They, it, was the right size and it was Davey's car and some of his wallet ID didn't get totally roasted and so forth."

"Yes?"

"Well, they were also saying the stiff got so hot, the skin was black and crackly, and the teeth, how you make a positive ID in these situations is the teeth and the teeth had exploded. You get moisture inside fillings and teeth pop like popcorn. Your bodily fluids boil off and turn to tar. Your skull splits and your jewelry melts like ice cream at Death Valley."

Kiet placed his Red Dog burger in its foam-plastic box, a coffinlike receptacle, and retired it to the paper bag. He had suddenly lost his appetite.

Binh bit into his second Red Dog zestily and continued, "Well, you know, the toxicology hangup, I've wondered about that. What are they trying to prove? His blood type. Was he on drugs? Did he die of burning or lead poisoning? What's the bottom line?"

Kiet shrugged.

"Yeah, exactly. If they prove it isn't Davey, what do they really prove? And is it really proof? If it isn't Davey, where is Davey?"

"Is it not to your advantage if the pathologists declare the corpse to be somebody else? Are you not then removed as a person of interest?"

"That's the best-case scenario, Superintendent, but it won't wash. You're saying Davey whacked somebody so he could disappear from me and justice in Luong and I'd get blamed for it and locked up so I couldn't chase Davey, right?"

"Indeed."

"If I'm pure as the driven snow, how come I've gone underground? How come I never reported in to SPD after the burning, to tell my side of the story, to present an alibi?"

Kiet said nothing.

"I don't have alibi one. Zip, zilch. And if Davey's alive, where is he?"

Kiet said nothing.

"Tetwell tried and convicted me on a live news report from Chipperfield's lot, right?"

"I do not know."

"Superintendent, let's face the facts. Chick was jerking your chain. He was getting you out of his hair with a fake clue. I'm sorry, but that's the name of that tune. There wasn't enough unburned corpus delicti to determine who it was, so how can they say who it wasn't?"

Kiet said nothing.

Binh pointed at Kiet's paper bag and said, "Superintendent, you gonna finish your burger?"

Marge Mainwaring's condominium was four stories high, a geometrical hodgepodge of big windows and small balconies. It was built into a hillside and looked out upon a lake designated Sammamish. Kiet did not recall the Sammamish name from his tourism readings, but it had the lilt of an aboriginal tribe, native villagers who had perhaps in the 1800s and millennia before lived on the lake's shores, scooping a bounty of salmon and trout from its waters.

On this glorious day of blue sky and borderline warm temperatures—a "blistering" eighty-nine degrees at last report on the Yugo's radio—the turquoise surface of the lake of Sammamish was a bathtub of watersport toys. Sailboats, powerboats pulling skiers, skiers on powered skis, rowboats, canoes, kayaks.

Kiet wondered if any of the watersporters were native Sammamishites. He thought not. These water toys were costly, and surviving villagers were poor and long since relocated to reservations and city slums. The Native American had been done in by the cavalry. Luong's original inhabitants, its highland primitives, had been done in by French missionaries and their harsh Vatican God who did not take no for an answer, and by colonial settlers who donated smallpox and syphilis.

Kiet was out of the car, following Binh along flagstones and grass manicured like Enchanted Lakes Golf and Country Club's greens. He pondered the American natives and the Luongan counterparts, the similarities and the ambiguities. The ancestral dead of both cultures were adored by archaeologists and anthropologists. The scientists had research grants and never tired of translating stone carvings and sifting for potsherds. Living descendants, on the other hand, were the sociologist's and law officer's problems, regarded en masse as lazy drunken nuisances. Kiet didn't understand.

"Marge's real estate company was the broker for this project," Binh said. "They had to go to the wall to pull off a zoning variance on the height. See anything else in the vicinity that's taller than two stories? Marge said it was her firm's finest hour."

"Splendid."

"Her unit is fourth floor center, naturally."

"Naturally."

"Dynamite view. Sweeping."

"Of course."

Binh pressed a button. Marge's voice emanated from a speaker, raspy and hard, like an aircraft transmission. A buzzer buzzed and the door unlatched.

"Security," Binh said, leading Kiet to the elevator. "You can't be too careful these days."

"Yes," Kiet said. "Indian attacks."

"Huh?"

"Never mind."

In the elevator, Binh said, "Superintendent, do you think you'd be able to, you know, find your way back to the model home by yourself?"

"Probably."

Binh winked. "Just in case, you know, tonight's the night."

"Say the word and I disappear," Kiet said.

"I owe you another one," Binh said.

Marge Mainwaring greeted them in sandals, filmy slacks, and silken robe. Kiet had seen that robe at the cinema, worn by Japanese geishas who fell in love with John Wayne and other American leading men. She was holding an empty wine glass.

"Gentlemen, gentlemen. Three-fifty-nine on the dot, and they say that people of the mysterious East have no concept of time. Come in. Bamsan, dear, I was peeking out the window and I did not see my car."

"It sort of had a warranty problem," Binh said. "The wheel bearings were kind of rattling. You'll have it by Friday."

Marge sighed. "That's twice I've had it in for warranty work."

"Don't build 'em like they used to," Binh said, nodding his sympathy.

Kiet scrutinized Marge's condo. Oriental furnishings and decorations were everywhere. Buddhas, Japanese screens, framed calligraphy, a fantasy wonderland of ceramic dragons, heavily lacquered tables with mother-of-pearl inlay, thronelike wicker chairs, jade figurines, and brass bric-a-brac. South and Southeast Asia were represented, as well as the Indian subcontinent. The arrangement was cluttered and geographically random. Carved knickknacks he recognized as Vietnamese and Cambodian, antagonists for centuries, were side by side on a tea table made in China, historically anathema to both. Marge's residence looked like a Hickorn curio shop.

She pointed at a bamboo trolley. "Please dig in. Don't be bashful. I must confess, I've had a head start."

On the trolley were vegetables sliced as thin as daggers, whole-grain crackers, and crustless white-bread sandwich triangles with pinkish puree centers. Binh's refugee camp comment, albeit vulgar, was insightful. On a trolley leaf were bottles of white wine.

Marge refilled her glass and raised it. "A light, cool libation for torrid weather. *Salud!*"

Kiet and Binh poured wine, clinked Marge's glass, and sipped. Binh said "mm," and finished his with a gulp. Kiet feigned a second sip. He could not comprehend the Occidental fetish for soured grape juice. The French, especially, had inserted cachet and insufferable snobbery into the unnatural and related acts of bottling spoiled juices and, years hence, being cowed in expensive cafés by sissy-boy sommeliers.

Binh kissed his fingertips. *"Magnífico,* Marge! Nineteen-eighty-six cabernet sauvignon is my all-time favorite."

"Captain Binh?"

Marge's eyes were dreamy, her cheeks flushed. Kiet pretended to sip and said, "Splendid."

"Shall we retire to the deck?" Marge said, leading them.

She was not unsteady, but Kiet sensed she was working very hard at sobriety.

Kiet sat in a non-Oriental aluminum-and-vinyl chair on a narrow wooden balcony. The railing was also lumber and through the slats Kiet could see the lake and the Cascade Mountains at the horizon. As Marge had promised, the breeze was marvelous.

"Two appointments canceled," Marge said. "I came home very early."

Ah, Kiet thought. The spoiled-grape glow on her cheeks.

"The extra time shows in the food preparation, Marge," Binh said, waggling a translucent carrot slice. "Labor Intensive City."

Marge threw back her head and laughed. "No, no. I bought the food as is at a deli. I've been dusting, straightening up, and nipping. Lord, had I taken a stab at precision veggie slicing, I'd be the stabee. I would have bled to death before you arrived. My domestic skills are minimal."

"Your detective skills are polished," Kiet said. "To have a report so promptly on Keedeng Choi."

146

Marge slapped herself on the forehead. "Oh, I just remembered. I forgot my listing book at the model home and I know I'll be receiving calls. Bamsan, be a precious and run up there for it."

"Well," Binh said, standing slowly and reluctantly, "the Choi situation——"

"Not to fret," she said, cooing, hooking her arm to his. "You said you assigned Captain Binh to handle this. He can brief you. Forgetful me, I'm helpless without my listing book."

She trotted him out the door and sat inside on a bamboo sofa with loose cushions. She patted the cushion beside her and said, "Binh, bring your wine and come on in. Too much fresh air isn't good for a person, and the sun's behind us. It's warm but we won't fry."

Kiet went inside hesitantly. Marge asked him to freshen her "drinkie-poo." He poured wine, white wine. Not white, he was thinking, not technically. It was a chromatic median of water and urine, sensory emphasis on the latter.

He gave it to her and sat beside her, on the cushion she insistently slapped until he did.

"Keedeng Choi, please."

"Do you practice tai chi chuan, Binh?"

"No."

"Noncontact karate is a slang definition. I don't like it. Tai chi is much much more. It's spiritual."

"Travelogues of China, Taiwan, and Hong Kong," Kiet said, remembering. "People in parks in the morning. Slow-motion dancing and fighting."

"I practice Taoist breathing methods too, body-soul holism, feng shui, and heart-mind consulting. Thanks to Seattle's cosmopolitan nature and relationship to the Pacific Rim, these teachings are available. I've studied under gurus and transcendental masters. I believe the East has a clarity and an opportunity for genuine enlightenment if one only opens his or her mind. Don't you think so?"

147

"Yes. Of course." He had not an inkling what she was saying. Breathing methods and body-soul something? Marge's gurus and masters did not seem entirely dissimilar to Chick Chipperfield and Ken Bolling.

"But acupuncture and raw fish? Not for this gal," Marge said. "I'm not too keen on Buddhism, either. It has good points, but shaving your head and celibacy, uh-uh, that's where I draw the line. You're looking at me as if I'm a candidate for the loony bin. Don't pay any attention. I chatter like a magpie when I've had a glass of wine or two. Honestly, is Bamsan on a spy mission?"

Her hand was on Kiet's thigh, nearer the hip than the knee. "Sorry," he said. "Classified data. Superintendent Kiet would rightfully court-martial me if I repeated sensitive information."

Marge faced Kiet, leaning into him, the hand on his thigh pressing and kneading. "Binh, it must be terrible to be from an underdeveloped country where there is no such thing as a career path unless you have high-level connections."

"Excuse me?"

"Superintendent Kiet is half your age and he commands your police department. You are as capable as he and you're stuck in a dead-end job."

"I am?"

"Binh, do you plan to spend the rest of your useful life working for a precocious lecher?"

"Yes."

"God! That's what drives me so crazy about Asian men. I admire your serenity, your spirituality, and at the same time I'm annoyed because you're not racing headlong up the ladder like a Harvard M.B.A."

"Superintendent Kiet is ambitious."

"He isn't you," Marge said. "Do you understand?"

"In recent days I haven't understood much," Kiet said, although he did understand what she was doing with the

148

hand that was no longer content to squeeze and stroke his thigh.

"You aren't home in China. Nobody'll know. A traveler seeks what he has to seek in his travels. In my interpretation, this is in harmony with Confucianism."

"Folk dancing and cathedrals," Kiet said in vain, weakening fast, and adding without conviction, "No time Binh— Kiet will be—"

"No, he won't," Marge said. "My listing book is in my purse. I'd lose my keys and my wallet before my listing book. Bamsan is on a snipe hunt. He'll be tearing that house apart, room by room."

Kiet could not inquire about the snipe creature. Marge's tongue was in his mouth and his resistance was nil. He was at a stage where his only protest might be lack of time. But that was not true. Otherwise, his resistance would not have so effortlessly vanished.

Marge deftly unzipped and unbuttoned him and he, less assuredly, uncinched her robe. They rotated together off the sofa onto a thick, soft area rug Kiet had not previously noticed. A busy pattern. Persian? Expansionism of the Asian theme? Stupid, silly, to wonder. He closed his eyes. He saw Quin. Quin. Her face. Her glowering face imprinted on his eyelids. His shirt was off, flesh laid bare for a lightning bolt. Just deserts.

Marge wore gauzy pajamas under the robe. She had peeled the top over her head, displaying Luongan-like breasts, lemons in size and shape and firmness. Quin. Kiet yarded down the bottoms, a delicate seam ripped, and Marge cried, "Henry, you brute!" Kiet froze, afraid that he had harmed her. Marge shoved his wrists and the dainty pajama cloth in his hands to her bent knees and over, to her ankles and feet and off.

Her legs wrapped around him like constrictors. She cried and beat his back with bony fists and begged Henry to quit hurting her. Time was irrelevant. They were done and sepa-

149

rated, sprawled, gulping oxygen. Had Binh bagged his snipe?

"Give me two drinks and—" Marge said. "I'm sorry."

"I'm an adult and I am stronger than you. I could have established control. I could have said no."

"Do you smoke?"

"No," Kiet said.

"I used to. Two packs a day for years. I couldn't kick the habit until I took a Zen-holotropic behavior modification course. We meditated and said mantras for a week. God, am I dying for a weed! Is a cigarette after sex ingrained in your culture, Binh?"

"Yes, if you smoke."

"Were you thinking of someone else?"

Kiet nodded yes. "And you, of your Henry?"

She sighed, stood, and began retrieving her clothing. Excellent idea, Kiet thought. Binh would soon deduce that snipes were out of season.

"He was my college lover."

"A Chinese named Henry?"

"Chinese-American. I've never gotten him out of my system. He treated me like trash and dropped out of school when I told him I thought I was pregnant. He joined the navy and I never saw him again. Ironically, it was a false alarm. My plumbing's screwy and I can't have children. That sailor uniform of Bamsan's, he's cute and twitchy. I was on the verge of succumbing to the horny little toad."

Kiet did not reply.

"Feeling guilty?"

"Yes."

"That's touching, truly, truly, but yours is a macho society."

"My guilt isn't cultural. It's personal."

They were fully dressed and Marge's arms were around Kiet. He reciprocated. She said, "I envy your lady. I guess you're curious why I came on to you like gangbusters."

150

"Mildly," Kiet said, smiling.

"You." She punched his tummy playfully. "Bamsan has the notion he and I are going to be a panting, sweating item because he reminds me of Henry. He does—of the Henry of days gone by. You remind me of how Henry would look today."

"You've hated Henry for years?"

"Love-hate, Binh, does quirky things to the libido. I had a Dorian Gray fantasy that he had aged badly. You're no spring chicken and you're out of shape. You're also a hunk. You are him twenty years later, better preserved than he deserves to be."

"Did you pay me a compliment?" Kiet asked.

Marge laughed. "I'm not sure myself. There's a second reason why I came on like a whore. It happened this morning. Very very very personal. Don't ask."

"Keedeng Choi, please."

"On to business. Fine. We might regain our composure and fool Bamsan."

Kiet and Marge took seats on the ends of the sofa. She said, "Mr. Choi is ambitious and he has a good business head on his shoulders. Are you going to tell me why he is so important to you?"

"No."

"Can't blame a girl for trying. Well, Mr. Keedeng Choi is a hard-driving, ambitious entrepreneur who is not afraid of taking chances. You people are incredibly industrious. The kids. The valedictorians of half the high schools in King County this June were Vietnamese. We're all going to be working for you people in a few years."

"Choi is Luongan. I am Luongan. Driving ambition in a Luongan is the consequence of a mutated gene."

"Oh, you know what I mean. I'm speaking in general about that Chinese part of the world. Choi's Luong Square mall, near the International District, was completed last winter. His occupancy rate has averaged sixty percent. Not good, not bad. Not good because you have space gathering dust instead of rent dollars. Not bad if and only if you can avoid a negative cash flow."

"Excuse me?"

"Outgo exceeds income. Choi was mortgaged to his ears with bank loans and personal paper. He couldn't raise another dime, particularly since he extended himself by opening the Hickorn Café. He's certainly making money there, but it's a drop in the bucket in comparison to his Luong Square obligations. He's a wheeler-dealer who bit off more than he could chew. So it appeared.

"Lien-holders were circling like vultures. Nobody wants foreclosed commercial property dumped in their lap. It is a giant pain. Your tenants are usually behind on their rent and things are generally chaotic. Everybody breathed a sigh of relief when Choi caught up on his payments."

"When?"

"Two to three weeks ago. Five hundred thousand dollars."

"His benefactor?"

"My contacts couldn't trace it. Choi plucked half a million out of thin air."

Marge's intercom buzzed. Binh was downstairs. Marge apologized profusely, said she had her listing book all the while in the bottom of her purse, you know what a mess women's purses are, and pushed a button, admitting him to the lobby.

She fluffed her hair and said, "You look okay. Zipper zipped. Clothes on right side out. Me?"

"Splendid."

"Good. By the way, have you reminded Bamsan how it is to his advantage to list his villa through me?"

"Soon," Kiet said.

Binh knocked on Marge's door.

She fluffed her hair again and whispered, "We look as innocent as babies."

"Indeed."

152

Marge let Binh in. He glanced at her and then at Kiet. His face blanched an unnatural hue of Caucasian beige.

Not a word was spoken until Marge, desperate to make conversation, stammered the beginning of her Keedeng Choi story.

19

Binh stopped at a convenience store and bought a six-pack. He gave Kiet a beer, and they drank, Binh's can wedged between his legs as he drove. Drinking and driving was probably illegal in America, Kiet thought; an additional violation in their accumulation of crimes and civil indiscretions.

He was, however, unconcerned about law and order. Binh had not said a word to him, had employed the silent treatment. Kiet felt so small he was surprised he could see over the dashboard.

Eventually, as the Yugo struggled up the hill to Swan Lake Acres, Binh opened his second beer and said, "I'm not going to ask you point-blank what transpired while I was gone, Superintendent, because I think too much of you professionally and personally to put you on the spot in the context, you know, of where you'd figure you'd have to lie to me."

"I wouldn't lie to you," Kiet lied.

"Superintendent, sometimes I wonder how you made it in police work. You can't fib worth a shit. Marge had sweat on her upper lip, for Christ's sake, and your ears were the color of a tomato. C'mon, out with it. Please. You owe it to me."

Kiet was boxed into a corner. No escape. He would tell everything, sans graphic detail, and hope that their friendship would endure. But how? His lips would not move. It was as if his jaws had rusted shut.

"Superintendent, you gotta spit it out sooner or later."

Kiet nodded.

"Marge set it up for you to soften the blow, right? So I really don't see what your problem is."

"Excuse me."

Binh swigged his beer, two long gulps worth, and sighed. "I hate being patronized, you know. I really fucking hate it. Marge is too nice a person, I guess, to dump me on a one-to-one basis, not until I've been prepared for a big-time let-down. So whip it on me, okay? I'm not a child. She sent me on a snipe hunt so she could dump me by proxy."

Kiet closed his eyes and thanked the pantheon of deities, none of whom he believed in. He knew he was unworthy of this pardon. "Yes, Marge did mention you."

"What, what? What did she say?"

Kiet said, "She characterized you as a 'precocious lecher.' "

Binh smiled. "Oh yeah? What else?"

"Nothing substantive," Kiet said truthfully. "We should analyze and interpret 'precocious lecher.' "

"Well, that message has been loud and clear since day one. I haven't been listening because I haven't wanted to hear. The bottom line is that from her situation she's robbing the cradle."

"That was the innuendo."

"I don't get it, Superintendent. In the States, foxy older ladies on the arms of studly young guys, it's a status symbol for the women and the guys get super poontang. Beaucoup worldliness and experience at their disposal. May-September is in vogue."

"Marge Mainwaring is a professional woman," Kiet said.

"Perhaps a handsome, dashing foreigner, a far younger romantic interest, would damage her career. People would presume that she had purchased a gigolo and no longer regard her seriously as a businesswoman."

Binh smiled again. "Yeah, Marge has a real head on her shoulders. My timing's off by a year or things could be radically different."

"Excuse me?"

"Next year is Marge's twenty-five-year high-school class reunion. Wouldn't we be an item? The girls she hated would be staring daggers through her. Drop Dead City. I'd be the man of the hour, Superintendent. Well, we can still be friends and don't think for a minute I'm giving up, either."

Binh's machismo and vanity and immaturity had shown through, had preempted the crisis. Kiet thought of Quin. A squadron of butterflies launched in his stomach. She was not as shallow as the lad and himself. Nor was she gullible. At least she is a trained and dedicated nurse; she will amputate my genitals with a sterile instrument.

"Are you thinking what I'm thinking, Superintendent, that Choi pocketed a chunk of our twenty million?"

"A finder's fee," Kiet said. "A commission. Yes. Choi promised me the name of the La La Consulate—Davey Peterson liaison."

"He doesn't produce a credible name, he's our boy," Binh said.

"Today is Wednesday," Kiet said, hesitating. "Isn't it?"

"It is," Binh said. "In Seattle. In Hickorn, Thursday."

"I shall revisit Mr. Choi on the upcoming Seattle Friday," Kiet said. "A fair and reasonable deadline."

"He's anticipating you delivering my ass on a silver platter. You coming alone is gonna be a big-time disappointment to him."

"Mr. Choi shall have a name for me or he shall be the name."

"Right on," Binh said. "Where are you rendezvousing?"

156

"Our choice, Captain, yours and mine. Impromptu."

"I hear you," Binh said. "I smell an ambush too."

"A Luongan who would palm off endives as Luongan cuisine is untrustworthy."

"Amen," Binh said. "Speaking of cuisine, let's eat."

They detoured and ate dinner at a Bill's Blitz Burgers—double-meat cheeseburgers, jumbo french fries, milkshakes: The Super Bowl. The dismal monotony of jail food, Kiet thought. No difference, be it fish chunks and rice or greasy chopped cow meat. If you had to eat it or starve, you were serving a sentence.

The model home door had been repaired. They went inside and Kiet peered out a sliver of daylight separating drapery panels.

"What's wrong, Superintendent?"

"Did you sense we were being followed?"

"Nope. I'm recovered. Cured. Did you?"

"Yes."

"Where, when, description of vehicle?" Binh asked.

"No," Kiet said, shrugging. "A sensation, not an observation."

Binh laughed. "Galloping paranoia. Same same what I had. It's gotta be a virus. You hungry, Superintendent?"

"Captain, did we not finish dinner minutes ago?"

Binh rubbed his flat stomach. "I should've had *two* Super Bowls. One just didn't cut it. The big disadvantage of American food is that you eat and an hour later you're starving again. I'm gonna make me a peanut butter and jelly sandwich. Can I fix you—"

"No!"

"Okay, okay. Don't get testy. How about turning on the tube? The remote's on the coffee table."

Kiet picked up the remote control device. On it were no less than twenty-five lozengelike buttons, their functions denoted by numbers or words or peculiarly abbreviated words such as DSPY and CHAN. No thank you.

He activated the wood-cabinet console television receiver manually and called toward the kitchen, "What do you want on?"

Binh returned, biting into his sandwich. Gelatinous fruit product and the disgusting brown matter oozed from between slices of wheat bread. Kiet shuddered.

Binh said, "Channel hop. Now's kind of the dead zone after news and before prime time. Slim pickings."

Slim indeed, Kiet observed. A situation comedy on film so old the sky was green. A dowdy game show contestant straining to place Spain in its correct continent. A perky young man and woman interviewing celebrities.

"Hold it," Binh said. "Look."

Binh was pointing animatedly at a commercial. The scene was a catastrophic automobile accident. The camera concentrated on a car that had rolled onto its roof. The driver-victim was hanging upside down by his seat belt. Sirens wailed and lights flashed. A man with an oily voice and the face of Heinrich Himmler was handing in a document and a pen. "A release of all claims," said the voiceover. The man on the scene was an insurance adjustor. The voiceover implored the victim (and the accident-suffering television viewer) to not be victimized further. Legal representation was but a phone call away, a 1-800 number and a conveniently located Baxter Blenheim Pacific Rim Legal Services branch office.

"Small world, huh?" Binh said.

"We shall contact Mr. Zane tomorrow," Kiet said. "We are paying him to represent you. In light of Marge's comments on Choi, Zane might have recommendations."

"He's my attorney, yeah, but the retainer will tap out pretty soon. I doubt if Doug's boss would keep us as charity clients. Rim Legal, I have a hunch, isn't into pro bono. Could you check the mailbox, Superintendent? Maybe there's some virgin plastic waiting for us. I've got peanut butter on my hands."

Contamination, Kiet thought. Hepatitis, typhoid. He advised Binh to wash with soap and hot water, and went to the mailbox. There was one piece, a plump envelope addressed to B. KIET. Printed on it in bold letters was: The Favor of a Reply is Requested.

Kiet took from the envelope a document, a fancy certificate that vaguely resembled a bond. It was an unconditional guarantee of award to B. Kiet in the amount of $10,000,000. He hurried inside and gave it to Binh, soiled hands or not. "Dare we hope?"

"Uh-uh. This is bat guano, a sucker play. You have to mail it back to them and they would really really appreciate it, you know, if you ordered mucho books and magazines."

"A lottery?"

"Sort of. We could send it in"—Binh paused—"but, hey, how's our luck been running lately, right?"

Kiet did not reply. He tore the $10,000,000 certificate into tiny pieces.

20

"Superintendent, do you burn with that hot spark of desire?"

Kiet tensed, blurting, "For Quin and Quin alone."

Binh lowered his newspaper and laughed. "Cool it. I wasn't accusing you of cheating on her.

"Thank you."

They were having breakfast the next morning in the Yugo, at a Bill's, an identical selection of First-and-Tens (ham, egg, American cheese on, contradictorily, an English muffin), a leaden deep-fried cake of diced potatoes called a Long Bomb, and plastic-foam containers of untitled black coffee.

Kiet had laundered the slacks and shirt he wore on the flight in machines provided at the model home, an automatic clothing washer and dryer. He would not freeze in sandals, slacks, and lightweight shirt if the forecast of another ninety degree Fahrenheit day was accurate.

Binh was in vibrant beer commercial splendor. A creature was stitched on the pocket of his pullover shirt. His pants were pleated and baggy. This nondisguise was perhaps the best disguise, Kiet thought. His adjutant looked like the rakish young bachelor he was, not a murdering, duck-assaulting, golf-course-despoiling person of interest.

" 'Do you burn with that hot spark of desire?' is what I'm reading. Look."

He was quoting a red-ink caption in a full page advertisement for Ken Bolling's Thin 'n' Rich Dynamic Development Seminars. Paragraphs tantalized the masses to partake of the power of scientifically researched, integrated personal development concepts. Mind turbocharging. Moneyless buying of real estate. Direct mail marketing. Memory improvement. Body slenderizing through exercise and consumption of Cuisine By Ken.

Like an antique silver frame, the text of the advertisement bordered a photograph of the health and wealth swami. Tanned and handsome and white-toothed, Bolling was in tennis whites, arms folded, pinkie ring conspicuous as an amulet. To his left was a Mercedes-Benz, to his right a BMW, to the rear palm trees and a dwelling that rivaled in design and scale the Enchanted Lakes Golf and Country Club clubhouse.

Mr. Bolling, by popular demand, was revisiting the Seattle area this weekend—Friday, Saturday, and Sunday—to conduct seminars for the overflow crowds who were turned away last weekend.

"We were not washed away in an overflow," Kiet recalled. "We were pursued by goons. We ducked into the seminar to escape. Empty seats were plentiful."

"Yeah, and that's not the end of the bullshit. Get a load of his bio. Ken Bolling put himself through college selling direct mail stuff out of his dorm room. He made his first million in real estate before he was thirty. Once he weighed four hundred pounds. He developed the diet and exercise regimen that brought him down to the sinewy one-hundred-seventy-five-pounder you see today. His books on dynamic development are best-sellers. He doesn't have to sacrifice his business income to teach seminars. He does this because, and I quote: 'He wants to help everybody in America who wants to help themselves.' Jesus, I'm gonna lose my breakfast."

"He achieved none of that?"

"I'd bet my next ten years salary he didn't, Superintendent. Guys who peddle these high-pressure seminars and tapes and whatnot, yeah, maybe they're rich, but it's the hustle that got them rich, not the situations they're selling themselves as experts on. Bolling bought that mansion and those cars by pimping his six- and seven-hundred-buck packages. He screwed me out of a hundred, right?"

Binh wiped his mouth on a Bill's Blitz Burgers paper napkin that had been printed with a polka dot pattern of ovoid American footballs and said he'd give Doug a buzz. He went to a pay telephone attached to a side of the hamburger kiosk, talked for a minute, and waved to Kiet.

"Doug says he has to see us ASAP," Binh told Kiet. "He says he has news for us. He says we could be in danger."

Ay-ess-ay-pee? "How are we in danger?"

Binh raised eyebrows and his free hand, a mime's bafflement. "He won't say on the phone. He says we ought to meet somewhere conspicuous or in total secrecy. Doug votes for conspicuous. If we're being tailed, total secrecy ain't gonna show on any map. Doug says he recommends a tourist thing. Doug says Seattle's crawling with tourists in July. Nobody'll take a potshot at us in a crowd of thousands."

"Ah," Kiet said. "At the cathedral or a folk dancing performance?"

Binh relayed Kiet's request, then said, "Doug says he thinks Seattle has a cathedral, but all we're gonna see there is worshippers and archbishops. As far as folk dancing goes, he hasn't heard of anything since *lambada* was in."

"Where, then?"

Binh conferred with Doug Zane and wrote down Zane's

162

directions. He looked at Kiet with wide eyes and said, "Under the flying saucer."

The flying saucer was the Space Needle, a 600-foot-high restaurant atop a futuristic pedestal. It *did* appear to Kiet to be a hovering alien spacecraft. It was flat and circular, walled with glass, and kinetic, although one rotation per hour was not warp speed.

The Space Needle was the guiding landmark of the Seattle Center, a public enjoyment compound two miles north of downtown. Seattle Center was home to a theater, an opera house, two indoor stadiums, one outdoor stadium, cafés and shops, carnival rides, a large fountain, renowned exhibition halls of science, and tourists and pigeons underfoot.

Doug Zane awaited them by the Space Needle's massive steel feet. Tourists queued to ride the elevator. Kiet said, "Yo, dude."

Zane grinned. "Bitchin'. The man's polishing his Queen's English. I got lost last night, running around in circles hunting that tract house you're guarding for Marge."

"It does look like a UFO, Doug," Binh said, gazing straight up.

"Awesome, isn't it? Use your imagination. Elvis could be up there hovering in it. He made a movie here, you know," Zane said.

"When?" Kiet said eyes widening.

"In sixty-two or sixty-three. *It Happened at the World's Fair*. The Center was built for the World's Fair in nineteen sixty-two."

"Interesting," Kiet said. "Fifteen years before his death."

"Sorry to get your hopes up, big guy. The King hasn't been positively seen for three or four years. Drive-up windows at hamburger joints, there's your best shot at a sighting."

"Your news, please."

"For what good it'll do you, you'll have a two to three hour jump on the official announcement. A press conference is set for noon."

"Please thank your dentist for the advance notice," Kiet said.

"Not my dentist," Zane said. "My hairdresser."

Kiet groaned.

Zane twirled around like a drunken ballerina in army boots. "Dougie had his locks sheared yesterday. Do I look different or do I look different?"

Perhaps two millimeters of long blond hair trimmed, Kiet thought. He detected an intangible change in Zane, though, a peculiar ambiguity in his manner. He was giddy, yet serene.

"Listen, her roommate dates a guy whose roommate works in the M.E.'s office. I remembered the connection, so I went and got a haircut I didn't even need. Once I buckled up and peeled out in this private eye mode of mine you guys laid on me, hey, Marlowe and Hammer, those dudes can eat my dust. The narrative hook is embalming fluid."

"Excuse me?"

"Embalming fluid. Formaldehyde or whichever thing they embalm stiffs with. That's the chemical that had them scratching their heads, that they finally isolated in analysis. Morticians pump the blood out and embalming fluid in. If there hadn't been that ultrahot fire, a first year pathology student would've doped it out in five seconds flat. But when you're dealing with a glob of tar and ash and goo——"

"Yes, yes," Kiet said. "The corpse is not David Peterson, Jr.?"

"Gets my vote," Zane said. "Davey had significant cause to fake his own death. He has your twenty million and as your basic deceased person, he will never again be hounded by the gendarmes of the world."

"Yeah," Binh said. "I'm not exactly fainting from shock. After what he pulled on me at Disneyland—well, he's one sneaky little son of a bitch. His clothes, a poached car, his ID on the body. Makes sense to me."

164

Kiet said, "Or Davey was indeed murdered, then embalmed, then burned and shot. The embalming step was a red herring."

"Jesus, Superintendent," said a frowning Binh. "The situation's already complicated enough without tossing in new wrinkles."

"I wouldn't dismiss his theory," Zane said. "There could be other cooks stirring the broth. Your airport Cro-Magnons and the alleged surveillance. The money's the key. Reach the twenty million smackeroo pot of gold at the end of that rainbow and you'll nab your alleged bad guys."

"Well, you know, supposing it isn't Davey, where's that leave me?" Binh asked.

"The thing is, nobody knows if it's Davey or not. They can't charge you with murder-one but you're still . . . what's that term?"

"Person of interest," Binh said, sighing heavily.

"Yep, that's it. They'll be anxious to talk to you and because you're an alien, they might just hang on to you until things clear up, or set bail that's twice Luong's gross national product. What's that legal term when they nix bail? High flight risk.

"In addition, you're up against the Enchanted Lakes golf vandalism you allegedly committed killing Davey. Enchanted Lakes membership reads like a *Who's Who*. There are too many golfers around here for too few golf courses. On a nice day on a desirable course, you'll never get on without reservations. The trashing of the thirteenth green fucked up tee times royally. There are influential dudes out and about who want a scapegoat.

"And don't forget the duck. Public opinion is a powerful force. We'd have to move your trial to Tasmania or someplace to seat an impartial jury."

"My trial?"

"Hypothetically speaking."

"The danger you alluded to on the telephone?" Kiet asked.

"Also hypothetical. When there's doubt who one of the players is, maybe other players feel they have to make adjustments. Sorry. I didn't intend to alarm anybody."

Binh shook his head. "Regardless of what I do or how the situation changes, I'm still up shit creek without a paddle."

"In a leaky kayak," Zane said. "Listen, gents. I've got to boogie on back to the ranch. My ear'll be flat on the ground. I get wind of a new development, you'll be the first to know. Call me often. Lay low. I'd better not know where you'll be. Somebody puts the heat on me, I can't guarantee I'll be a stand-up guy. You can never be sure how big your gonads are until somebody's got their paws wrapped around them."

"I know the perfect lay-low place," Kiet said.

21

Kiet told Binh where to drive, told him what he thought they could accomplish. Binh said groovy, except let's kick in a touch of your basic fine-tuning, for it'd be super-pointless if we were gonna step on our own peckers before the situation got off the ground, let alone fly like a big hairy bird, right?

Kiet hadn't the foggiest notion what Binh said. The only phrase that stuck was the reference to damaged penises. He thought of Marge, he thought of Quin. He nodded grimly and authorized his adjutant to repair the shortcomings however he chose. Binh said can do and stopped at a hardware store, which was of course a strip mall tenant.

He came out with a bag and said that it was for the bread, *fini money,* Insolvency City, but that the expense was well worth it. Binh drove. Kiet inspected the contents of the bag: clipboard and notepad, steel measuring tape, two International Harvester baseball caps. He reined in his curiosity en route to their destination, Mrs. David Peterson, Sr.'s home.

"Captain, are we parking here?"

"Right out front, like we own the joint? You betcha. Adjust your cap and slip it on, Superintendent. You take the clipboard, I'll hold on to the tape."

They went to the living room window. Binh pretended to measure it and said, "All clear. Nobody home. Draw some lines and squares and stuff and jot down numbers, Superintendent."

"My compliments to your ingenuity," Kiet said. "In the event we are challenged by a neighbor, what are we doing?"

"Storm windows. Winter's coming. This is the Great White North. You have to insulate against blizzards and stuff."

"We are employees of the International Harvester window company?"

"Nah. You see these caps everywhere and that's all the store had. Walk into any tavern in America and there's at least one guy wearing an International Harvester cap unless he's wearing a John Deere cap. Nobody'll bother us. Were you figuring on entering from the rear?"

Kiet did not request a translation. "Yes. Greater privacy."

They worked their way to the backyard, window by measured window. On the patio, Kiet said, "Mrs. Peterson is at work at the Boeing airplane company, but we don't have unlimited time to snoop. I suggest we begin with Mrs. Peterson's and Davey's bedrooms."

Binh was studying the Peterson house. "Okay. If Davey's alive and she's communicating with him, she could have an address or phone number taped under a dresser drawer or something. It should've sunk in after you interviewed Mrs. Peterson, you know, how she wasn't torn up mourning like she ought to have been. Eeenie meenie minie moe. Catch a Peterson by the toe. When he hollers, let him go."

"Excuse me?"

"An old American rhyme for when you can't make up your mind in a situation. I'm deciding between the patio sliders and the door that goes into the laundry area and garage. They're both pushovers. The laundry door wins."

"Not that it is any longer relevant, but can you estimate how many American laws we are breaking?"

"I don't know," Binh said, reaching for his wallet. "Three, four, five, depending on whether we take anything with us. Tack them on to the rest, the ones we're innocent of and the ones we're guilty of. Hell, I quit keeping score. It's too damn depressing."

Kiet sighed and said, "True."

Binh withdrew a depleted credit card, kissed it, and said, "We dance our last dance, doll."

He inserted it in the garage/laundry room doorjamb, a traditional entry technique of Western burglars. There was a dark Nissan or Toyota in the garage. A door led to the kitchen. Opaque draperies and curtains were shut in vain against the summer heat. Kiet could see the kitchen cabinets and countertop in silhouette and shadow. He smelled yesterday's dishes and food scraps.

A hallway bisected the house lengthwise. Binh said as they explored it, "These crackerboxes, they built them pretty much same same. One bath, two or three bedrooms. Bathroom on the left, bedroom on the right. That's Davey's Mom's. Bed made neatly. Photo on nightstand. Can't see who, but who else would it be but her baby boy, right?"

Kiet said, "The second and last door on the left is Davey's. It's locked."

"His mom maybe has it sealed off like a shrine. Let's check it out first, okay? I'd feel kind of funny tearing her room apart and the only thing we come up with is a vibrator. Allow me."

Binh slipped the door with his invalid plastic, walked in, switched on the light, and whistled.

Kiet followed. A bed covered by a plain blue bedspread was pushed into a corner adjacent a wardrobe closet. Bookshelves were mounted above the bed, lined with what appeared to be computer literature and operation manuals. On tables at the two free walls were computers, keyboards,

169

monitors, printers, software, telephones, and additional technical books. He said, "Impressive."

Binh sat at a table, in a padded swivel chair. "Impressive's putting it mildly, Superintendent. Didn't I say Davey had more computer hardware than the Pentagon? This chair is first cabin too, nice and soft and ergonomic. You know, supposing our boy's still among the living, well, he's gonna be a zillion miles away, like in Rio, and there aren't gonna be clues recorded on paper. Him and his mom are probably maintaining contact on the computers. They've got to be."

"Mrs. Peterson did not strike me as a computer enthusiast," Kiet said.

"You don't have to be a nerd to run a computer these days. How's this scenario grab you? Davey teaches his mom the rudiments of computer operation, devises a password and code system, and they chatter like magpies on the keyboard. There's a knock on the front door, an SPD detective following up on the murder case for instance, she signs off, and the evidence goes bye-bye forever, on account of you can't fingerprint or do a handwriting analysis or trace the watermark on electrons that are hopping and spattering like water droplets in hot grease on tiny, little silicon chips inside these gadgets while Davey, he's been keyboarding his mom from a laptop computer on Copacabana Beach and the shifty little bastard, when his mom signs off, he folds the screen and continues soaking up rays."

Binh the electronics wizard, Kiet thought. "The money?"

"Easy as pie for Davey. No sweat. Remember, he's awfully slick at wire transfers of funds."

"Indeed," Kiet said glumly. "How do you propose we extract clues from the machines?"

"Well, uh, right off the top, I'd say we find the on-off switch."

Binh pawed the sides and back of the computer and the detached keyboard as if searching an arrestee. Kiet leaned in to assist, his hand on top of the monitor.

170

"Jesus, I hope it's not a turnkey model. I can't diddle a key cylinder with a bank card."

Kiet lifted his hand. "Captain."

"Did you find the magic button?"

"No. Never mind." Kiet scanned the room again, dropped to his knees, lifted the bedspread, and grasped an ankle.

"Holy shit!" Binh said, swiveling and diving, grabbing the other ankle, which was kicking and jerking.

They pulled in unison, dragging Davey Peterson out onto cheap, abrasive wall-to-wall carpeting. He was skidding along on his nose and his eyeglasses, thick as telescope lenses, were hanging by an ear.

"Ow, goddamn, that hurts! Ow!"

Binh gave Davey's ankle an extra yank and said, "Hurt? Hurt! You don't know what hurt is till you've had umpteen ducks and mice pounce on your back and beat the living shit out of you."

"Captain."

"I'm sorry, I'm sorry," Davey cried.

Kiet released his ankle, lifted him to his feet by a wrist, and pushed him onto the bed. "Relax a minute, gather your wits, then we shall have a long chat."

"I intend to cooperate."

"Tell me one thing, Davey," Binh said. "Tell me—"

"Captain."

"—one thing. Was an ex-frat brother of yours actually a producer on 'The Dating Game'?"

Kiet groaned.

Davey sniffled, blinked, and put on his glasses. "Honestly, of my multitudinous lies, it was a uniquely total prevarication. What fraternity house would pledge me? That and the remaining partial evasions were impelled by the survival instinct, an imperative essentially beyond my conscious control."

"Swell," Binh said. "Peachy keen. I'll bet you had your fingers crossed too."

"The neckless creatures at Seattle-Tacoma International Airport, did they belong to you?" Kiet asked.

"Yes. I hired them. I hypothesized that you would pursue the money and entertain the possibility that I had staged my own murder."

"Thanks loads," Binh said bitterly. "You know what a person of interest is?"

"I *am* sorry, but I surmised that the authorities would ultimately ascertain that the body was not me. My goal was to buy time."

"Who is the dead person?" Kiet asked.

"I don't know. My university interim was brief. Before I yawned my last yawn of boredom and forsook higher learning, I cultivated friendships and acquaintanceships. For a consideration, an impecunious medical student liberated a laboratory cadaver and concomitantly eliminated its existence on paper. He will someday be a fine surgeon and gifted as he is administratively a superb department head."

"Jesus H. Christ," Binh said. "Invasion of the body snatchers."

"Were the goons bought from acquaintanceships too?"

"Yes."

"Jocks," Binh said. "Football studs. Gotta be."

"Darren and Dirk could have had outstanding college careers and employment in the National Football League. They had, however, been discharged from the squad for infractions. A combination of steroid abuse and congenital psychosis had rendered them dysfunctional. They were talented linebackers with commensurate lateral range and quickness. They blitzed on *every* play."

"Blitzing," Kiet said. "Quarterback assaulting."

Davey Peterson nodded. "Some men dream of finding a cancer cure. They dreamed of sacks and nine-yard losses and the quarterback's helmet and decapitated contents, rolling on the turf. You, sir, rapidly became evangelized by American football."

172

"Excuse me?"

"Your sweatshirt and stocking cap at the airport."

"Where are our pals, Dirk and Dork?" Binh asked.

Davey saluted Kiet. "My kudos on the Oklahoma City ploy. Fortuitous it was for Darren, who has emigrated to the Sooner state. Your trickery made him especially irascible. He barhopped to a legendarily rough saloon. A fellow patron had the temerity to say hello to him. Darren mopped the floor with him. I envision sawdust and spat tobacco ground into his facial pores. He took on all comers. A southwestern college football scout was among the survivors. He made Darren's bail and signed him to a letter of intent."

"How about Dork? Has he been following us?" Binh asked.

"No. I was compelled to discharge Dirk. Aside from football, he is overemployed in most endeavors. I gave him an airline ticket to Oklahoma as severance pay. Darren recommended him for a transfer scholarship also."

"You were following us?"

"Yes. I exposed myself to substantial risk by leaving the house, even in the dead of night. I could not risk revealing my identity to hirelings. Darren and Dirk knew my name but not my newsworthiness or contrived death. They read only the sports pages and only until their lips grow sore. I too assumed disguises. I have false identification and the car in the garage is registered to the namesake of my bogus driver's license and allied documents."

"Did you or your employees break into Captain Binh's Swan Lake Acres residence?"

"No. I was never informed of that address."

"Then who did?" Binh asked.

"How many residential burglaries does the Seattle metropolitan area have annually?" Kiet asked Davey.

"Thousands and thousands."

"Okay, I'll accept random, but how did you and the goons pick us up on surveillance and why?"

"I'll answer your two-part question in the sequence the

subquestions were posed. I directed Darren and Dirk to patrol the airport for you or Superintendent Kiet. I didn't know where you were, but took the calculated risk that you would send for your leader. You spoke glowingly of him. I had created a plethora of problems for you. It was plausible that a prudent man would seek help."

Kiet and Binh blushed, did not look at each other, did not reply.

"My presupposition was accurate," Davey said. "They invariably are. Expect no false modesty from me."

"Your crazed linebackers trailed Binh. They tried to follow him and me. Were they going to kill us?"

"No. Their intent was a secondary component of the second subquestion."

"Superintendent, as you can tell, Davey talks like a Philadelphia lawyer who's been spindled through these computers. You have to stay on his case or you can't understand a damn thing he's saying. He wears his 171 IQ on his sleeve."

"Sorry. You've hit upon a significant personality flaw I constantly strive to rectify. One-*seventy*-one. No. They were ordered to observe you and protect you."

Binh laughed. "Protect us?"

"From arrest. Your movements were vital to me for ulterior inducement, but rest assured, Binh, you were my friend and I was and am tremendously shamefaced for what I wrought upon you."

Binh shrugged and looked at his feet.

"How did you know where I was?" Davey asked Kiet.

"We didn't know you were at your mother's home. We burglarized it to search for clues to your whereabouts. A brilliant piece of misdirection by you."

"Thank you. Isn't this the last place in the world a genius criminal would escape to with his ill-gotten millions? My question should have been phrased: How did you know I was under the bed?"

"The television monitor was hot," Kiet said.

174

"When we have visitors, I access the crawl space from the garage. You came in that way and I was so exceedingly engrossed in my work that I didn't hear you until you entered the kitchen. I have a hidey-hole in the crawl space that you would have to definitively search for."

"What work were you so exceedingly engrossed in, please?"

Davey smiled wanly. "Your syllogisms have been excellent. Would you care to hazard a guess?"

Kiet hesitated.

Binh said, "Allow me. You're under your bed or under the house, getting eaten by spiders, right? Given your druthers you'd be *on* a bed in a Copacabana luxury hotel getting eaten by a couple of *chiquitas*, right?"

Davey closed his eyes and moaned, "Yes. Unequivocally yes."

Binh looked at Kiet and rubbed thumb and fingers together. "He'd be there if he could afford to. Our money's vamoosed and Davey's hunting for it electronically."

"Money," Kiet said. "Of course."

"Money," said Mrs. David Peterson, Sr., from the doorway. "The root of all evil. And it don't grow on trees."

22

"With or without crushed potato chips?"

"With, with, with," David Peterson, Jr., said eagerly.

"Oh, I know for you it's *with,*" said Mrs. David Peterson, Sr. "How long have I been cooking for you? I'm asking our guests."

They were seated in the cramped dining room. A counter divided it and the alcove of a kitchen, where Mrs. Peterson was preparing lunch. Davey had phoned her when he realized intruders were in the house. She had immediately driven home and upon discovery of Davey's discovery had phoned her supervisor at the "Lazy B," her slang reference to Boeing, and said she had come down with cramps and was taking a half day of sick leave instead of just an hour to let the man in to shampoo the carpet.

"With," Binh said. "Please."

Kiet watched in mounting horror as Mrs. Peterson spooned a cup of whole cow's milk into a bowl that already contained a can of cream of mushroom soup, a can of peas,

176

and a can of tuna fish. Mrs. Peterson had said it was nearly noon and that a revolting turn of events was no excuse to miss a meal. Davey had poutingly said he wasn't hungry, and his mom had said, now, now, the worst time in the world to skip your vitamins and minerals is when you're under stress. Davey had acquired an instantaneous appetite, had loudly smacked his lips, when she said she would fix his favorite seafood dish—tuna chip casserole.

"Superintendent?" Binh said.

Seafood? Seafood was fresh shrimp dredged from the floor of the Ma San River, fried in sesame seeds and peanut oil. "With."

"Good," said Mrs. Peterson. She poured potato chips into another bowl and crushed them with her hands. "Tuna casserole without chips is like cake without icing."

"I can imagine," Kiet said.

On the counter was a television with a screen the size of a paperback novel. Davey rotated it away from his mother and adjusted the rabbit ears. "Don't give me dirty looks, Mom. The news is coming on."

"That's all right, son. Since I've had to go to work, I've lost touch with my soap operas anyway, but one of these years, if I scrimp and save my pennies I'll be able to afford a VCR."

"Jeez, Mom."

Mrs. Peterson, cigarette hanging from her lips, stirred a portion of the potato chips into the first bowl and placed it in a microwave oven. "The secret of microwaving this recipe is to brown it off under the broiler afterward, before you sprinkle on the rest of the chips. You can't tell it from oven-baked."

"Davey, how did you receive the assignment to computerize Luong's fiscal agencies?" Kiet asked.

"I do free-lance programming. I advertise in regional computer journals. I was contacted by a Luongan intermediary who arranged an interview with a Luongan consular officer who came up from Los Angeles. The meeting was mutually satisfactory. I am supremely qualified and my low overhead allows me to undercut competitive bids. In two weeks I was notified that my proposal was accepted. I flew to Hickorn and completed the task in six weeks."

"Some task completion," Binh muttered.

"In normal circumstances, I could have installed working programs in four weeks," Davey said. "The hardware was hand-me-down garbage, obsolete floppy disk PCs and clunky minis. I couldn't believe it. I would not have been dumbfounded had they been coal-fired. Alternative power might have facilitated my work by a week. Your electrical network was a formidable hindrance. I'd have a program on line and it'd crash. The brownouts and power surges were incredible, bizarre."

"Yes, yes, we realize that conditions were not up to your usual standards," Kiet snapped.

"I'm sorry," Davey said. "I should not criticize. I loved Luong. The people are beautiful and warm."

Binh nudged Kiet and said out of the corner of his mouth, "This from a guy who had to go on the streets of Hickorn and pay for beautiful and warm."

"The intermediary, please."

"I cannot remember his name."

"David Peterson, Jr., your nose is growing," Mrs. Peterson said, making herself heard over the hum of the microwave.

"Jeez, Mom, I met him a grand total of twice."

"If your father was alive, he'd take off his belt and strap your hide raw."

"Ah jeez-o, Ma, dang, stop it, lemme alone!"

Peculiar, Kiet thought. A schizoid flip-flop of vernacular. From the hyperintelligent humanoid in a science fiction movie to a preschooler chastised for soiling his pants. He knew that the relationship of Western mothers and sons was strange and smothering, often to the extent of purchasing an automobile for youngsters still in adolescence. The Petersons seemed almost that abnormal.

178

"Davey, relax," Kiet said. "The name, please."

"I dunno. I'm lousy at names. I hear it again and I'll know it."

"I saw the bird once," Mrs. Peterson said. "He came to the house. I ain't saying all you Chinamen are sneaky like lots of folks say, but this one, he was shifty as all get out. He had a widow's peak and gray hair. He kept his brows furrowed like he was worrying nonstop. Like to of drove me to distraction."

Kiet and Binh looked at each other. Kiet looked at Davey, "Keedeng Choi?"

"Yes. Choi. That's his name."

Lunch was served. Kiet could not look at his. Fortunately he did not have to. The noon news was on and the Davey Peterson autopsy was the lead story. The mother-son bickering had preempted the press conference. The camera shifted to the reporter for her summary.

"Well, there you have it. In a terse, joint statement by the chief county medical examiner and the Seattle chief of police, the fiery, bullet-riddled corpse on Enchanted Lakes' unlucky thirteenth green—"

"Bullet-riddled," Davey said, snorting. "I shot the cadaver once with Dad's old .22 revolver."

"—has authorities baffled. The presence of embalming fluid—"

"Land o' Goshen," said Mrs. Peterson. "Bullet-riddled!"

"Jeez, mom."

"Yum," Binh said. "Great tuna casserole."

"Shhhh," Kiet said.

"—asks more questions than it answers. Is David Peterson, Jr., dead or alive? Is he in hiding with a stolen fortune? Or are the charred remains his? And where are the mysterious Luongan policemen, Kiet and Binh, and the church leader from their homeland, and what is their role? Only one thing is certain in this situation, a live Davey Peterson is certainly a person of interest. This is Annabeth Marie Tetwell-

179

Moodey reporting live for the 'Nooner Action News Hour.' "

"Davey's a person of interest," Mrs. Peterson said. "Is that a way of saying he's in a jam?"

"Indeed," Kiet said.

"They'll lock me for car theft for starters, Mom. Jeez, I had to walk all through a mall parking lot to find a four-wheel-drive car with keys in it so I could take the cadaver through the woods in that dumb golf course. It was the closest wooded area to that mall."

"A shopping mall parking lot has many cars," Kiet said. "A splendid choice."

"Jailhouse queers will take turns on me in the shower."

"David Peterson, Jr., you stop your whining and you stop using language like that around your mother! I've been protecting you instead of throwing you to the wolves, so you treat me with more respect."

"Sorry, Mom."

"These fellows, I read people pretty good, I think they want to help you, but they want their money. How's your lunches?

"Super," said Binh, who had cleaned his plate.

"Splendid," said Kiet, who had transferred the malodorous muck to a side of his plate. "Filling, though. I cannot swallow another bite."

"Yeah, it does stick to your ribs. I've been taking a big gamble hiding Davey. They could toss me in the pokey too. I'm doing it so he can get back the money he stole that somebody else stole from him. I wouldn't take a penny myself. I want Davey to recover it so he'll have a bargaining tool, you know, restitution to finagle him a lighter sentence."

"Sensible," Kiet said.

"Copacabana," Binh said. "Davey, somebody's on the beach spending like there's no tomorrow."

"He won't tell his own mother who bamboozled him," Mrs. Peterson said to Kiet. "Like I said to you at South End

Lanes, Davey's a genius, but you could sell him the Brooklyn Bridge."

"You'd make fun of me if I told you how it was taken, just like you're doing now, only worse. I'll find the money."

"Are you fellows taking my boy with you?" she said, looking at Binh. "You're a bounty hunter, aren't you?"

"No, ma'am. No sweat. Not to worry. We have a nice place where we can stay until the situation is resolved."

"Davey, will you cooperate and work with us to recover the money?" Kiet asked.

"Yes, sir."

Mrs. Peterson said, "I'll cover the leftover casserole with foil. Don't forget to remove it before you reheat it in a microwave."

Kiet looked at Davey. "Can we count on you? Can we trust you?"

Davey wagged a finger. "You can, yes sir. I'll even give you a sign of good faith."

Kiet leaned toward Davey, who whispered in his ear, "Ken Bolling."

23

They debated whether to delay until dark before moving Davey and a dusty straw suitcase his mom had packed for him and computer equipment Davey packed himself. Binh said that they should bug out now, not sweat prying eyes, he had a plan. Kiet cautioned that a chance spotting of Davey by a neighbor, a mere sideward glimpse, would be their ruination. Davey had applied his disguise and said he was unafraid to depart immediately. Kiet evaluated his disguise of contact lenses (and furious blinking) and the stucco-work application of acne cream, and said that while he might readily deceive a law officer with a wanted poster, people in an adjacent yard might not be fooled, splendid as his masquerade was.

Mrs. Peterson concurred with Kiet, remarking that discretion was the better part of valor. Stick around for dinner, she said, and she would whip up a Davey favorite: tomato soup, grilled cheese sandwiches of processed American on white, lettuce wedges, and for dessert, lime gelatin with baby marshmallows and fruit cocktail. Kiet abruptly said that it would be unfair not to listen to Captain Binh's proposal.

Binh walked them through it and by doing so accomplished his objective. They straightened the bills of their International Harvester caps, raised the overhead garage door, measured the opening, drove out Davey's surveillance car, backed in Mrs. Peterson's Plymouth Volare, fussed with their cap bills while consulting the clipboard, drove the Volare out, backed in the Yugo, and pulled the door downward and shut. The cover story, Binh said, was that they were measuring for automatic garage door openers.

Mrs. Peterson said she'd kill for one of them push-button doohickeys. Late at night, coming home from bowling, when it was rainy and windy, doing it manually was no bowl of cherries.

Davey told his Mom that he'd buy her one someday, state of the art, and it wouldn't be financed by dirty money. A VCR, four-program fourteen-day memory, the sky's the limit. Kiet and Binh busied themselves recinching the seatbelts that secured the computer equipment as mother and son sniffled and hugged and kissed.

Davey climbed into the rear floor of the overloaded Yugo on hands and knees above the floor hump. Kiet cloaked the lad with a blanket his mom said in a hushed voice Davey had had since he went from crib to his first bed. Kiet said he would take good care of boy and blanket. Mrs. Peterson also gave Kiet the casserole leftovers with a reminder about the foil and the lightning storm they'd have if they forgot and microwaved it as is. Kiet said he would be especially careful in the company of microwaves.

They drove to Swan Lake Acres. But for complaints about leg cramps and the Yugo's harsh ride, Davey proffered no conversation. Kiet and Binh let him be. The combination of the boy lamenting into floorboards and the flimsy automobile's acoustics was peculiar. Each whiny grievance echoed like an animal tortured in a tunnel. They could chat later. At length.

"Oops," Binh said at the foot of the model home cul-de-sac.

"Two cars in the driveway," Kiet said. "One old and one new."

"The old is Marge's eighty-two Celebrity. The new is an Infiniti. It's a prospect or a family of prospects. Dandy wheels, an Infiniti Q45, the big sedan. *Mucho dinero.* California plates. We'll hang loose. It won't be long. That unit's slightly overpriced and they haven't had a written offer."

Binh drove to the vacant lot. To his amazement and Kiet's, the copse of alders was unchanged, undiminished, relatively pristine. Two days had gone by, Binh said, two days in a go-go yupscale subdivision, and the lot hadn't been prepped for construction. We're talking stranger than fiction.

Perhaps it has been set aside as a nature preserve, Kiet suggested. There's a thought, Binh said. They can hang some birdhouses. The government won't permit swan trapping, no biggie. You can entice them with room and board, right?

In deference to Davey, Binh climbed the curb slowly. They had no money for dental emergencies. They parked in the miniature forest, walked to the observation post Binh had discovered Tuesday, and sat on the ground.

"Davey," Kiet said. "Talk to us."

"I think I had told you that I was a Ken Bolling student," Davey said to Binh.

"You lost a ton of weight as a result of it," Binh said, nodding.

"A form of aversion therapy," Davey said with a humorless smirk. "I willed myself to maintain Ken's diet regimen. Have you ever tasted Cuisine By Ken. It's a rip-off and it tastes like dog poop."

"Marginally palatable when stir-fried and seasoned," Kiet said.

"Gross," Binh said.

"You lose weight because the prospect of eating is repugnant. His motivational package was simplistic, but repetition brought forth a modicum of enthusiasm. His get-rich-quick appendages were ludicrous, but they appealed to my baser instincts. Not specifically the real estate and mail order schemes, mind you, but the promise of something for virtually nothing. His sales seminar, at which I succumbed with pitiful resistance, was peopled with mirror images of me. No, they did not have IQs of 171, but they were underachievers and dropouts, men and women who had done little with their lives and were steadfast in the resolve that they would do little else unless the sky turned gold and rained nuggets onto their laps. These are the people who spend too much on lotteries and feel cheated when they don't win. They never win at anything but that does not stop them from cutting corners and chasing rainbows. My IQ is double theirs, but I am one with them, a symbolic brother."

"I have an irrational fear that Keedeng Choi and Ken Bolling are symbolic brothers," Kiet said.

"They are and I am to blame," Davey said. "My free-lancing had been small scale, enough to pay Mom a few dollars for room and board, and to buy more computer gear. I was afraid to risk failure and I was ashamed of how I looked. I'm no Mel Gibson today, but I can live with myself. The rah-rah aspect of the program gave me the confidence to accept the Luong job. I knew all along that it was self-delusional, but I didn't care. The continuing yammer of big money and quick success made me grabby."

"Are you blaming Bolling for stealing our money, escaping Captain Binh, and burning and shooting the dead body?" Kiet asked.

"No. He is at fault for bringing out the sociopath in me. He is as transparent as a soap bubble. If Ken Bolling could do it, who couldn't? The monster in me is restrained by a two-dollar padlock. Don't misunderstand. The monster isn't a bloodthirsty fiend. The monster is a lazy seeker of comforts and undue rewards."

"Well," Binh said, staring at the model home. "I know I feel better."

"Your mother's reaction to Bolling?"

"She never knew. She is not stupid, but she is not informed either. Her field of interest is bowling to soap operas to supermarket coupon sales. She saw my Cuisine By Ken in our freezer. I said it was a new test-marketed product that would appear only sporadically in the freezer case. I didn't tell her about my matriculation in his program. No! She'd ridicule her boy, me a genius, the pupil of an oily, pimplike pedant."

"The Choi-Bolling brotherhood, please."

"We were finalizing the Luong deal during the apex of my Ken Bolling's Thin 'n' Rich Dynamic Development Seminars, Incorporated enthusiasm. I rhapsodized intemperately to Choi."

"Speaking of intemperate, Superintendent," Binh said. "I don't know what's keeping Marge, but I'm sure becoming parched. Marge has a prospect for thirty minutes plus and she's got him. She'll hammer away at them till Wednesday if need be and they're not gonna walk until she has a John Henry on an earnest money agreement."

"Parched," Kiet said. "Indeed."

"I'll buy," Davey said, digging in a pocket.

"You have to buy," Kiet said.

Binh took the money, said please don't continue till I'm back, there's a market three miles down the road, you'll see me in ten minutes max. They saw him in nine minutes, eight minutes and fifty-five seconds after the sickening thud of Yugo striking curbing. Binh distributed icy bottles of Rainier Dry and bags of potato and corn chips, sodium maintenance on a hot day being as vital to good health as adequate fluid levels.

"I presume that Keedeng Choi enrolled in the Bolling seminar program," Kiet said.

"Unfortunately he did," Davey said. "He was spellbound by Ken and his philosophy when he visited me in Hickorn."

"Holy shit," Binh said. "Visited you in Luong?"

"Choi went to Luong to see you while you were computerizing us?" said a stunned Kiet.

"Bearing a proposal. He was in the country for two days. I saw him only at night and alone. He traveled on a forged passport. Choi and Ken had developed a friendship. Ken and I hadn't. We were acolyte and guru, period. Ken is headquartered in California—"

"Big surprise," Binh said.

"Ken concentrates on the West Coast, so he appears in Seattle often. Following a seminar, Choi and Bolling met, and I was the subject of a conversation. Choi may have enrolled in Ken's advanced postgraduate seminar that he sells for about a thousand dollars. Ken's aloof on a personal level. However it happened, it happened. Ken praised Choi's initiative in orchestrating my deal with your Los Angeles consulate, although he voiced disappointment at the pittance Choi negotiated as a middleman fee. Ken says that to be satisfied with peanuts is antithetical to his teachings. He told Choi that computers and money can interact in lucrative ways. The pump was primed. Choi flew to Hickorn the next morning.

"I'll be candid. I was halfway into the project. Not a minute went by that I did not also consider the interaction of computers and money. I had no concrete plot. I had theoretical plans to program in a fund transfer capability. But to where? I had no money-laundering support. I had no accounts in European or Caribbean banks. Keedeng Choi was the other side of the equation.

"My Luongan superiors insisted on layers of data entry codes. The numerical obfuscation would effectively protect the network from thieves without, but not from within."

"Rats in the grain silo," Kiet said.

"Yes. The mass of numbers required to transact from the pay telephone required twenty minutes instead of what should have been five minutes."

"Poor baby," Binh said.

"I had the access codes and Choi brought an electronic receptacle, a money-laundering destination."

"Compliments of Ken Bolling?" Kiet asked.

"Yes. He sells his courses for six hundred to seven hundred dollars each. Roughly thirty thousand subscriptions equal the twenty million dollars. Converting twelve billion Luongan zin into U.S. dollars was problematical. The zin isn't a kingpin in world currency markets.

"Choi came through. He knows everybody. We made a bargain with a man in Bangkok. My first stage at the Honolulu telephone was to transfer the zin to him. He transferred dollars to an interim account I had surreptitiously established in the Luongan National Bank for that purpose. We were in and out in seconds. The Bangkok broker made money and I presume Choi received a kickback from him besides."

"Who was to receive what?"

"Choi received five hundred thousand dollars. Ken Bolling and I were to split the rest."

Binh whistled. "Nine and three-quarter mil apiece. Not too shabby."

"Did Choi confess having financial troubles?"

"No, but I sensed it. I regarded the scam as an adventure. Ken Bolling is an old pro at scams. Choi was desperate. His cut came off the top, a direct deposit from the Luongan National Bank dummy account to Choi's numbered account in the Cayman Islands. I transferred the balance to Bolling."

"Your cut?"

Davey shook his head and ate a potato chip. Kiet noticed that the large bag in his lap was nearly empty. The lad was no drinker, especially in comparison to Binh who belched

188

and opened his second, but he was indeed a junk-food afi-cionado. "Ken Bolling has it. I was stupid, naive. That's why I wouldn't spill my guts to Mom. A genius of 171 IQ, and a sleazeball swindles me."

"You transferred the nineteen-five to Bolling's account and trusted him to reimburse you?"

"Sad but true. He has some outstanding computer minds working for him. I transferred the money into his offshore account. The money trickled into his general business account over a space of ten days, then his offshore account terminated. It does not exist, nor did it ever exist. I hack into it and boot up a blank screen."

"Trickled?"

"Thirty thousand trickling drops of rain," Davey said.

"A large puddle," Kiet said. "You are telling us that Ken Bolling converted our money into thirty thousand fictitious sales?"

"Astounding but true. He's accessed world-class program-ming talent."

"Wait a second," Binh said. "Bolling does beaucoup busi-ness with plastic. You'd be able to trace phantom credit card numbers, no sweat. Leak the information and the IRS'll have him by the shorts."

"No. The transactions were recorded as cash and money order. No credit cards. His seminars are around thirty percent cash and his TV sales are fifteen percent money order. He entered the noncredit activity lump sum, x number of cus-tomers at x dollars per day. He spread the transactions re-troactively from the time of entry to the first of the year. Thirty thousand buyers lined up at a weekend seminar is not credible. I surmise he notified the IRS about the revenue that erroneously did not appear on his quarterly returns. A new accounting system and the bugs weren't out of it yet. He paid the back taxes and penalties."

"Pretty damn slick of Bolling," Binh said. "They can't nail

you for anything else, you know, like Al Capone, they sick the IRS on you and your ass is grass."

"Bolling is involved in other criminal activities?"

"I know he is."

"You cannot prove it?"

"Not yet. I haven't accessed his systems, but I'll die before I give up. He disperses his monies and he flits from software to software. The minute I think I'm going to crack him he changes systems."

"Bolling stiffed you cold?" Binh said. "Not penny one?"

"He pretended he didn't know me. He said that if I continued pestering him and disrupting his seminars, he would report me to the police. I think he already had in the form of an anonymous tip to my mom."

"You didn't phone her from that downtown penthouse suite?" Binh asked.

"No. She phoned me. Ken was conducting a seminar at that hotel. He refused to see me. I was blue. A cab driver arranged the ladies."

"Hey, they can cheer me up any ol' time," Binh said.

"I made the mistake of becoming drawn into an argument with Mom and hanging up on her. She is extremely adept at getting under my skin. I should've refused to talk to her and checked out instantly."

"The money for your penthouse and lady friends, please? It must have been very expensive."

"Expensive and fun," Binh said.

"Choi."

"Marge has been in there an awfully long time, Superintendent. You don't suppose her and a guy—"

"No," Kiet said. "She isn't the type."

"Choi split his half million with you?"

"No. I went to him to ask him to influence Bolling. He said he would. I was naive to believe him. Why should he? We weren't connected on paper. He endlessly pointed out that he had gone to Luong incognito and that we were never seen

190

together. He gave me a few dollars to placate me. Three thousand dollars was my total share of twenty million."

"I wonder why Ken Bolling continues to take his seminar carnival on the road if he is worth twenty million and perhaps much much more," Kiet said.

"The precepts of dynamic personal development," Davey said. "Ken wouldn't be satisfied with twenty *billion.*"

Doug Zane drove into the forest hideaway. Kiet looked at Binh. Binh shrugged and said, "Every convenience store in the world has a pay phone and I had an extra quarter."

Zane got out of his car, lifted his wraparound sunglasses and said, "Whoa, as I live and breathe, Amelia Earhart. Binh, your directions were boffo."

"Who's he?" Davey asked Kiet.

"Captain Binh's attorney."

"Davey had a court-appointed attorney," Binh said. "Worthless as tits on a boar."

Doug Zane gave Davey a business card.

"I've seen your commercials," Davey said. "The one where the victim is hanging upside down by his seat belt is hilariously entertaining."

"Bitchin'. Dougie and his merry band of shysters aim to please. You'd love the one with the dumb schmuck who isn't represented by us in a courtroom in a wheelchair and wrapped from head to toe in tape, just him against a boxcar load of insurance company shysters."

Binh gave Doug a beer. "Shocked?"

"At Davey arising from the dead? Not hardly. This thing has gone umpteen light years beyond goofy. Who was the alleged dead body who was allegedly you, Davey?"

"A medical school cadaver."

"Wild and crazy," Zane said. "Are you my client or what?"

Davey looked at Binh, who gave a double thumbs up. "Rim Legal is aces. They sprang me from the Anaheim jail in nothing flat."

"Cash or charge? I can't show my face at the office without a retainer."

"Do you take Visa?"

"Can do," said Zane, who went to his car for a charge plate. Davey signed for six hundred dollars of legal aid. Binh filled Doug in on events.

"Where does that leave the concerned parties, namely you guys?" Zane said. "This just gets fucking weirder and weirder. I *love* it."

"Hey," Binh said. "Bandits at three o'clock."

Marge Mainwaring came out of the model home with a couple in their thirties. The threesome was all smiles. The woman wore shorts and halter top, the man Bermudas and tank top. They both wore sunglasses and thongs, and were of bronze skin coloration.

"California tacky," Doug said.

"Surf's up," Binh said.

Marge shook the woman's hand, then the man's. Rather ceremoniously, Kiet thought. Marge stapled a Sold banner diagonally over the For Sale sign staked in the lawn. She left in her Celebrity, the California expatriates in their Infiniti.

"There goes our safe house," Binh said.

"Great pad," Doug said.

"Let's enjoy it while we can," Binh said, sighing.

A note to Binh was on the coffee table:

> Bamsan,
> Be a dear and dust and plump the pillows and polish the tables and counters. Spray wax is fine. The Fergusons are just up from San Diego and will be renting until they clear. Which should be within days. They're as good as gold. They'll be moving in this weekend. Thanx.
> —XXXOOO
> Marge

Binh wadded the note and flung it into the fireplace. "I guess I know where I stand with her. I'm a law enforcement chief executive, a foreign dignitary, and she's treating me like a goddamn houseboy."

I thought I was the chief executive and you were a person of interest, Kiet thought. He said, "Captain, please, no hasty judgments. She is simply requesting a favor. You are on guard duty on the premises. I sense time urgency. She wishes everything to be right so her sales commission is not jeopardized."

"Do you think so, Superintendent?"

"Indeed."

"Yo, boys and girls, gotta run," Zane said, pointing at his watch. "I have an appointment in the vicinity and I'm overdue. Davey, take care. Dougie's in your corner and copacetic is the name of that tune."

Davey was setting up his computer apparatus on the coffee table and did not seem to hear. A preoccupied Binh waved to Doug without looking at him and said to Kiet, "I suppose I'm overreacting. Yesterday, using your usual rational and logical approach, you explained how I'm spinning my wheels with Marge. My brain buys it but my heart doesn't. And it pisses me off that we have to vamoose by the weekend. Tomorrow's Friday, you know. Where are we gonna stay?"

"Do not despair, gentlemen," Davey said. "Do not pack your bags."

"Excuse me?"

Davey's computer was in operation, its television monitor layered with lines of words and numbers. He held up a small, black ring binder. "See this? It's my little black book. Some guys have girls' names in them. Maybe someday. Mine's filled with access codes."

"To hack into computers?" Binh said.

Davey tapped the monitor. "You accumulate codes. You communicate with like twisted minds. You play touch and go on the computer bulletin boards, the outlaw sort. What you are seeing is the state of California's motor vehicle registrations. I memorized the license number on the Infiniti. See the cursor? A Ferguson person is the registered owner. San Diego address."

Davey pushed a key and the screen went blank. He consulted his little black book and typed a cryptic row of characters. The screen filled.

"Jesus," Binh said. "There's Ferguson again. Credit?"

"A routine credit check that I am billing to a Seattle bank. Mr. Ferguson, we can see, is an aerospace executive. Nine chances in ten he has taken a job at Boeing. Mrs. Ferguson is a securities broker. Combined income in the low six digits. Four star credit. The Rock of Gibraltar."

Davey was talking primarily to himself. The glow of the cathode-ray tube bathed his face. The chalkiness of the acne medication lent him an eerily pastel tone. Kiet mused, Man and machine as one.

The screen format changed. Davey said, "I'm in as a credit bureau employee, not client. Addition here, deletion there. These prefixes and abbreviations are elementary. That should suffice."

Davey turned off the computer. Kiet asked, "Suffice what?"

Davey smiled and said, "I destroyed the Fergusons' credit rating. Defaults on auto loans, personal bankruptcy, chronic credit card abuse. The realtor will run a routine credit check and to her dismay learn that they are staggeringly unqualified. The credit report will be found to be in error, an error that will require several days minimum to remedy. Our sleeping accommodations will not be disrupted in the short term."

"Damned if you aren't a genius," Binh said, laughing. "I'll bet you could hack into the Pentagon if you worked at it."

Davey beamed, loving the praise. He feigned a yawn and said, "The Pentagon is easy easy easy. Beginner hackers practice on the Department of Defense."

"Ken Bolling should be America's Minister of War," Kiet said.

"They call him Secretary of Defense, Superintendent."

Davey said, "I'll continue night and day."

"Thank you," Kiet said.

"Running morphemic and numeric permutations in access mode."

"Of course," Kiet said. "But can you tell us anything else about Bolling? Uncomputer data, as it were."

Davey shook his head.

"He is seminaring in Seattle this weekend," Kiet said.

"That's right, he is. He has a girlfriend his wife doesn't know about. She lives across Puget Sound in Bremerton. He comes in Thursday, spends the night with her, and takes the ferry back across sometime Friday. Choi told me. He's a gossip."

"Luongans gossip," Binh said. "It's in our genes and chromosomes."

"Ah," Kiet said.

"Does that help?"

"Ah," Kiet said.

24

Kiet finished the *Bremerton Sun* and began reading the *Seattle Times*. This would be his fourth trip into the *Times*. He told himself without conviction that the surveillance wasn't an utter waste, that at least his English reading proficiency was improving. He said, "Perhaps I am the savant, not Davey."

Binh had given up on hard news and was pretending to read shoppers. "It's far too early to throw in the towel, Superintendent. Like a bad penny, he'll turn up. Your comment that Davey and his 171 IQ is so narrowly channeled into computers, I think, is valid. He doesn't see the nose on the end of his face. He didn't connect Bolling's teepee creeping in Bremerton as an opportunity to get up close and personal to him. But 'savant' is too strong, you know. 'Dipshit' is fairer. And as far as our concern that he might split from the model home, well, number one, we have his wallet; number two, he's got no wheels and out there in suburbia without the Metro you adore, he might as well be on a desert island;

number three, he's pumped again about nailing Bolling on his computer and he's in a trance in front of the screen; number four, he knows if he jerks us around once more, we'll call his mother."

Binh took a deep breath, replacing oxygen depleted by logorrhea, got up and looked outside yet again at cars lining up for the next eastbound crossing. They had taken the first Seattle boat this Friday morning, the five-forty-five. The cross-sound cruise on a Washington States Ferries ferryboat to Bremerton, a shipyard city, was twenty miles and sixty minutes long, on water substantially smoother than the Soft Springs Motel waterbed. It had been a gorgeous morning of turquoise sky and a sea so flat and glossy it could have been waxed. Conifer trees and the Olympic Mountains back-dropped Bremerton and its resolute gray naval fleet.

They bought coffee and rode outside, alternating between the bow deck and the stern deck, while the Seattle skyline stayed in view. They had bought muffins at the snack bar to feed seagulls who glided alongside and picked torn pieces out of the air. For one glorious hour, they were sightseers, visual adventurers, not persons of interest or detectives. Most of their fellow travelers were weekday commuters who worked at Bremerton's Puget Sound Naval Shipyard. They regarded the childlike pair with bored amusement. Kiet heard "Japanese tourists" when they queued to disembark.

Four hours and four boats to Seattle had passed, four hours of scrupulous yet discreet perusal of every pedestrian, bicyclist, and vehicle passenger. Kiet watched the walk-ons. He had delegated vehicular traffic to his adjutant.

Binh sat down and sighed. "Zilch, zip."

"When is the next sailing?"

"Ten minutes. I know, I know, they really start lining up in the last ten minutes. I should be out there, faking like I'm you know, feeding the pigeons, but it's slack."

"I trust your judgment."

"I wish I did. Our judgment, I mean. This is a long shot situation, you know."

"Indeed."

"We're relying on a rumor. Bolling could have broken up with her. She could have moved. He could have driven around through Tacoma or he could have taken the Winslow ferry instead of the Bremerton. What's the odds, right?"

"Right."

"And if by some miracle we make him, what do we do?"

"In your vernacular, play it by ear."

"Ad-libbing could get dicey. I wish to hell we had a game plan."

Kiet looked at the passenger ticket window, then at his newspaper.

Binh sighed. "Okay, I'm gone. Same tune, different verse."

Binh returned in seconds, eyes wide, whispering, "We were right on the mark. I knew it. He's here. In a car. The boat's loading."

"You are certain?"

"Well, pretty sure. He was in a bad-ass Caddy Seville, black with black vinyl top and black glass. I'm guessing an expensive rental. No ten-buck-a-day Yugo for Ken Bolling. The glass is super dark, but I saw his driver's window roll up and I sort of saw part of his face."

Kiet suppressed a groan. "Sort of part?"

"He was touching his hair, primping. I saw his pinkie ring. I'd know it anywhere."

Kiet jumped to his feet. "Let's go."

They boarded and took the stairs to the car deck. It was the eleven-twenty and Kiet gauged it a third full. They quickly found Bolling's Cadillac and waited several cars behind. Unlike the morning load of shipyard workers, these riders were casually dressed, chiefly tourists who headed upstairs. The ferry labored from its mooring, engines howling, propellers churning a wake of greenish foam.

"Okay, Superintendent, the ball's in our court."

198

"Your eyes are superior to mine. Is he still in his car?"

"Beats me. Hey, unless my eyes are playing tricks, I detected a flash of light."

"In the car? I see nothing."

"Yeah, I lost it too. Okay. Bingo. He lit up. His window's down an inch and smoke's wafting out."

"No Smoking signs are prominently posted."

"Bolling obeys his own rules."

"His four doors are presumably locked. How?"

"Power door locks gotta be standard equipment on this buggy. I think I see what you're driving at. The switch is on or near the driver's armrest. First we have to get that window down."

"Ken Bolling transcends mortal law, yes, but how would a humble deck employee of Washington State Ferries know?"

"Gotcha," Binh said, smiling. "You and me, we're getting positively psychic. I'll do the honors. You situate yourself to ride shotgun, okay?"

Kiet sidled to the right-front door, slowly. Binh was shouting at Bolling, an obsequious coolie's grin plastered on his face. So sorry, sir, too much loudness of motor and wind, lower your window, I have to say, thank you, sir, rules prohibit smoking on the car deck.

At the "the," Binh's hand darted downward and unlocked the doors. Kiet swooshed into leather aside Ken Bolling. The left-rear door slammed and Binh was also in the car.

Bolling reached under his seat. Kiet reached under Bolling's seat, grabbed Bolling's pinkie ring pinkie finger, and bent it backward. Bolling yelped. A hard object clunked on the carpeting. Binh was leaning above Bolling, clasping hands around his left bicep, denying his free hand the floor and the clunking object.

Kiet increased pinkie pressure and said, "Ten degrees further and we shall hear a disgusting sound. Up with me, slowly, quietly, obediently, please."

Kiet raised Bolling's hyperextended pinkie with his left and felt for the clinked object with his right. It was hard, cold, and peculiarly small.

He gave it to Binh and said, "My firearms expert."

Binh laughed and rested the barrel on Bolling's ear. "A Browning .25, Jesus, pearl-handled, nickel-plated, no less. A pussy pistol, too cute for words. You ought to have this strapped to a lace garter, Bolling."

"Advantage to you," Bolling said, gritting his teeth. "Ease up on the finger, will you?"

Kiet released Bolling's pinkie and sniffed. "I have been trying to identify the smell of this automobile, Mr. Bolling. Leather. Tobacco. Perfume. Ah, I have it. Boutiques in a mall."

Bolling butted his cigarette in the ashtray. "This is not a potluck abduction, I take it."

"We have seen you on television, Mr. Bolling," Kiet said. "We attended a dynamic development seminar."

Bolling permitted himself a tight smile. "Dissatisfied clients, eh? Believe it or not, you're a rare breed."

He flexed his pinkie-ring hand and looked at Kiet. "Cheap shot. I practice what I preach, champ. I'm fit. I aerobicize and can play singles from sunup to sunset and I've been known to work out on the heavy bag. You and me, one on one, my pleasure. But it's your serve. How can we conclude this little tête-à-tête before it turns ugly? A refund is no problem. Circumstances considered"—the Bolling smile came and went faster than a camera flash—"I won't even require a receipt."

"We are Luongan police officers, Mr. Bolling."

"Boat people? I could've guessed. Luong is in that little corner of the world. Listen, I've had Asiatics like yourselves come to my seminars. Their worldly possessions are on their backs. I thrive on David and Goliath stories. They sell. You people, I'm no commie, but beating the French at Dien Bien Phu and chasing them out of your country, I relate the story, sell them on having their own personal Dien Bien Phu

200

against mediocrity. I turn their lives around, give them confidence, and direct them to unlimited potential."

"Splendid," Kiet said. "Admirable. We three are boat people for the next thirty-five to forty minutes. What, please, are boat people by your definition?"

"That's what in the States they call Indochinese refugees who fled in boats to escape communism, Superintendent."

"Of course. Vietnamese, primarily. They are courageous and desperate, but your 'boat people' inflection was condescending."

"No, no it wasn't," Bolling said. "You're twisting my words so that I come off as a bigot, calling you niggers or such. You couldn't be more wrong. My program is geared to every race, color, and creed."

"We are sidetracking, Mr. Bolling. I said we are Luongan. Please make the correct association. You are not a stupid man."

Binh stroked Bolling's ear with the gun barrel.

"You're policemen?"

"Yes."

"I don't have anything to say. I'm entitled to due process."

"Due process. Of course," Kiet said. "Captain, the printed card you carry in your wallet that you brought home after your stint with the District of Columbia constabulary."

"My Miranda card, Superintendent, but you made me stop Mirandizing suspects at home."

"Yes. You were misleading them. They did not necessarily have the right to an attorney or the right to remain silent. This is America."

"Yeah, but the States is kind of out of our jurisdiction."

"No matter. Recite to Mr. Bolling. Soothe his anxieties."

"Save yourselves the effort, boys. Direct confrontation of problems is a tenet of dynamic personal development. I'd greatly appreciate it if you would kindly state your business."

Kiet said, "Davey Peterson, Jr. Keedeng Choi. Twenty million dollars embezzled from the kingdom of Luong."

Bolling smiled at Binh's reflection in the rearview mirror and said, "Davey Peterson rings a bell. Say, you're the loose cannon who the papers say may not have killed him since he may be alive and responsible for the stunt."

"Keedeng Choi," Kiet said.

"Who?"

"Our twenty million dollars, please."

"Your English has a funny accent, champ. I didn't understand a word."

"Captain."

Binh cocked the hammer. "It's a baby slug, Superintendent. It won't even come out the other side of his pointy head. The ferry's super noisy. Nobody'll hear the shot."

"Answer my questions," Kiet said.

"The gun's unloaded," Bolling said.

Binh ejected the clip and examined it. "Son of a bitch."

"You wouldn't have shot me. You aren't the types. My girl is world-class in bed but she's a paranoid ditz. She gave me the gun, insisting that as a celebrity I'm in need of protection. All threats to my life and limb should be like you boys. I'll live to be a ripe old age."

"Mr. Bolling," Kiet said slowly, to emphasize patience, "we will hound you until our money is returned. Give it to us now and we will take it home in such a state of euphoria that we might not pursue criminal charges."

"Do you propose to investigate and arrest me? I'm squeaky. I pay my taxes. I *overpay* my taxes. I have money. I want more money. I will have more money. Dynamic personal development is the art of becoming rich and never being satisfied with what you have."

"Pardon my funny accented English comprehension, but I believe you confessed."

"Read anything into it you like, champ. My books are open to the harshest scrutiny."

"Laundered so splendidly that they sparkle," Kiet said.

"You're real live cops? All right, let me give you a tip, free, gratis. In your country, what's a big, stressful crime day, a double-parked elephant? In my country, it's no sin to be rich and irregardless of how you acquired your wealth, if you're germ-free on paper, you're clean. No fed or state or local gendarme would waste five seconds taking a lick at Ken Bolling. You know what turns them on? Drugs. Nose candy or horse. They'll tear mattresses apart from here to Zurich hunting laundered drug money."

"Thank you for the law enforcement advice," Kiet said. "Our money, please."

Bolling shook his head. "You boys are slow on the uptake. Let's make a deal. Seats are available for tonight's seminar. Attend and I'll give you each a free program."

"I bought the program," Binh said. "It's bullshit."

"Through proper cooking, the Cuisine By Ken Salisbury steaks can be palatable, however," Kiet said.

"All right, be difficult. I'll spring for my advanced post-graduate seminar. My students are repaid in knowledge and insights a hundred fold."

"Twenty million dollars," Kiet said.

Ken Bolling glanced at his watch. "My last offer. The boat docks in twenty minutes. Be out of my car in fifteen or I scream rape."

Binh had been damping his anger by playing with the gun, cocking the pistol and pulling the trigger.

Bolling said, laughing, "That clicking is like the Chinese water torture you're famous for. Too bad we haven't more time. You'd crack me."

Kiet opened his door and smiled. "We already have."

25

"Go figure, Superintendent. Seattle, a city of hills. Were they boobs, you know, there'd be a year of *Playboys'* worth, going from the ferry dock up through downtown. It's like climbing the Matterhorn, they synchronize the stop lights north and south where it's flat, but east and west, we must be looking up at a twenty-degree grade. The lights take until the Second Coming to turn green."

Kiet was distressed too; his beloved Hickorn was as flat as Western rock music. Their car might indeed tip over backward. He looked out at the natives on the steep, steep sidewalk. Adaptable folks, he thought. A compensatory lean was built into their strides. He identified a stench he had not initially recognized: the Yugo's clutch that Binh had been riding was blistering.

His adjutant was likewise a flatlander, so Kiet forgave the mechanical abuse. The light changed green and they rattled through the intersection. At the next street Binh impulsively turned right. Baritone horns bleated.

Binh stuck his arm out the window, his middle finger saluting. "Jesus, Superintendent, don't flinch. They'll think we're weenies. Neither one of those trucks would have dared clobber us. Their employers would suspend the drivers and there goes their meal tickets. The sooner we steer south, the better. This tin can might even hang together till Luong Square.

"Nice fake you put on Bolling, by the way, saying we'd quote-unquote cracked him. He's a slick boy, too sharp to tumble for it, but you sort of got us out of his car without our tails dangling between our legs. We saved face."

"Perhaps we have cracked him."

"C'mon. How?"

Kiet shrugged.

"Superintendent, it pisses me off severely when you play inscrutable. To *them,* fine. To me, uh-uh."

"I am sorry, Captain. I am not playing. Bolling said something that caused an itch I cannot quite scratch. I cannot isolate what it is. A reply, a reaction, a denial."

"Should the muse smack you upside the head, share, okay?"

"Okay," Kiet said. "Yes."

They drove through the International District. Previously referred to as Chinatown, Kiet recalled from his travel literature. Chinatown would be a misnomer today, he observed. Chinese held the majority, yes, but Japanese, Korean, Lao, Vietnamese, Thai, and Cambodian entrepreneurs were represented also. The International District was indeed international. Erase parking meters and chimneys from the sketch and they could be in a cosmopolitan section of Hickorn.

They were en route to Luong Square out of curiosity, to see what five hundred thousand U.S. dollars had saved. Ten minutes later, on a fringe of the International District they came upon a two-story mall of ground-level stores and upper offices. The building was an unimaginative, wooden frame box, stucco-finished and flat-roofed, subdued in comparison to the brick facades and neoclassical fakery of the newer suburban malls, and, Binh said, as Luongan as an Exxon station.

"No criticism of Mr. Choi's architectural tastes," Kiet said, "but I do not see the money."

"The land it's on, Superintendent. The prices land in the Seattle area goes for, you'd think there was oil underneath. I'll park catty-corner to that dry cleaners. I'll back in so we can have a look-see from the car. With in excess of six hundred Luongans in Seattle and us kind of hometown celebrities, someone's bound to recognize us."

"No argument," Kiet said.

"Busy place," Binh said. "See anybody you know?"

"No."

After ten minutes, Binh said, "Well, could be that they didn't immigrate from Hickorn. They may have come from Obon or the farm villages."

"They?"

"Yeah, come to think of it."

"Shall we?"

"Yeah," Binh said, getting out. "Why not? What do we have to lose but our freedom?"

Binh parked the Yugo in a yellow zone by the Hickorn Café. He stayed behind the wheel, on alert for parking enforcement police. The alley door to the restaurant was wide open to dissipate heat. Kiet walked into a clamor of pots, pans, and jabbering kitchen drudges. He found Choi in his office, an afterthought of a cubicle partitioned between a sink and a walk-in freezer.

Choi was at a desk the size of a checkerboard. He laid down a menu and pen. "Kiet."

There was no space for a swinging door. Kiet pulled a shower curtain shut behind him. He said, "Elegantly unpretentious. Hickorn master chefs surely do not create their

206

masterpieces concealed by the privacy of a shower curtain. We are unsophisticated. The Seattle yupster tabloid that adores you could devote a headline article to Choi and his shower curtain."

"You were to contact me regarding Captain Binh. I expected you to make an appointment."

"I am contacting you. What is the tongue your kitchen employees speak? It isn't Luongan. I haven't been gone so long I've forgotten my own language."

"Vietnamese. Lao. Cambodian. Tribal dialects. Is Binh amenable to a deal? I concede that confusion about the identity of the corpse has altered his status to nebulous, but he is not out of trouble. Surrender to the custody of my important police friends and yours truly is still his best option."

"I again thank you for your generosity. Captain Binh thanks you. The liaison you promised to deliver to me, please?"

"I have narrowed the suspects to a handful. Of the six hundred and seventy Seattle Luongans, three hundred are adults. Nobody has stepped forward to admit guilt, so I have been confronted with a difficult screening process that has consumed every waking minute outside of my humble café and landlord responsibilities. Bring Binh in to me now, Kiet. I'll deliver our traitor in a day or two."

Kiet groaned. "Choi, you are the liaison."

"Ridiculous! I am the first Luongan you encounter in America and I am your culprit. Doesn't that defy probabilities? Isn't it an improbable coincidence? A detective doesn't solve crimes by coincidence, Kiet."

"True. Nature abhors a coincidence, Choi. You are no coincidence. I just came from Luong Square. An impressive accomplishment. You have vacancies, yes, but there is a supermarket, a tropical fish store, a passport photographer, a jeweler, and two restaurants downstairs. Upstairs, you have a doctor, a dentist, a realtor, and an herbal medicine healer. The tenants are Vietnamese, Choi. Vietnamese customers widely outnumber non-Vietnamese. No, excuse me. I made a mistake. In the spirit of accuracy, the tropical fish shop is Thai.

"Earlier in the day, Captain Binh and I were referred to as boat people, refugees from communism. Indochinese living in America are refugees from communism whether they paddled into the South China Sea or not. Luong is landlocked and noncommunist. You won a lottery and came to Seattle. How many of our countrymen are actually in Seattle, please?"

"I believe you know, Kiet."

"Aren't you lonely?"

"No. I have friends of every persuasion. Ironically, if I had not been a community of one, I would be an object of discrimination. Our Indochinese neighbors look down upon us because we are the smallest nation. Americans view Asians as a homogeneous race who either destroy their balance of payments or live in refugee ghettos on welfare and drain their tax revenues. I, a community of one, am an oddity."

"Explain your myth of a Luongan community numbering in the hundreds, please."

Keedeng Choi smiled. "A myth easy to establish and perpetuate. The locals accept any amount I say. I am a Luongan example, the only example. They like me—us. They're happy to assume there are more since they do not have to buy Luongan cars and read of Luongan street gangs."

"A warped and confused and cynical philosophy," Kiet said. "You give the natives too little credit."

Choi shrugged. "I intend to maintain the ruse. There's an American saying. If it ain't broken, don't fix it."

"The Luongan economy is broken, Choi, and it requires fixing. We are not bankrupt, but the twenty million dollar rumor you heard was correct."

Choi picked up his menu and pen. "It is a shame that the

208

youthful computer genius got away with it. I wonder if he is alive, enjoying our money."

Kiet tore the menu out of his hand and said, "He is not enjoying five hundred thousand dollars of it."

"Don't be rude. What are you implying?"

Kiet sighed. "Offshore banks, David Peterson, Jr., Ken Bolling, et al."

Choi's naturally furrowed brow furrowed. It looked to Kiet like a contour farm. "Are you playing a word association game, Kiet? You have me at a great disadvantage. You win."

"Please tell me why you are so anxious to have Captain Binh thrown in jail."

"You phrased the question as an insult. It's beneath my dignity to answer."

"It was not a question. Regardless, I shall answer for you. Captain Binh is arrested, tried, and convicted of murdering Davey Peterson and desecrating a private golf course. The conviction certifies Peterson's death. The secret of the twenty million goes to the land of his ancestors with him. The Kingdom of Luong needs her twenty million, Choi. I appeal to you as a citizen and a patriot."

Kiet paused, yielding to Choi, who did not reply. Kiet waited, looking at him. Choi accepted the challenge of a staring duel. It was a mismatch. Choi averted his eyes in seconds. Kiet held his gaze. Five minutes passed, then ten. Choi began perspiring. He cleared his throat and picked up the menu.

Kiet ripped it to pieces. "Choi, this is not the moment to be inserting price increases on grilled endives. Speak to me."

"I have one thing to say, Kiet. You are violating my rights."

Kiet threw up his hands. "Rights! Due process! Everybody I interview today is making capricious demands."

Choi straightened up in his chair and attempted a watery, blinking gaze. "I'm losing my patience, Kiet. I have work to do. I'm going to call my influential friends—"

"Pathetic bravado, Choi. On your feet."

"No."

Kiet got up. "You refuse to talk to me here. We'll talk elsewhere."

"You're not in Hickorn. You can't."

Kiet took Ken Bolling's pistol from his pants pocket and pointed it at Choi. "Come."

Choi's mouth twisted and he inhaled deeply, as if staving off nausea. He focused on the nickel-and-pearl Browning, and his mouth contorted further into a smirk. "Kiet, in Hickorn you were a legend, a police officer who never carried a gun. Is that a *real* gun?"

"This is America. Everybody is armed. Come."

"You can't storm into my café and kidnap me."

"I can indeed. I already have, haven't I? I am deputized by the Seattle Police Department. I am not kidnapping you. I am bringing you in for interrogation."

"I don't believe you."

Kiet flashed his wallet badge and said, "Are you resisting the order of a duly appointed law officer? The baby slug would not even exit the other side of your head. Your multiethnic kitchen is noisy. The shot would not be heard."

"I'll come, I'll come," Choi blurted. "On one condition. That you release me before the dinner hour. My patrons expect me to perform at my grill."

"Of course," Kiet lied.

In exchange for a pledge not to misbehave, Kiet pocketed his weapon and generously waived deployment of handcuffs he did not have. Outside, on the sidewalk by the yellow zone, Binh was grinning inanely.

"Guess what, Superintendent."

The Yugo was gone. Kiet looked left, then right, and saw it turning the corner, nose in the air, tethered to a tow truck.

"Captain——"

"You'll never believe what happened. This meter maid came by."

"Excuse me?"

210

"Meter maids. They drive around in these little putt-putts and write tickets and put them under a windshield wiper if you're illegally parked or your meter's expired. They chalk tires so you can't run out and reload the meter all day long, right?"

"Seattle's parking police policies are doubtlessly fascinating. Where is our Yugo going, please?"

"To some impound lot. No sweat. Good riddance. Tow and storage fees are Chick Chipperfield's problem. Marge's Town Car's supposed to be done today, you know. We'll catch a cab and have ourselves a boss set of wheels again."

"Captain, were you not to be vigilant and move the car if it was approached by parking police?"

"Well, I'd intended to till I got a load of Penny. Superintendent, I'd never in my life seen a woman who looked dynamite in a uniform, not before Penny."

"Penny?"

"Penny's my meter maid."

"Splendid. Your own personal meter maid."

Binh winked. "It kind of worked out that way. She climbed out of her putt-putt and started to ticket the Yugo on account of it being in a loading zone."

"Which you were to remove from jeopardy."

"Hey, she'd've thought it was mine. Gross-out City. I wouldn't've got to first base with her."

"No. I imagine not."

"While she was writing it up we talked. She's also a Virgo, you know. One shot in twelve. It's an omen."

"It is a coincidence," Kiet muttered. "One thing presumably led to another."

"Sure did. She's just radioed for an impound on Second and Blanchard Streets, so a tow truck was in the vicinity."

"Fortuitous."

A passengerless taxicab appeared. Binh waved and yelled to it.

"Where are you taking me for questioning, Kiet?"

211

"Headquarters."

"Seattle Police Department headquarters?"

"Yes."

"Are you lying to me?"

"No," Kiet lied, clamping onto Choi's forearm.

"You are lying. This is all too informal. American police follow strict procedures. I have a feeling that you're abducting me on a whim and a hunch. That's the Luongan way."

Kiet smiled, clapped a palm on the top of his head, and guided him into the taxi. "Now that you mention it, I'm homesick too."

26

"Christ Almighty," Binh said to the mechanic. "You promised us we could have the car Friday and today's Friday."

"I didn't promise nothing. You said Wednesday, the day you brought it in, and I said how about Friday around fourish, which ain't a promise. It's a guesstimate. That control arm you bunged up, it's on *national* backorder. Dealer's got it on the hot line outta the factory, Dearborn, back there somewhere. Would you believe Tuesday?"

"This is a totally unreasonable situation," Binh said.

Unreasonable? Kiet thought. The delay seemed very reasonable, very Luongan.

The mechanic yawned. "That's the way the cookie crumbles."

Binh sighed. "Well, okay, we'll settle for a loaner."

The mechanic's eyebrows lifted to his hairline. "How long did you say you was out at sea?"

"A rental?" Kiet suggested.

The mechanic pointed to a side of his station. "You're in luck. One just came in."

"Oh no," Binh said. "No way."

"Don't let the California plates fool you. It's in tip-top shape. Most all of them go one way, down there to up here."

"No," Binh said. "Out of the question."

"Yes," Kiet said. "Perfect."

The mechanic's eyes volleyed between Kiet and Davey Peterson's driver's license. He mulled visual discrepancies, then phoned in Davey's credit card number. It validated.

"Close enough for government work," he said.

Kiet signed 'David Peterson Jr.' with flair. The mechanic gave him the top copy.

"Impossible," Binh said. "Im-frigging-possible."

"Not unless you don't downshift on hills and pay attention to your mirrors," the mechanic advised.

"Power steering, power brakes, automatic transmission, air conditioning, which I permitted you to turn up as high as you wished despite my aversion to artificially cooled air," Kiet said, breaking a long silence.

They were off the freeway, climbing the hill to Swan Lake Acres. Binh replied, "It's still a big, ugly pig of a rental moving truck. I've got a confession for you too; orange is *not* my favorite color. My date with Penny is royally screwed. I can't take her out in . . . this."

"You'll improvise, Captain. You're ingenious."

"Don't patronize me, okay?"

"I didn't seize the truck opportunity to deny you sex with the parking constable, Captain. It is a flawless cover. What could be more chameleonlike than a moving truck with California license plates at a Swan Lake Acres home?"

"Well," Binh said. "Yeah, I guess you sort of have a point."

Keedeng Choi, sandwiched in the middle, finally piped up, "I think I am going to regret disregarding my instincts."

214

"Excuse me?"

"Running away and screaming for help when you shanghaied me."

"Damn lucky for you, you didn't, Choi," Binh said, affecting a hard-boiled snarl. "The superintendent is a crack shot. Even with that fruity pea shooter, he could've drilled you at twenty paces. You'd've been dead before you hit the pavement."

Choi gulped. "You aren't deputized. You aren't taking me to a police station."

"No shit, Dick Tracy," Binh said.

Choi craned his neck around Kiet. "This is an expensive housing development. There aren't any police stations in the area."

"You're right, Choi. French châteaus yes, police stations no," Kiet said.

"French châteaus," Binh said. "Reminds me of history class in school. I received high marks in history. The French revolution. What was that guy's name—Robespierre? The guillotine and stuff like that."

"What is it you want from me?"

Kiet groaned. "Choi, we want what you refused to provide at your café. Pertinent conversation."

Choi's voice rose. "You're kidnapping me to a remote area to torture me. You can't. I have rights."

Kiet sighed. "You and your imaginary rights again. No. No torture. Merely conversation. Perhaps you wouldn't speak to me in your office because of the cramped quarters and the kitchen noise. You couldn't concentrate. Where we are going there will be no distractions."

"You can't do this to me, Kiet."

Binh pulled into the model home driveway. "We already are. Be cheerful. We have a surprise for you."

Davey Peterson was at his computer, childhood blanket on his lap, bewitched by the glowing tube. Letter and number combinations of five were plummeting down and off the screen too fast to read.

Keedeng Choi's mouth fell open.

Binh tightened his hold on Choi's arm and said, "You look like you just saw Amelia Earhart. Now will you give us a statement?"

Choi shook his head no.

"Fine," Binh said. "No problem. Go ahead, dig your hole as deep as you want."

"Davey," Kiet said, laying a hand on his shoulder, startling him.

"I didn't hear you enter." He took off his glasses and cleaned them with his shirt. "I had to trade the contacts for these before my eyes fell out. Constant VDT monitoring is as beneficial to what remains of my vision as ammonia eye drops. Mr. Choi. You have Mr. Choi."

"A reunion," Kiet said. "A reunion of two old friends who have been apart too long."

"The superintendent's a sentimental fool," Binh told Choi.

"Davey, any progress?"

"No," Davey said, turning back to his screen. "I'm imputing random alphabetic-numerics. The twenty-six letters and the ten digits arranged in every possible five-character mode. If that fails I will move to six-character."

"When will you be done with the fives?" Kiet asked.

"On a Cray mainframe, weeks. On this PC, providing I allocate time to procreate, my grandchildren may solve the problem."

"Procreate," Binh said wistfully. "Penny."

"Why bother?" Kiet asked.

"I think I have stumbled upon Mr. Bolling's financial abode. I require a password to enter. I may become lucky in the manner of a lotto winner who defeats odds of five million to one. What other avenue do I have?"

"So you are on the front porch of his home, knocking, but he is ignoring you?"

"Essentially. Conceptualize it as follows. His home is a medieval fortress and you are on the wrong side of the moat. The password lowers the drawbridge."

"And?"

"The gates are constructed of thick timbers. They are barred with iron straps."

"You batter the gates?" Kiet asked.

"Not feasible. Fanatical soldiers await with swords and spears. Other troops are up in the battlements, pouring cauldrons of boiling oil on you and picking you off with crossbows."

"You fall in the moat," Binh said. "You're up to your ass in alligators. The bottom line is you die."

"Ah," Kiet said. "You lower the drawbridge, entrench on superior ground, entice them to come out to join you in battle. You decimate, pillage, and plunder."

"An exemplary analogy," Davey said. "You have articulated the solution."

Kiet looked at Choi. "Before we can ambush the enemy and sack him, we must lower the drawbridge before its hinges rust together. Talk to us, please."

"What are your plans for me? What's in it for me if I talk?"

"No deals," Binh snapped.

"One deal," Kiet said. "A fair trial in Hickorn."

"That is no deal," Choi said, sneering.

"Of course," Kiet said. "What do you have to gain? We have already kidnapped you and are preparing to torture you. What is the advantage of reforming into a helpful, patriotic Luongan?"

"Release me now, Kiet, and I promise I won't lodge a complaint with my powerful friends."

"Mr. Choi," Kiet said. "We haven't searched you, so we do not know whether your passport is on you. If not, Captain Binh and I would be pleased to burglarize your house tonight."

"I always have my passport on me. So what? You have no arrest and extradition papers."

"We haven't arrested you. As you so insightfully stated, we abducted you. We're going to book space on an airplane and escort you home. I am a guest police executive. I have a waiver to carry my firearm through the airport metal detectors onto the airplane. Resist or cry for help and I shall have to shoot you."

"Superintendent, what you can do, you pull your badge, yell, 'stop in the name of the law, scumbag' or something like that, real loud so you have tons of witnesses, give him a five meter head start, then nail him. *Pop pop pop.* Three rounds minimum. Two in the chest, through the ticker, one in the noggin."

"Thank you, Captain."

"They'll be looking for me. It'll be splashed in the papers tomorrow. You'd be stupid to take me to the airport. I'm a celebrity. You won't proceed beyond the check-in counter before ten officers are drawing a bead on you."

"Thank you for the warning. Captain, we should perhaps lay low until the heat is off. Is that the correct jargon?"

"Well, you're getting better, Superintendent. Yeah, not a bad idea. The crawl space."

"Splendid."

"Crawl space?"

"Underneath this unit," Binh said. "You know, that two or three feet between dirt and the floor joists. It's fairly dry this time of the year. We'd let you up twice a day or so. It shouldn't be more than—what, Superintendent?—a month, maybe, and you're on the back burner, mediawise. You'll adapt to the situation pronto. The only hassle I can think of is maybe the spiders."

"Spiders?" Choi asked.

"Those suckers they have down below this unit, they're so big they have tattoos. They're shy, though. Not to worry.

So long as you don't sit on them, which tends to piss 'em off."

"I don't know anything about computers or Bolling's business," Choi said.

"Simply speak to us about anything you and Bolling spoke about," Kiet said.

"He's a braggart, a megalomaniac. He always talked about himself. Does reinvoicing mean anything?"

"It could," Davey said.

"He said he could move millions as if change from pocket to pocket. He could appear like a billionaire on the books or a pauper. He said he could perform legerdemain by adjusting the price of each seminar upward or downward."

"That is a form of reinvoicing," Davey said. "Retroactive reinvoicing. Reinvoicing as a money laundering scam, for example, entails buying raw materials through a dummy foreign subsidiary at a low price and reselling to the parent company at a much higher price. Taxable profits are proportionally reduced."

"Bolling has already reported the income and paid taxes on it," Kiet said.

"He reports quarterly and the second quarter just ended," Davey said. "He may not have paid his second quarter taxes yet. He can charge the seven hundred dollar seminars at three hundred and offload the cash before the IRS knows it exists. Assuming he is swindling others too, he could be choking on his cash flow."

"Must the drawbridge be lowered for us to ambush and loot his offloaded cash flow?" Kiet asked.

"Regrettably," Davey said. "Otherwise he can offload from the back door and we'd never be the wiser."

"The password, how is it chosen?"

"The parameters are arbitrary," Davey said. "Sometimes it's personal, sometimes it's abstract."

"The personal you can link to the user," Kiet said. "The abstract you cannot. Which would Bolling employ?"

"He's not stupid," Davey said. "Abstract."

"Isn't a personal password kind of like a private joke, something really familiar to you, but secret to others?" Binh asked. "Kind of like vanity plates on a car?"

"It can be."

"Bolling has a humongous ego," Binh said. "We could have us an Achilles heel situation. Choi?"

"He was distant," Choi said. "We did not swap intimate details of our private lives."

"He talked about nothing besides your criminal conspiracy?" Kiet asked.

"We lapsed into general conversations, but Bolling was a master manipulator of the spoken word. He kept the topics neutral and extraneous."

"He didn't dwell on his own life, except that he was onward to being a trillionaire. I can accept that," Kiet said. "Did the conversation ever focus on you?"

"Past the initial amenities, no. He confused me with Vietnamese."

"Can't blame him for that," Binh said.

"He asked me how I felt about the communist takeover in 1975. I said I did not care as long as the Viet reds didn't march into Luong. He told me his Dien Bien Phu motivational story no less than five times. He hates communists, but he admired the dedication of the Vietminh."

"Stop," Kiet said, beginning to pace the room. "In 1954, during the first Vietnam War, the French War, the French mobilized a garrison in a remote valley surrounded by impenetrable hills. They were inviting the Vietminh to attack. They anticipated an infantry assault, which their airpower and artillery would chew to pieces. The Vietminh accomplished an impossible feat. They brought artillery to the hilltops, piece by piece, inch by inch. We know how the story ends."

"Yeah," Binh said. "So?"

"The French ego. The white European colonial arrogance."

"Okay." Binh was pacing behind Kiet, snapping his fingers. "I know what you're driving at. Hey. The French commander, something about him, right?"

"I'll complete the thought. Ken Bolling's sidelight, not incorporated in the motivational story he fed his students," Choi said. "There were outposts, strong points, dug in on the hills, outside of the garrison. The French commander named them for past mistresses. They fell early to the Viets, but Bolling admired the general's panache."

"Beatrice. Isabelle," Kiet said. "*Lycée* history class is too far in the past to remember the others."

"Davey," Binh said. "Bolling's Bremerton chippy, what's her name?"

Davey had already cleared his screen and was typing *L-I-N-D-A*. "Enter," he mumbled, cuffing the enter key with the heel of his hand. "Do it! Cowabunga! Yes! We're in."

Kiet looked at the screen and read aloud, " 'Fiduciary code, enter, and press any key.' Fiduciary code?"

"Cute," Davey said. "He's saying come and get it if you can. Basically, you have to input a secondary password."

"Marie," Binh said. "Sandi, Joyce, Janet, Nancy, Renee, Naomi, Becky. Hey, Davey, whip 'Penny' on your machine."

"Futile," he said. "Bolling rewarded us for our psychological ingenuity once. He won't twice."

"The gates," Kiet muttered. "The gates. Lure the rascals outside."

Brakes screeched. A car door slammed hard. Binh herded Choi and Davey and Davey's computer into a bathroom.

Marge Mainwaring burst in, sputtering, "You have your nerve, you—Binh. And Bamsan."

"Yes," Kiet said. "Us."

"Marge, you're looking ultra foxy tonight," Binh said.

"Where are they?"

"Who?" Binh said.

"Who?" Kiet said.

"An owl imitation," Marge said, slumping into an over-stuffed chair covered in velvet not unlike optional upholstery in midpriced family sedans. "That's all the hell I need."

27

"I thought I was *such* a good judge of character," Marge lamented. "They fooled me. Did they pay you to hide them and get rid of me? Oh, God, strike that! Me and my big mouth, I've caused you to lose face. I wouldn't intentionally do that in a million years."

"You can make it up to me, Marge," Binh said, leering and winking.

"You wouldn't, would you? Binh," she said to Kiet.

"Excuse me?"

"Hide them. Sneak them into a spare bedroom out of the goodness of your hearts. I wouldn't be in a snit if they hadn't deceived me so convincingly. I'm not excusing my gullibility, but you should have seen them. They could have taken anybody in. Malibu Natural was the look. Toss on what isn't in the hamper and hit the beach."

"Surf's up," Binh said.

"Casual, natural, rumpled—hah! From knees to Marc's pecks, and Jenny's flat breasts, they were Ro-day-oh Drive.

Jen and her Junior League, Marc blowing Pro-Am smoke. Pebble Beach in a foursome with Arnold Palmer's cousin. God, they were smooth! I fell hook, line, and sinker. Damn you, Marge, you sap!"

"Pebble Beach foursome? Pro-Am," Kiet asked. "Is that golf? Golf is a wonderful and vigorous sport."

"Pebble Beach, Palm Springs. Golfing as pseudoroyalty at play. Those despicable Fergusons, they're no better than Bonnie and Clyde. I ordered a rush credit report to expedite the closing. You would *not* believe those two chiselers."

"You can't judge a book by its cover," Binh said.

"Those two bunco artists wouldn't qualify in a trailer park," Marge said.

"Reprehensible," Kiet said.

"Driving by on the road, I glanced over and saw the moving van with Cal plates, and put two and two together. I thought the Fergusons were squatting. I thought it was a schtick to legitimize homestead rights. You can do anything in California. They have some cuckoo laws."

"Well," Binh said. "We were responding to your note, you know, maid service on the joint before we hit the road. Our law enforcement leadership conference has been extended indefinitely. We were going to find an apartment we could afford the damage deposit and first and last months rent on, if there is such an animal, and rent some furniture from whoever would be willing to rent to dusky foreigners."

"I'm sorry, Bamsan," Marge said. "I was thinking of myself and my commission. There are times when I'm a horse's butt."

Guilt, Kiet thought. Binh could tap in and bubble it to the surface like a shaman divining water.

A horn honked.

Marge went to Binh, kissed him on the cheek, and said, "Got to run. The Ferguson deal is down the toilet. You fellows stay as long as you want. Ciao."

She fluttered fingers at Kiet, who nodded neutrally in

224

return, as platonic as could be. Binh looked outside as she drove off, then said, "The truck van blocked my view. I couldn't see who she was with."

"Perhaps a sales colleague."

"No sweat. Thanks to Penny, Marge didn't raise my blood pressure a click, didn't once make my heart go flutter-flutter."

"Splendid."

"Penny," Binh went on. "That wide leather belt she had her radio clipped to, it gave her a wasp waist. Superintendent, she's got a body that won't quit. Nice disposition too. Great personality."

"Captain, excuse me, our guests in hiding."

Binh retrieved a sullen Choi and a sneering Davey. He said, "Superintendent, we have to stash them in the same room again, we'll have to drug them or we'll have a cat fight on our hands."

"Drug," Kiet said. "Drugs. My Ken Bolling itch. I can scratch it."

"Huh? Oh yeah, right."

"His itching powder was not 'boat people' or 'Dien Bien Phu.' He boasted that laundered money attracted law enforcement attention if it were suspected as earned in the sale of narcotics."

"Yeah?"

"Captain, what is America's paramount drug agency?"

"Well, with dope so prevalent these days, every town with a police force that amounts to more than a part-time redneck cop on a motorcycle behind a billboard with a radar gun has a dope squad. *Número uno,* though, I guess you'd have to say, is the feds, the Drug Enforcement Administration."

"Davey, can you ram the fortress gates?" Kiet asked.

Davey Peterson flipped through his little black book, furiously *thunk-thunked* the keys, tongue protruding from a corner of his mouth. Davey obliterated the Ken Bolling text and replaced it with different graffiti. To Kiet, this display and its predecessor could be ideograms carved onto temple walls.

"Ho hum. Slightly more stimulating than hacking into the pentagon," Davey said, bobbing in his chair, pleased with himself. "Slightly with a lowercase *s.*"

Binh whistled. "Ninety seconds. Not too shabby."

"How shall we best proceed?" Kiet asked Binh.

"Are you into headquarters?" Binh asked Davey.

"I've accessed their e.m. on their director's password."

"Awesome," Binh said.

"Ee-em?" Kiet said.

"Electronic mail," Davey said. "We can send memoranda from the desk of their illustrious leader to the hinterlands. That's the beauty of e.m. You can log on any time of the day or night. The branches pull up the documents the next morning."

"And shit their knickers if we play our cards right," Binh said. "How about we issue a directive warning branches nationwide, calling all cars, as it were, that Mr. Ken Bolling through the legit cover of his traveling road show is primarily engaged in narcotic trafficking and/or laundering drug proceeds, blah blah blah."

Davey *thunk-thunked.* Binh critiqued, "Okay, not bad. We need some buzz words. Mafia. Mafioso. Organized crime. La Cosa Nostra. Make that LCN. When I was in D.C., the wiseguys, the button men, the whole evil spectrum was LCN. One humongous, monolithic LCN. The feds, it was a code they invented, you know, macho and secret and clubby. Every hotshot in the field on the make to fast-track, LCN is gonna be his battle cry."

"Impressive. However, today is Friday, Friday night," Kiet said.

"Yeah. DEA agents operate around the clock, but, yeah, universally, offices are kind of dead on weekends. Immediacy is what we're talking about. Front Burner City."

226

"Anonymous phone tips," Kiet said. "The vigilance of public spirited citizens."

"Not to worry," Binh said. He produced a telephone directory. "The blue pages. Government listings. Bolling is stroking the masses at some motel near the airport. We ought to be able to light a fire under a narc in that jurisdiction."

"Everybody, every agency eligible," Kiet said.

"Can do," Binh said, jotting phone numbers and narrating, "Seattle Police Department Narcotics Section. King County Sheriff's Department Drug Enforcement Unit. Washington State Patrol Marijuana Hot Line. Hey, why not? Grass leads to the hard stuff. Last but not least, the Federal Bureau of Investigation."

Binh volunteered to make the calls. He made them eagerly, hamming, in a mix of voices. Nodding-off junkie, rival Fu Manchu druglord, outraged citizen, man in the street eyewitness.

"Bolling's wired seven ways to Sunday, Superintendent. An hour from now he'll have himself a load of big-time heat. A blast furnace'll feel like Greenland in January."

"Captain, you have a potential career as a linguist."

"Huh?"

Binh had been juggling the rental truck key from hand to hand. Kiet said, "You may go out on your date. You have my blessing. There is nothing more you can do."

"Yeah, thanks. Big ugly set of wheels or no big ugly set of wheels, Penny's a doll. I gotta go for it. But, hey, you'll have to watch our fine feathered friends by your lonesome."

Binh looked at their guests. Davey was joined to his computer by soul and blanket. He would be no trouble. Choi was on the couch, arms folded, pouting. "Is there a toolbox in this house?"

"Yeah. Basic stuff. Screwdriver, hammer, nails, pliers."

"Before you leave, please nail the windows shut in a bedroom. We'll install Choi there. I'll sleep in the hallway with blankets and pillows."

"Will do," Binh said. "The Fergusons won't mind. I'll relieve you when I get home."

"My compliments on the spider ploy," Kiet said, lowering his voice to a whisper. "Psychologically ingenious of you."

Binh shrugged. Pride reddened his face. "No biggie. Choi's a weenie. Weenies are afraid of spiders. That's an automatic."

"How will you explain your mode of transportation to the parking constable?"

Binh's eyebrows lifted. "I guarantee you one thing, whatever it is it'll have to be a whopper. Superintendent, I have to ask. Davey hacked the department dry. How could you afford to fly to America to rescue me and the situation?"

"Irrelevant. We shall soon have our stolen money."

"Jesus," Binh said, eyes moistening. "You went on the street, didn't you, to Chinese shylocks?"

The moment was becoming too tender. "Think nothing of it. We have been after those characters for years. I entrapped them. After we are in Hickorn, a priority shall be to arrest them on usury charges."

"You know," Binh said, sighing. "I hope we can wrap this fiasco up pretty damn soon."

Kiet nodded. A wave of euphoria almost knocked him off his feet. Why? Then he realized. Binh had obliquely confessed homesickness. He had not yet gone native.

28

Doug Zane came by at midnight. "This kooky case, you and Binh, you've made an insomniac out of Dougie. Besides, I caught an earful that'll turn you on. What are you and the boy wonder up to? Computers, they're all Luongan to me."

Kiet had been looking over Davey's shoulder as numbers flickered and danced on the screen. He updated Zane.

"Bitchin'! Egg sucking extraordinaire. How many bucks have you glommed so far?"

"Twenty-two million and change, diverted as it offloaded and transferred circuitously to the Luongan National Bank," Davey said. "We're, alas, approaching the end of the string."

"On the radio, they had a report on your man, Ken Bolling," Zane said. "He's in the slammer."

"Evidently his one alloted telephone call was made to his computer custodian instead of an attorney," Kiet said. "They're stampeding out of the fortress, across the drawbridge, and we are picking them off as if shooting fish in a rain barrel."

"Yo, time out. Too late in the day for metaphors and things," Zane said.

"Computer lingo," Kiet said. "They are transferring funds. We are decimating, pillaging, and plundering them."

"You have a profit of two million," Zane said. "You don't know where the overage came from. It ain't yours is what we know for sure. You and Binh, don't you dudes do anything legal?"

"Consider it a service charge," Kiet said. "A fee for the aggravation of recovering the loot."

"Consider us done," Davey said. "They've keyed confirmation codes at their destinations and have drawn blanks. They are cognizant that something is rotten in Nassau. The foul odor has drifted to Willemstad and Zurich. They have discerned our proverbial hand in the proverbial cookie jar, but the contents are depleted if not exhausted."

"Money laundering inside humor," Kiet told Zane. "Your earful, please."

"The embalming fluid thing, the police narrowed it down to a med school cadaver. No mortuary is likely to pull a Dickensian grave-robbing stunt. Otherwise they'd be out of business and in the pokey. Do not pass Go, do not collect two hundred dollars. The med student Davey hired did it himself. He collapsed like a pawnshop accordian and confessed. Didn't Davey hear what I said?"

"He is computer hacking," Kiet said.

"Yeah, computer nerds, they go into trances, don't they? They have these out-of-body experiences. The gendarmes searched David Peterson's home. His mother swung a dust mop at a dick, knocked his glasses off before they subdued her. She took the Fifth, but they tore the house apart and have figured that just maybe Davey's amongst the living. They'll be breathing down your necks before you can say nolo contendere."

"The source of your earful? Your dentist or your hairdresser?"

"My dermatologist."

Kiet groaned.

"He's been giving me stuff to clear up my complexion. School's still out on that. We got to shooting the breeze. He flies gliders. Sailplanes. This dude, he's one-quarter owner on one with—those suckers are *expensive,* you can grasp what they'd cost if they had engines—an associate dean at the medical school. The dean's catching a skyful of flak on the cadaver thing. He's typing up his resume."

"Davey," Kiet said, shaking his arm. "We are going to Luong tomorrow. Thai Airways flies every day from Seattle-Tacoma to Bangkok, via Tokyo. You and I and Binh and Choi shall be on the plane. I do not want you to worry. Your cooperation will be influential, particularly since Luong has made a profit. I shall insist that you receive a suspended sentence."

"All right. You've been fair with me so far. I won't resist. I can't go home. Mom will kill me. It's my fault our house was searched. Mom hates housework. Jeez, she'll hate straightening up afterward. But how do you propose to pay for the tickets?"

"Captain Binh's credit cards are maximum'd out and I doubt if yours have adequate limits."

Davey nodded. "I'll key in the card numbers and pay the bills. No problem. But isn't that stealing?"

"Indeed not. It is a legitimate business expense."

"You guys are beautiful. I could be disbarred for being in the same ZIP code area you're in," Zane said. "Hey, isn't that Chef Choi?"

Keedeng Choi was seated in the center of the sofa, arrogantly and silently, arms folded tightly at his chest, the mien of a deposed emperor.

"Mr. Choi has not yet embraced the spirit of our mission," Kiet said.

Doug Zane went to him, leading with a business card, saying, "'Rim Legal. We're up and down the Coast, but you're thinking, whoa, what good's Dougie when I'm on the other side of the globe? God invented fax machines for this kind of thing. We're never more than a document apart, you and me, attorney and client."

Choi ignored him with the imperiousness of a medieval Chinese dynast.

Zane said, "A cash flow pinch isn't anything to be ashamed of, you know. It's like head lice. You can't help it. One day you're afflicted. Yeah, I'm required to take a retainer and I realize that the restaurant game is topsy-turvy. I have a charger plate out in the car, so bread needn't be a factor. What do you say? No defendant should be without legal counsel."

Choi had nothing to say. Doug Zane, attorney-at-law, did not exist.

"Do not worry regarding his rights," Kiet said. "I will appoint him a lawyer before his trial."

Zane got up, shaking his head, saying he was already five minutes late to another commitment and that he'd see them off at the airport in the morning. He closed with a question that may or may not have been rhetorical: If the state of Washington *does* pull my ticket, what the hell do you have to do to pass the bar exam in Luong, because it sure as hell sounds like I'd be practicing in Oz?

Captain Binh and the rental moving truck rumbled into the driveway—when, what time of the declining night? Kiet pulled aside a drapery and saw sunrise, an orange fire warming a charcoal blue sky. Davey had not moved from his keyboard; the hacking was done, yes, but he was equally engrossed in electronic bulletin boards, pulling them up, reading, then *thunk-thunking* his own comments. How genius nerds gossip, Kiet thought. Keedeng Choi was immobile, true to an evident vow of silence. Kiet had not slept. Who could sleep? Bamsan Kiet was going *home*.

Binh walked in, disheveled and beatific. He was holding a newspaper. "Superintendent, what a night!"

"Do not elaborate. I comprehend. A leer is worth a thousand words."

"You know, these moving trucks, they have a bunch of those heavy quilted blankets they throw in back for you to tie around your wood furniture so it doesn't bang into stuff and get bunged up."

"Yes."

Binh winked. "Lay them out flat, stacked up, and they're real soft and slippery, same same a mattress. But, hey, I'm putting the cart in front of the horse."

"Excuse me?"

"Telling my tale backasswards, end to beginning, *Z* to *A.*"

"Oh?"

Binh took a deep breath and said, "We parked in this lot up the highway from the motel Bolling was huckstering at and watched the show from the truck, that I told Penny was a standby paddy wagon in case the raiding parties hauled out an overload of scumbags their squad cars couldn't hold, which dovetailed swell with what I told her about me being on special assignment with the local agencies as far as Golden Triangle heroin interdiction was concerned, all of this Penny related to intensely on account of her already passing the exams and being on the waiting list for SPD's next training class, and the fact that I was in on the raid situation beforehand, well, she never had been in on anything in advance as a meter maid and, you know, and while the outcome was anticlimactic, pardon the pun—"

"Captain, I understand Ken Bolling was arrested."

Binh gave Kiet the newspaper. "Hot off the presses. Check the headline. You gotta love it."

Kiet read the headline aloud, "INFOMERCIAL PERSONALITY ARRESTED IN MELEE."

"You should've seen the cop cars, Superintendent. They had enough dope-sniffing dogs in them to stock a Westminster Kennel Club show. They couldn't barge right in to Bolling's seminar, of course, but they were there in the event of probable cause."

"Bolling was arrested on what charge? Punctuate your sentences, please. Time is not of the essence."

Binh sighed. "Disorderly conduct. Assaulting a police officer. Et cetera. Between the newspaper story and what I learned sniffing around after the confrontation, I guess it was quite a scene. Bolling was alerted during the lecture that cops were nosing around and demanded to know what was going on. The police were evasive and Bolling kind of lost his cool. He called them thirty-grand-a-year losers. This one detective, I think he was county, he told Bolling that he'd shelled out seven hundred bucks for his package last February and that it was garbage. There wasn't a damn thing in it he didn't know already. He said the subliminal tapes gave him a headache and that nobody but an idiot would sell you real estate for no money down. He lost ten pounds, but only because Cuisine By Ken gave him the runs. Bolling came down off the podium swinging and what you'd call your basic donnybrook ensued."

"Salisbury steak," Kiet said, looking at the paper. "Ah, a small headline in a bottom corner. CREMATION KILLING ON LINKS TAKES STRANGE TWIST."

"It's getting warm, Superintendent. Big-time warm. Warm as in *heat*."

Kiet told Binh about the twenty-two million and said, "Get some sleep. We're going home."

Home to Quin, he thought.

"Sleep," Binh said. "Who can sleep?"

29

Saturday. Their flight departed Seattle-Tacoma at 1:30 P.M.
Kiet did not want to be too early, loitering—waiting an
excessively long time—an exposed and stationary target for
law officers. Nor did he want to be late. Miss the flight and
they would have to reschedule the following day, thus multiplying the risk of recognition in the high-visibility environ-
ment of an airline terminal.

En route to the airport, they stopped at Keedeng Choi's
apartment to pack him. Kiet escorted Choi inside, restricting
him to one bag and five minutes. To Kiet's surprise Choi
rented a studio in a bland building in a middle-income neighborhood. No other celebrity chef in the world lived as modestly and frugally, he thought.

But upon examination, Choi's thriftiness proved logical.
His few possessions were arranged neatly and compactly,
underclothing in a single drawer, hangups at a side of a
closet, books and papers and miscellany in boxes. Keedeng
Choi and every trace of Keedeng Choi could be out in fifteen

minutes, Kiet realized. The guilt of the half million dollars menaced the man like a dark alley.

Kiet graciously carried Choi's suitcase out, saying, "Evidently you were not missed."

"Oh, I was missed," Choi said. "My employees are stealing me blind. They complain endlessly about low wages. They'll rob my till and larder, and report me missing when they are good and ready. Vietnamese and Cambodians resent working for a Luongan, you know. They think we are inferior to them."

"Ingrates," Kiet said, attempting without success to calculate how many people could be paid slave wages how long on five hundred thousand American dollars.

At the airport they parked the moving truck in a load-unload zone, a hundred feet from the doors nearest Thai Airways. The zone was aggressively policed. As they entered the terminal a towing vehicle had already hoisted the truck's homely orange nose.

Marge Mainwaring was at the Thai counter. Kiet halted his entourage on the entrance ramp. Marge, eyes red, an unhappy person, went to them, jaw set, heels clacking on the tile.

Kiet was not inclined to ask her how she knew they were leaving. He had a pretty good hunch, and ample discussion topics of an unpleasant nature loomed anyway. He said, "A sudden late-breaking emergency development in Hickorn."

"How did you know we were leaving?" Binh asked.

"Kiet, that wasn't a complete sentence. Where is my Lincoln?"

"Uh," Binh said.

"Why do you look familiar?" Marge said to Choi.

Keedeng Choi nodded to her curtly and strode briskly toward the concourses.

"Superintendent."

Kiet held Binh's arm.

"What did he call you?" Marge asked Kiet.

"Bamsan," Kiet said to Binh, "it is a nice day for a stroll. The outside weather is bad for our companion's condition, however."

"I get it, I guess," Binh said, taking off after Choi.

"Will you please tell me where my car is?"

Kiet gave her the approximate location of the gas station. "A specialist. The dealer subcontracted to him."

"Can I believe you?"

"No, but the repairs are paid for. Honestly."

Marge looked at Davey. "You look familiar too? Haven't you been in the paper?"

Davey blinked and gulped.

"No, why should you have been. I'm going crazy. Binh, come here for a minute."

Marge dragged Kiet by a hand to a row of chairs that were bolted to the floor. Kiet, off balance and sidling, directed a stare at Davey that said "imitate a statue."

"Your woman at home," Marge said, "is she astute?"

"Excuse me?"

"Does she know her man inside out? Does she read him like a book."

"Yes."

"Whenever you look at me, whenever, I mean, after you-know-what happened—in the Chinese cultures, do you have a saying that compares to our 'you look like the cat who just swallowed the canary'? I don't mean smart-assed and smarmy. I mean embarrassed. Expecting to be chased out of the house with a broom. That type of look on your face."

"Several sayings. They are stories. We Luongans love parables. Unless we, individually, are the moral lesson of them."

"God help you, Binh. Your cheeks are bulging and yellow feathers are sticking out of your mouth. Is she violent?"

"I do not think so."

"Well, that's a break for you." Marge's kiss was wet, intimate, lingering. Her grip on his saddlebags was painful. She said, "Keep after Bamsan about listing his villa with us. It's for his own good. And—thank you for exorcising Henry."

She was on her feet, striding up the ramp and outside, pulling facial tissue from her purse. Davey had not budged. His lower jaw was hanging and his eyelids were humming-bird wings. We shall play Cupid for the lad, Kiet decided. Perhaps a surplus lady friend of Binh's. Despite past inconveniences, a profit of two million Yankee dollars (less expenses) merited a suspended prison sentence and a matchmaking effort.

Doug Zane came in an adjacent set of doors and sat beside Kiet. "Are we talking the last act of *Casablanca* or what? Dougie can dig a pinch of melodrama so long as nobody gets mushy, you not remotely resembling Ingrid, no offense."

"You and Marge Mainwaring, when and to what extent, please?"

"The morning I chauffeured Binh to her place for the Lincoln."

"Captain Binh said that you struck an immediate friendship."

"Affirmative. Marge and I both got to work late that day."

"One thing led to another," Kiet said.

"The Oriental thing she has, that hang-up, I felt like a jerk for exploiting it. Binh clues me in and I ace him out. Mr. Nice Guy, huh?"

"I am reasonably confident you are a Caucasian."

"Funny how those things work out," Zane said. "Remember me telling you I took a year of Japanese in college?"

"Yes."

"Marge is waltzing me around her pad. You saw it. How would you describe it?"

"Asiatic Flea Market."

"There you go. So I tell her how interested I am in the Orient, which isn't a total lie, not after I met you and Binh. Where is he?"

"On counterintelligence duty."

238

"Kore ga watashi no pasupoto desu."

"Excuse me?"

" 'Here is my passport' in Japanese. Hey, I got a C in the class years ago. I don't remember much. I call her my little *omuretsu*. *Omuretsu* is omelet. I couldn't remember 'flower' or 'sugar plum' or anything sexier, so *omuretsu* was it, take it or leave it. The *kore ga* thing—she went nuts."

Kiet groaned.

"Hankachi o otashi mashita yo. You've dropped your handkerchief. Marge did, carnally. Whoa. Cease and desist the eyeball laser thing, Kiet. You're wilting my nose hair. Under oath, I admit a one morning stand was foremost in my dirty little mind. You Asians and your chivalrous attitude toward women, if I didn't know better, I'd think you and Marge had something cooking. Couldn't be, though. No way. You're a couple of decades too old for her."

"I am?"

"She's a complex lady. Her principal hang-up is young guys, not Oriental guys. Henry, her inaugural lover, while Chinese, was young. She was young too, yeah, but she's chronologically frozen. Her age, past or present, is irrelevant and immaterial. She's gone out with younger guys and she's gone out with Oriental guys and Binh's theory of young *and* Oriental had solid underpinnings. Problem. She buys the theory herself, which makes it too cold and clinical: I am what I am, therefore no spontaneity. But here I come from off the wall, a young round-eye dude who shocks the hell out of her by speaking pidgin Japanese. Get it?"

"No."

"Me neither. Not exactly. We're talking substance over form. Results. Marge is one nifty lady. Kiet, she sends me over the moon. I'm hanging on to her. You won't tell Binh, pretty please?"

"Our secret."

Davey said, "Pardon me, gentlemen. Our flight was announced."

Binh returned as they were getting up. "Doug, hi. Superintendent, you'll never guess what happened."

"Concerning Choi?"

"You got that right. Every sky marshal and port authority cop in the terminal is in his face. He saw I had the outside exits cut off, so he tried slipping through security. He had to run his suitcase through the metal detector on that little conveyor belt they have, and the bells and sirens went off like a three alarm fire. They pulled a gun out of his bag. It looked like a twin of Bolling's pussy pistol."

They were walking, nearing the security point that separated them from their boarding concourse, a Boeing 747, and home. Keedeng Choi, in the company of numerous uniformed men and women, was spread-eagled against a wall. Assuming the position, Binh would say.

"I planted it at his apartment," Kiet said. "Choi was untrustworthy, an escape risk. I was going to discard the gun before we passed through the security point, of course. In the meantime, we needed to worry about him fleeing in one direction only. Outside exits, not pathways to airplanes."

"He was gonna pull what we pulled on the goons," Binh said. "Sneaky."

"Indeed."

Doug slapped Kiet, Binh, and Davey on their backs, an expedient and masculine farewell, and walked toward Choi, business card extended. "Yo. That's my client you're pushing around. What's he allegedly done? Choi, you don't have to say a word. You have the right to remain silent."

Kiet lowered his basket from his head and placed it on the conveyor for X ray scrutiny. He jabbed a thumb at the brouhaha and said, "Terrorism. It is so senseless."

"Go figure," Binh said.